UP

BASCH
Degrees of 1

D0734763

EVANGELINE PARISH LIBRARY
VILLE PLATTE, LA.

WITHDRAWN

# DEGREES OF LOVE

# DEGREES OF LOVE

## Rachel Basch

W. W. NORTON & COMPANY
NEW YORK    LONDON

135757

EVANGELINE PARISH LIBRARY
P.O. BOX 40
VILLE PLATTE, LA. 70586

Copyright © 1998 by Rachel Basch

All rights reserved
Printed in the United States of America
First Edition

For information about permission to reproduce selections from this book, write to
Permissions, W. W. Norton & Company, Inc., 500 Fifth Avenue, New York, NY 10110

The text of this book is composed in Janson
with the display set in Letter Gothic Bold
Desktop composition by Lane Kimball Trubey
Manufacturing by Quebecor Printing, Farifield, Inc.
Book Design by Chris Welch

**Library of Congress Cataloging-in Publication Data**

Basch,  Rachel.
    Degrees of love / by Rachel Basch.
        p.    cm.
    **ISBN  0-393-04625-7**
    I.  Title
    PS3552.A784D44    1998
    813' .54—dc21                             97-40319
                                                      CIP


W. W. Norton & Company, Inc., 500 Fifth Avenue, New York, N.Y. 10110
http://www.wwnorton.com


W. W. Norton & Company Ltd., 10 Coptic Street, London WC1A 1PU


1 2 3 4 5 6 7 8 9 0

For David, for everything,
and
in memory of our Caroline,
who was with me as much of this
was being written

23.95    1198    ovigham

# Acknowledgments

I am deeply grateful to my sister-in-law Maria Gould Cronin for so generously lending me her expert medical opinion, as well as the kernel of this story.

Writers usually thank foundations for granting them the time to write. My "foundation"during the writing of this book was my children's daycare provider, Heidrun Morgan. Her loving care of my children quite literally freed me up. My many thanks to Sarah Sturgis, Patti Noone, Sarah Halper, Asia Martin, and Lorrie Jones, women whom my children and I came to rely on during the long process of making this book.

I am indebted to my parents, Norma and Sheldon Basch, for stepping into the the domestic fray that heralded more than a few deadlines, and more important, for raising me to embrace challenge. And thanks to my brother and sister-in-law Fred and Susan Basch for their abilities at jollying up the niece and the nephew.

I had the good fortune (and sense) to marry into a family that has, for me, doubled as a vast and voluble cheerleading squad. Sally Gould, Forrest Gould, Maria Gould Cronin, Geoff Cronin, Peter Gould, Joan Gould Kelley, John Kelley, Claudia Kupervaser, and F. J. Gould have been tireless in their suspension of

disbelief that there really was a book, as well as in their willing-
ness to sweep my children off their feet so that I might work.

My thanks to the attorneys Linda Medeiros and Zoe Manos
for their legal expertise. I am indebted to the social workers
Stephen Thermes and Cindy Gerstl for illuminating the child
welfare system for me. My appreciation also to Cindy and to
Cathie Petrosky for taking into account my own children's welfare and treating them to long afternoons far from my desk.

The writers Tricia Bauer, Bill Bozzone, Bonnie Friedman, and
Anna Monardo all shepherded me along the way. Their generos-
ity in sharing information, offering advice, and providing encouragement continues to be invaluable for me. My writing students
have been a gift. Communing with them weekly fueled the
process. Jill Edelman taught me about mothering with equal mea-
sures of insight and compassion. My thanks to her is unending.

My writing life turned around one hundred and eighty degrees
the day I met Alice Martell, my literary guardian angel, my agent.
I continue to be awed by the commitment my editor, Jill Bialosky,
has demonstrated toward this book. Her rigorous guidance in the
rewriting of this novel was indispensable. Ted Johnson, the copy
editor on this book, also deserves my many thanks.

There is no way to properly thank my family for stomaching
the chaos that was the sometime byproduct of living alongside a
work in progress. Nathaniel and Hannah have gone from toddlers to readers in the time it has taken me to complete this project. Along the way they cheered me, consoled me, and thankful-
ly, engaged me in real life. They have endured much and have
done so with stunning equanimity. My respect for them is limitless, their presence in my life my greatest joy.

My husband David Gould has supported me in every sense of
the word. He has read and reread and reread my work and
brought his prodigious editing skills to bear. He has lavished
upon me the great gifts evident in his own writing: passion, truth,
humor, confidence, dedication, and patience.

# BOOK ONE

# Lily

The caseworker wasn't there yet, and technically, Lily told herself, she wasn't late unless the caseworker knew that she was late. Jack, of course, knew that she was late. She could see him looking out the living-room window. He'd probably just put away the vacuum and had not yet laced up his tan bucks.

She could say that she had spent the last five miles of the ride home from the hospital behind . . . a thresher, a tractor, a backhoe? Or she could explain that for the past ten days she'd only left the hospital when she was sure that Katie was sleeping deeply enough that she wouldn't wake soon but not so deeply as to be in danger of slipping off into some other realm; and to leave Katie there this morning, after she'd waked up but before the doctor had made her rounds, had been difficult. Or she could tell the truth. She was dreading this interview with Mrs. Thoms from the state's Department of Social Services, almost as much as she had dreaded the daily debridement of Katie's burns. On her way home for the first time in over a week, she had stopped once for coffee, once for half a Xanax, and a third time for a pack of cigarettes, which she had later tossed unopened into a trash can when she stopped again to fill the Subaru with gas.

"Mom, Mom." Their seven-year-old, Ben, came running out to the driveway as Lily was pulling up the emergency brake. Brakes, gates, safety straps—she always remembered them now.

"That lady's going to be here any minute, Mom." Ben allowed himself to be kissed when Lily stepped out of the car and even reciprocated with a one-armed hug.

"I missed you, buddy, a lot."

"I missed you too."

"You look nice."

Ben looked down at his navy-blue shorts and white golf shirt. "We're supposed to," he said, looking up now at Lily's brown T-shirt freckled with bleach.

"I know. I'm going to change."

"How's the little?" he said, studying her face for a moment, then bending down to pull up a fat weed from between two squares of slate on the front walk.

"Good. She misses you and Greg."

"Will she still have the bandages on when she comes home?"

Lily stopped walking and looked down at Ben, engrossed in uprooting a whole family of weeds now. "Her legs look much better. A little pink, that's all. Nothing like before, no blisters, nothing like that."

Ben had walked in while Jack was changing Katie's bandages that first night, after the doctor in the ER had sent her home. He'd seen the tops and sides of his baby sister's feet and the front of one leg bubbling with green, fluid-filled blisters. By the time Jack carried her into the Shriners Burns Institute in Boston the next morning, Katie's feet were swollen and she was running a fever of 104. The doctor who admitted her at the Shriners cursed under his breath as he picked threads of macerated gauze out of the oozing blisters. Not nearly enough Silvadene ointment had been applied by the emergency room physician at their local hospital, the one who'd negligently released Katie from the ER, the one who'd later filed the report of possible abuse.

Jack was waiting for them just inside the house, behind the screen door. Through the mesh, Lily could see that he had dressed himself to match Ben, with navy pants instead of shorts. She imagined that Greg was similarly clothed.

"The Von Trapps," she said.

"Who's that?" Ben asked, sidling up to her.

"Christ, Lillian," Jack said wearily. "It's five past."

"I know," she said, fingering the blond curls at the back of Ben's head.

"You're just lucky you didn't pull into the driveway after her."

"I am lucky." Lily took her hand from Ben and squeezed the trigger of the door handle. "I'd say we're all lucky."

He'd done a good job of cleaning. The wood floors were free of any sign of the outdoors, of the dried grass and sand of summertime, of the three children who usually lived there. Jack had polished the dining-room table and cut some peonies from out back, and he'd bought a new high chair and placed it here, in this room where no one in her right mind would feed a sixteen-month-old, but where there were no hot plates or grills or burners, only mahogany and porcelain and glass.

She wondered what he'd done with the old high chair. She hoped he'd thrown it out. On some afternoon in the spotless future when she was rooting around in the basement for somebody's ice skates, she wouldn't want to stumble across that cheap tray with its brown half-moon where the pot must have landed, molecularly rearranging the plastic so that it had begun to fold in upon itself.

The high chair was still functional. The tray still slid across the arms, probably even locked in place. Lily thought that there must be an unfortunate mother in town who could have used it. But she would have hated for that woman to sit night after night feeding her kid rice cereal, staring at the scarred tray, to come to the inevitable conclusion that the chair had once been used by another mother as a means of punishment or even torture.

Lily wondered if Mrs. Thoms would want to see the chair. "Incongruities in the mother's story . . . combined with the presenting injuries . . . necessitate further inquiry in this case," the ER physician's report had stated. She'd want to see the kitchen, "the site." "She'll want to see that you've corrected the problem, installed safety devices, grasped the acute seriousness of the situation," Linda Polowitz, the hospital social worker, and seemingly their only advocate in this whole mess, had said.

Lily hadn't been in the kitchen since the morning of the accident. When they'd come home from the emergency room, Lily had taken Katie, all bandaged and full of Demerol, upstairs. From there she could hear Jack cleaning up—the pot, the eggs, the empty juice glass that had been swept off the counter when Lily had very nearly thrown Katie into the sink to immerse her leg in cold water. When the boys got hungry, Jack fed them. When Lily was thirsty, she ran the tap in the bathroom. And on her endless tour of the house that night, she closed her eyes each time she found herself at the kitchen doorway.

Almost every night at the hospital, she'd dreamed about the kitchen, not her kitchen exactly, but one she knew as well or better, one she could find her way around in night after night in her sleep. The kitchen in her dreams was not so much an amalgam of all the kitchens she had worked in as it was a reduction, an essence.

Each night in her dream, she followed the path of thick, black rubber floor mats from the reach-in at Allison's where she had worked during high school, to the walk-in at L'Hermitage, past the proof boxes at the Hilton, around the grinding Hobart from their own shop, all the way to the storeroom at the Wiscasset Way, where she'd first met Jack fifteen summers ago, and where, on the nights he was left to close up, they would scrub each other with stiff towels in the ancient metal shower, drenching the wooden shelves piled high with worn banquet cloths and yellowing monkey dishes.

Invariably the cries of the babies on the burn unit or the screams and curses of the older children would wake her. She'd lie on the narrow cot, hungover with failure and fatigue after a night spent filling never-ending orders in a strangely silent, cold kitchen, and she'd whisper to herself that everything was really okay. Only a dream. Then, beyond the mound of her own blanketed shoulder, she'd see the metal crib with its caged top, and she'd remember where she was and why.

During those first few critical days the pigskin had to be changed every morning and every night. Lily would grip the bars at the head of Katie's crib as Dr. Wheeler lectured to the interns who crowded into the tiny room.

"The xenograft tricks the skin, keeps the granular skin from forming a scar." She'd try to do most of her talking before removing the bandages. "We're looking to make sure it's not dirty, to see if the skin is attempting to make a comeback."

Lily was grateful that Dr. Wheeler spoke softly. Katie often slept through the winding discussions of edema, lymphangitis, tachycardia, morphine. But as soon as Dr. Wheeler removed the bandages and the burns were exposed to the air, the baby would jerk from sleep into struggle. Her face wet with tears, she'd thrash her head back and forth against the pillow, again and again like a beating.

"Sing to her," Dr. Wheeler would murmur.

"Three little ducks that I once knew . . ." Lily could remember only that one song.

"Hold her down now . . . that's right . . . flush to the mattress," the doctor would instruct as she scraped with the metal tool.

"A fat one, a skinny one, a . . ." Lily would watch herself close in on Katie, her fist around her child's wrist, her bosom pressed against her baby's belly.

"MamaMamaMama . . ." Katie would cry, watering Lily's own dry mouth.

The whirlpool baths followed some days later, when the burned tissue began to separate from the underlying tissue. "Debridement. The eschar needs to be thoroughly sloughed off," the nurse would appeal to Lily, as Lily forced herself to carry Katie through the doorway of the room with the tubs.

"Submerge. Submerge the whole leg . . . just like that." The nurse would shout to be heard above the roaring of the jets.

Lily would sink her arms into the chaos of wound and water and metal. The nurse's freckled arm would disappear beneath the churning water.

"MamaMamaMama . . ." was Katie's sole unbroken plaint above the scrubbing and the roiling. The cure seemed so like the accident itself. "MamaMamaMama . . ." The same word for both mother and pain.

"Mummy, Mummy, Mummy's home," Greg, Lily's four-year-old, called down from the top of the stairs, where he had lined up a traffic jam of Matchbox cars along the base of the new gate Jack had installed.

"How's my guy?" Lily yelled out as she raced up the stairs so fast that Greg squealed. "Can you let me in?" she asked, looking at the locked gate.

"Oh, sure, Mum. It's easy. Look. Oh, wait, wait, wait. This is my tollbooth. First you have to pay me."

Lily uncurled his hand from its pudgy grip on an ambulance and pecked his palm with her fingertips.

"I missed you the whole time you were gone," he said, as he swung open the gate.

"I missed you, too." She hugged the top of his head and bent over and kissed his hair. "Maybe you should pick up some of these," she said, starting down the hall to her bedroom. "We wouldn't want anybody to trip."

"You mean that lady, right? The lady who's coming to talk to me and Ben about safety and stuff, right?"

"Right, honey."

Lily swung open her closet door and took a look. Jack had brought her something to wear last night when he'd come to see Katie in the hospital. After Jack had rocked Katie to sleep, singing "Mountain of Love," Lily had walked him downstairs and waited in the lobby while he ran from street-light to streetlight toward his parked van. She watched as he ran back with something dangling from a dry-cleaning bag. She wished she had gone with him. It was warm out and she would have liked to run fast, feet pounding the pavement, scot-free.

As she waited, she pretended she was in stride with him, that she could hear his breathing, see his chest rise and fall with something other than the weight of his anger. She forced herself to look around the lobby at the security guard and the two Shriners waiting to walk some red-eyed mother or aunt out to her car, and then she rewarded herself by looking past her own reflection in the glass door to the street again.

When she spotted Jack, she registered a kind of thrill that she momentarily mistook for love, but realized was envy.

"I'm not going to wear a dress," she said, as he emerged from the revolving door. He walked past her to one of the insistently cheerful orange vinyl couches and laid down the dry-cleaning bag. It was the blue linen dress she'd worn to Jack's father's funeral three years before and hadn't worn since. It looked to her like a dress for a funeral.

"It looks like a dress for a job interview," she said, lifting up the plastic.

"And . . ."

"I already have the job, and it's not at the Bank of Boston, which—"

"Fine," he said, heading toward the door.

"Thank you . . . for bringing it." She started to follow him. He was shaking his head back and forth.

"I mean, I'm sorry. Really, I'm sorry." She reached out to touch his wrist, but he shook her off and kept walking. "You've got to admit," she said, smiling, "it was sort of a Perry Mason thing to do. Don't you think?"

She laughed, but he didn't. She watched as he slipped into one of the sections of revolving door and turned out onto the street.

"How about this one, Mum?" Greg stuck his skirt-draped head from out of the front line of clothing in her closet. He loved to hide in there, walking slowly through the flannel shirts and corduroy pants and, in the back, the ridiculous cache of silk dresses that had belonged to her grandmother.

She usually hated for him to play in her closet. But the list of things her children did that irked her had been erased. She felt a vague gratitude toward Ben and Greg now, something more companionate than maternal.

Either Jack or his mother had brought the boys to the hospital nearly every day. They weren't allowed upstairs—risk of infection was too high on the unit. So they would sit downstairs with Lily at the big yellow table near the vending machines and show her their scorecards from miniature golf. They'd ask her again if she knew that Winstead Lake had been closed all because one dumb kid—the one who spent last summer telling about the *Titanic*—had got sick from drinking the water there. Ben was getting Mr. Rossi for second grade. The letter had been mailed home the other day. Nana wouldn't buy frozen pizza. Daddy was mad.

She would listen to them talk as if she were an invalid and they were describing a life at which she could only guess. There was a distance. She loved them, but didn't deserve them. She had been stripped of her rank. She couldn't imagine telling them what to do, let alone reprimanding them. And as she watched Greg now, walking in one pair of high heels all over the other shoes at the bottom of her dusty closet, she wondered if scolding wasn't a kind of bond, the constant affirmation of mother's and child's place.

"This one, Mum. This one is really it." Greg had pulled forward a long, flowered split-skirt dress she'd worn to her mother-in-law's on Easter.

"You think?" she said. He nodded.

She moved in toward the mirror beside the closet and took a long look, something she hadn't done in over a week. She seemed to have shrunk down from her five feet four inches and away from the seams and waistband of her summer-weight clothes. A week of fluorescent hospital sun had leached the olive from her skin. Her straight hair had grown beyond the edges of its bob. "Midnight tresses," her father had called them, back when she was young and her hair was long and truly black. Now, coarse white strands arced wildly across her head like so many dying comets.

"And these to go with it." Greg held up a pair of spike-heeled black velvet shoes she couldn't remember ever having worn. "These shoes would be purrr-fect," he said, in what she hoped was an unconscious imitation of herself and the way she sometimes exaggerated to punch up the relentless routine of dressing and grooming children.

"I don't know about the shoes," she said, tossing her shorts and shirt into the wicker hamper in the corner of the bedroom. She unzipped the dress that Greg had picked out.

"They're kind of . . ."

"Steep?" he offered.

She nodded. "I might fall over, and that wouldn't look very good."

"No," he said. "It wouldn't."

Looking good, sounding good, that's what the next hour or two was all about. "Act like you have nothing to hide," Linda, the hospital social worker, had said as they sat in her office on Friday.

Lily had looked over at Jack, willing him to return the glance, but he was looking down at his hands, picking at the Band-Aid on his thumb. He'd cut himself on the meat slicer at work.

"Attitude counts. Maybe it would help you to understand where they're coming from. Burns are the second most frequent cause of accidental death in kids age one to four. It takes one second for an adult to receive a full-thickness burn from water heated to one hundred and sixty degrees. Children's skin is thinner, so the exposure time is even less. Second-degree burns, certainly full-thickness burns, raise flags. Emergency room physicians are mandatory reporters. And splash burns can be tough to call."

Jack shook his head, and Lily could hear him suck his teeth.

"But she's going to be fine," Lily pleaded. "Dr. Wheeler's prognosis for her is excellent. Some scarring, some depigmentation." The threat was over. The infection that had coursed through Katie at the outset had been successfully treated. She had avoided a skin graft. They'd splinted her right leg and ankle into the position of function, and after the first week, they'd started her on physical therapy. For thirty minutes each day, the splint and the bandages were removed and Katie was forced to point and flex her feet, to move the burned skin over the bones in her ankles and toes. She was not expected to suffer any loss of contour or function on either of her feet or her right leg. "That's important, isn't it?" Lily said. "That she's going to be fine?"

"Since no one else was home at the time, they'll need to be reassured of the accidental nature of the injuries," Linda explained. "When all the measurements add up—her physical dexterity, the size and placement of the pot—you'll be golden. They'll be looking for a cause, a reasonable explanation for why the burns on the feet were more severe than the ones higher up on the leg, which sort of runs counter to gravity." Linda flashed them some kind of knowing smile.

"And will they be looking at the hack in the ER who's trying to cover his own negligence in releasing her?" Lily said.

Linda nodded vigorously. "Try to enter into this with a positive, cooperative attitude. I don't know this Thoms, which is good. She doesn't have a reputation for hostility or extreme idiocy or anything that precedes her. But understand, these caseworkers are not licensed. Few if any are MSWs. It isn't often that these people get to ride out to the burbs to check up on professional white couples with private pediatricians. All I'm saying is, don't make it any juicier than it already is. Put the BMW in a friend's garage, stow the mink in the basement—"

"It's a Subaru and a down coat," Jack said, cutting her off. "And when you say 'these people'—"

"Jack," Lily interrupted, "I think Linda is only trying to warn us that we might be dealing with someone who has an ax to grind, a paper pusher, a public—"

"I think we all understand what Linda is saying," Jack said, squeezing his bandaged thumb with his other hand. Lily looked across the desk at Linda, fairly certain that the older woman was unaware that Jack had stopped just short of calling her a racist.

"She'll want to talk with your other children. You have . . . two—"

"Boys," Lily said.

"Most likely she'll want to speak with each of them alone."

# Lily

"Mom. Hurry up. She's here," Ben yelled from downstairs. "She's coming up the driveway right now."

Lily could tell from his voice, the fast whine of it, and the slapping of his sneakers—first partway up the stairs, then thinking better of it, down the hallway to the front door—that he was nervous. Of the three children, he was the most like her. She supposed it was from having spent the most time with her when she was still herself, before she became so much of a mother to all these children. He had even called her Lily when he was a toddler, thinking it funny to refer to her the same way that his father did, to get the same response, the turn, the smile. He tended to be anxious, like Lily usually was. And she suspected that her uncharacteristic lack of preparedness was as alarming to him as his father's furious silence. Katie's accident had turned things inside out. Mother and father had swapped roles, and subsequently temperaments. Lily doubted Ben was old enough to know that this veneer of calm, this lassitude on her part, was really still a function of shock and fatigue, that her heel-dragging was the only hostile act that depression allowed her.

His father was another matter. The children were used to him being loud. He talked loudly, laughed loudly, made them laugh loudly. Lily could always tell when Jack was in a room with the kids—the steady buildup of squeals edging toward screams as he pressed Greg to the bathroom ceiling with one thick chef's arm, or dangled Katie's Barney over a whirling bowl of batter, or dashed when the phone rang, straight toward an unpeeled banana, cupping it to his mouth and ear.

Lily excused all kinds of lapses in Jack because he could make her laugh. His fuse was long, too long, she had often thought. It took a willful and heinous offense for him to lose his temper, and now he was angry all the time. His anger invited no response. He was not like Lily, who blew off steam in great verbal clouds on a regular basis, then stood back and waited to see what would transpire. No, Jack's anger was hard-boiled and resolved. After thirty-eight years of open-mindedness, he had received in Katie's accident definitive evidence, proving beyond a shadow of a hope, that life, in general, was an exercise in disappointment, and that life with Lily, in particular, was an exercise in agony.

"Hi, Ginny Thoms." The caseworker stood up from her place in the good chair in the living room when Lily came downstairs.

"Sorry," Lily, said, greeting the very young woman. "I just came from the hospital. I'm running a little behind, I guess."

"Coffee?" Jack said.

Lily looked at him in a panic. They hadn't worked this out. Was he offering some to the caseworker, or asking Lily if she'd made any, knowing full well that she hadn't? He was sitting on the couch with the boys on either side of him. That left only the piano stool for Lily.

"No thank you." Mrs. Thoms gathered up her long blond hair and laid it across the front of one breast like a shield.

"Tea?" Jack countered.

Lily spun the seat a few times to raise the height of the stool.

"Actually, a glass of water would be great. Ooh, goodness, did you make these?" With one hand she held her short denim skirt against the back of her legs and with the other she reached for a mini-muffin from a plate on the coffee table.

"No, we did," Ben said.

"You baked these all by yourself?"

"No, our grandmother did it with us. He's too young to use the stove or the mixer," Ben said, pointing to his brother. "And I'm not supposed to either," he added after a pause.

"We're all a little nervous," Lily said, as Jack reentered with the water. Prepare them, the hospital social worker had said, but whatever you do, don't coach them. Lily and Jack had spoken with the boys when they'd come to the hospital to visit the day before. As soon as Jack started talking, Greg had wandered to the far end of the lobby and begun to construct a teepee out of the various Shriners brochures: the burning house, the boy in the wheelchair, the time-lapse photo of the girl with the crutches.

But Ben had been confused. "What am I supposed to say?" He poked the plastic tip of a shoelace into one of the eyelets of his sneakers.

"The truth," Jack said.

"What if I don't know the answers?"

"Oh, buddy," Lily said, sinking down in the seat next to him. "It's not a test. Just a conversation."

"What about?"

"Our family," Jack said.

"Like how old everybody is and what grades we're in?"

"Yeah, mostly things like that," Jack said, slipping his hands into his pants pockets. "Maybe a few other things. I don't really know. We've never done this before."

"Done what?" Ben looked up at him.

"We've never gone through this kind of thing before, this interview."

"Does she want you and Mom to cater a party or something, and she like wants to know if you're good at it?"

Lily laughed. "No, sweetie. It's about Katie and her accident. I guess they just want to make sure we don't have a lot of accidents at our house." She stifled the urge to put her arm around him, knowing he wouldn't like her to do that here, in public. Instead, she lowered her elbows to her knees and cradled her chin in her hands.

"Who is this lady?"

"Mrs. Thomas."

"Thoms," Jack corrected.

"Is she like a doctor or something?" Ben asked.

Jack shook his head.

"Well, is she a policeman or a sheriff, or something like that?"

"Of course not," Jack said. "She's—"

"I'm sure she'll be very nice to you and Greg, and if she needs to talk to you at all, it will only be for a few minutes. Okay?" Lily said.

Ben shrugged and, after a while, looked up at Lily and smiled knowingly. "Let's just hope that Greg the dreg doesn't mess it up."

"I'd like to talk to each of you separately for a few minutes, and then maybe we can all talk together at the end, okay?" Mrs. Thoms took a sip of water, loosened the drawstring at the top of her woven knapsack, and pulled out a bent file folder.

"No, Daddy, I want to stay with you," Greg blurted out, nestling his head into his father's shoulder.

"Honey, you're not going anywhere, we're all—" Lily said.

"Greg? Is that right?" The caseworker leaned forward in her chair and smiled warmly. "How about if I talk to you and your brother together, okay?"

Greg shook his head and stuffed his face into Jack's lap.

"Come on now," Jack said firmly, trying to stand him up.

Lily didn't know what to do. Her inclination was to pick him up and hold him, but what if her physical interference was misinterpreted? She remained on the stool. Indifferent, uninvolved. Better that than getting caught in the crossfire of a tantrum and having it look as if she were battling it out with a four-year-old.

"Did I see a swing set outside?" Mrs. Thoms said, trying again. She nervously spun her wedding ring around her finger.

Greg didn't answer, and after a while Ben said, "Yes, in the backyard."

"How about if we go out on the swings, the three of us, for a few minutes?"

"Daddy, too?" Greg said.

"Well, Mom and Dad are going to stay inside—"

"No. I want my daddy to come, too."

"I'll give you a great big push, as high as the sky."

Ben shook his head and said softly, "He doesn't like to go high. He's only four."

Jack looked up at the young woman and said, "Maybe you could talk to my wife first, and by then . . ."

"Okay," Mrs. Thoms answered, this time hitting those two notes with a forced perkiness. "Is there somewhere we can go . . ."

"I'll take the kids outside," Jack said, picking up Greg.

"Twenty minutes should do it." The caseworker smiled anxiously.

Lily hooked the heels of her sandals around the footrest of the stool and tried to smile, too. They waited for the slam of the screen door.

"You look tired," Mrs. Thoms said, staring down at her chart.

"I've been sleeping with Katie at the hospital."

"And your husband?"

"Well, he's been here, with the boys."

"Oh, from what they said, I thought that a grandparent was watching them."

"Well, during the day, yes, my mother-in-law has come up—"

"Do you work?"

"Well, I did, up until about a year ago, up until about the time Katie was born. We had a gourmet shop and catering business in town."

"Boston?"

"Oh, no, right here in Winstead, down by the train station."

"Oh. And now?" Mrs. Thoms asked, looking straight at Lily, while fishing around in her carpetbag of a pocketbook for a pen.

"When Katie was born, Jack took a job with the Quabbin Group, running the executive dining room. It's a large company with benefits, and . . . it seemed to make the most sense at the time." Lily reasoned that the whole truth—they'd been forced to close Station Break after more than eight years because they could no longer make a living from it—was beyond the purview of a caseworker.

"Then you're home alone with the children all day?"

"Yeah, well, mostly. We still do some occasional catering. Well, Jack does, and I'm sort of, of counsel." Lily smiled.

Sometimes now she might ask Jack what he had cooked that week at work and he might tell her. It had been almost two years since they'd gone out to dinner and raced back home in a great white heat, stopping at the last open supermarket on the way. Jack would uncork a bottle of wine and Lily would reach for the large wooden cutting boards above the refrigerator. Slicing into the dewy meat of a summer squash or scraping the seeds from the inside of an ancho chili, Lily would feel a surge of adrenaline, as if a powerful engine had been ignited, and she and Jack were about to travel together far and fast. She remembered eating at Fenimore's in the Back Bay one night, then hurrying across town, without discussion, to buy live lobster. By the time they got home, the four-pound lobster had clawed a hole through the bag, leaving a trail of salt water from the car to the kitchen. She laid the magnificent thing belly side down on the cutting board and stroked its black hard shell with her left hand. As Jack swiftly brought down the blade of his knife, Lily flinched, almost imperceptibly. Life was too rich.

At two that morning she and Jack sat down at their own kitchen table, one plate two forks, and ate Lobster Wellington for the second time in one night. It was understood between them that they could improve on anything, that anything was possible. Cooking together, they had assumed an identity far headier than husband and wife. But now that the great engine of their creative life together had been cut, they were plummeting precipitously into impoverished territory.

"You must be bored, home all day," Mrs. Thoms said.

A warm breeze blew through the living room and sent the plastic-tipped cords for the blinds rattling against the windowsills. Lily shook her head. "Not at all," she said.

"Well." Mrs. Thoms shifted her tiny body in the overstuffed chair. "I assume you've taken the time to find out how all this goes . . . the initial report, the 51A, then my 51B?"

"Yes," Lily said, leaning slightly against the old upright and accidentally sounding a note. "We've spoken to a few people at DSS."

A few days after things began to "miraculously" turn around for Katie and it seemed that she wouldn't be needing a skin graft after all, Jack had received a letter issuing the formal complaint against them. He had spent most of the day on the phone with DSS, trying to find out who had filed the report. By the time he'd gotten to the hospital that evening, Lily had already been paid a call by the hospital social worker.

Linda had approached her in the playroom, where Katie was busy filling and refilling a plastic egg carton with slightly chewed plastic eggs. Lily stood up quickly and greeted Linda, sure that she had come for some informal play therapy with Katie. This place takes care of everything, she had thought as she watched Linda ease herself into one of the child-size red chairs.

"Do you like to go shopping with Mommy?" she asked. Without looking up at Lily, she continued in her remedial tone, "I'm going to need to interview you and your husband. It seems there's been some question somewhere along the line about Kate's accident. Standard stuff, you know. Sixty percent of the parents and guardians who walk into this place end up going through this. It's the nature of the beast."

Lily had replayed this scene again and again for the past week, trying to understand what had been said, what was happening, what could happen. But it was like the accident itself, really. To envision what had occurred during the few minutes in which she had left the kitchen that Friday morning, a leap was needed. A suspension of disbelief was necessary to comprehend that somebody could actually suggest that she had burned her baby. And something akin to a total conversion would be necessary for her to even begin to entertain the idea that she might now lose her Katie, not to this injury, but to the Commonwealth of Massachusetts.

Some part of Lily was stuck back in her bedroom, upstairs for longer than she should have been, that Friday morning. And the rest of her, the part that had motored on until the following Thursday, the day she learned that she was named as a possible child abuser, was frozen in the play therapy room on the third floor of the Shriners Burns Institute in Boston. The Lily that was on the piano stool now was like a figure trapped inside one of those cheap holograms the kids sometimes brought home in their goody bags after birthday parties. The context here was continually shifting, impossible to isolate.

"I make my report based on this interview and a review of the scene," Mrs. Thoms continued. "Then all your materials are looked at together—the hospital social worker's recommendation, although you do understand that she does not work for the state, your pediatrician, your priest, whatever."

Lily nodded.

"How long have you and your husband been married, Mrs. Keliher?"

"Sterne. I'm Sterne."

"Oh. You go by your maiden name," she said, as if it were an alias. "And you've been married . . . ?"

"Twelve years," Lily said.

"And these children are . . . all from this marriage?"

Lily nodded.

"How long at this address?"

"Six years."

"Do you have friends in town?" Mrs. Thoms asked, scribbling loudly on a form she had attached to a pink acrylic clipboard.

Lily wondered if this was a summer job. The caseworker reminded her of the self-important seventeen-year-olds who spent the hot months lifeguarding at the town lake.

"Of course," Lily said. "I mean, I can't imagine living any-where that long without making friends."

"And would you mind giving me the names and numbers of two for references?"

"No problem," Lily said.

Each night at the hospital, after she had gotten Katie to sleep, Lily had walked to the pay phone in the hallway outside the burn unit. She had talked to her brother in Chicago once, but her close friends she had called every other day. She had even cried to Julia. Her friend Ellen had worked out a rotating schedule of invitations for the boys, and in so doing had spread the story of the accident far and wide. It was the kind of story that mothers of young children are incapable of keeping to themselves. All the elements were so common, the very stuff of a weekday morning: the radio, the unmade bed, the eggs in the pot, the high chair, the baby. Lily had in the past been guilty of this same kind of talis-manic gossip, as if the act of telling and retelling somehow inoc-ulates the teller against similar tragedy. And so she had freely

endorsed the passage of this information, the story of the accident, but not this business with the state. That she had told to no
one.

"Family?" Mrs. Thoms asked.

"My husband's family all live pretty nearby."

"And how about you—parents or siblings nearby?"

The woman's assumption that Lily still had her parents irked
her. "I have a brother in Chicago."

"Church?" Mrs. Thoms asked, her eyes on her clipboard.

"Hmm?" Lily said, leaning slightly toward the caseworker.

"I need to know . . . the degree to which the family is connected to the community," she said, clearly reading from the
form. "I do know that you had a priest pay a call to your baby in
the hospital. Are you fairly active in your church?"

Jack's mother had insisted on having her priest visit Katie in
the hospital. She also now insisted on giving the man more than
partial credit for Katie's having avoided a skin graft.

"Oh, no. My husband, his family is Catholic. I'm Jewish."

The caseworker placed her petite hands theatrically over her
ears. "I'm sorry, I didn't mean for you to tell me your religion. That,
of course, is not a factor. Okay, so why don't we go into the . . ."
She paused while she shuffled through some papers on her lap.
"Into the kitchen, right?"

Lily rose slowly from the piano stool and led the way.

Mrs. Thoms gathered up her papers and her bag for the short
trip.

"What an interesting house," she said, following Lily into the
center hall, which separated the living room from the kitchen
and dining room.

"It's old. And it's in need of some work." From behind she
heard a misstep in the regular flapping of the young woman's
sandals. She turned to see Mrs. Thoms recovering her balance.
"Are you all right? It's these scatter rugs, I'm sorry."

Mrs. Thoms nodded and reembraced her stack of papers.

"I know they sell those pads for putting underneath, and I've been meaning to get some."

"It's very quiet back here."

"It's great for the kids, being so far from the road."

"You really don't have any neighbors, do you?" Mrs. Thoms said, stopping at the entrance of the kitchen to jot this down.

"Well, of course we do, we just can't reach out and touch them." Lily laughed. "I mean, down the road, as you came up, on the left, the big white farmhouse, they have two boys." Lily pointed out the window over the kitchen sink. "My husband just finished building a soccer goal. It's great for the kids—half the town's been back here playing soccer this spring, it seems."

Mrs. Thoms smiled and spread her paperwork and her clutch of pencils on the kitchen table. "I just have to find one other form here . . ." she said, beginning to sort the papers into piles.

Lily craned to try to read something, anything. But all that she could make out was that DSS didn't have high-quality copy machines. She straightened a few dish towels and fingered the spoon rest and wished that the phone would ring. Monday morning, ten a.m. What kind of people were these whose phone never rang?

In his effort to clean up, Jack had erased all evidence of the fullness of their lives. He'd stripped the refrigerator door of the schedules and appointment cards that had all but completely covered it during the school year. He'd stowed the stack of half-read newspapers and community bulletins somewhere out of view. There was no mail in sight, as if they were people who didn't receive even junk mail.

"So, why don't you just walk me through the whole thing," Mrs. Thoms said.

"Excuse me?"

"The day of the accident. Show me what happened."

"Well." Lily fingered the collar of her dress and leaned against the sink. "Well, it was the last day of school for both of my sons.

Ben was finishing first grade, and Greg, Greg's nursery school was having a family picnic that morning. I was supposed to make eight egg salad sandwiches. I'd done about half of them the night before, but I'd run out of eggs. So I was just finishing up the rest that morning."

"You were cooking?" Mrs. Thoms said, writing as fast as she could.

Lily nodded. "I had about six eggs—"

"How were you cooking them?"

"Well, I was hard-boiling them. I had them in a pot on the stove."

"Was it covered?"

"The pot? No. I was in a hurry for them to cook, so—"

"Can I see the pot?" Mrs. Thoms said, writing carefully on her form. "I just need to see the size of it, see where the handle is, to see if, you know . . . Katie weighs about?"

"Twenty-two, twenty-three pounds, I think. Well, at least before this week." Lily pushed the faucet arm back and forth a few times. The good short stockpot had been in the refrigerator, filled with leftover spaghetti and sauce. So she'd grabbed the ancient tin pot, the one Greg liked to use as a drum in his marching band. It was useless for anything but boiling water. "I'm pretty sure the pot is gone."

"What do you mean?"

"Well, my husband cleaned up. I think he just threw everything away. The kitchen was a mess. There was a glass on the counter that broke when I tried to get Katie's leg in the cold water.

"I think we're getting ahead of ourselves here," Mrs. Thoms said, pushing her chair back slightly from the round kitchen table. "The pot was on which burner?"

Lily pointed to the front one. The stove was old, and none of the burners were level. "It's the only big one that works. That other one in the back has been broken for, oh, I don't know . . . I mean, it's not dangerous or anything—"

"And this?" The social worker pointed to the stove guard that Jack had just attached. "Was this here?"

Lily shook her head.

The social worker scratched away with her pencil. "And the baby," she said, looking now right at Lily. "Where exactly was the baby?"

"She was eating a bowl of cereal in her high chair."

"Which was?"

"I'd say about over there." Lily walked across the kitchen. "I'd say about over here. I usually put it here. Well, I used to—with the back of it against this counter, so that she could watch me at the sink."

"Then what happened?"

"I ran upstairs for a moment to do something," Lily said.

"To do what?"

Up until now, in the emergency room, with Jack, and with the social worker at the Shriners, no one had thought to ask her what she was doing when she was out of the room, or even how long she was gone. "I had to make the bed," she said, doubting herself.

"The baby was still in the high chair when you left the room? She was alone?"

"Strapped in," Lily said.

"Eating?"

"She may have had a few Cheerios on the tray. I don't know. To tell you the truth, I really don't remember." Choking was the childhood accident Lily had, until ten days ago, worried about the most. When she'd left the room there had been only a few soggy Cheerios on the tray. Lily had taken away Katie's cereal bowl and her cup after both had been thrown to the floor twice amid peals of laughter.

What Lily had intended to do that morning was call in to Gwen Harrington's show on WXBO. Harrington's guest, a psychologist, was going off the air at ten. The microwave clock read

9:53. All she wanted was a few minutes to herself to run upstairs and make this phone call in relative silence, to bring up a point that no one had yet made in the two hours she had been straining to follow this vapid discussion of motherhood as she drove two kids to school and ran in and out of the car doing errands.

It had already been a bad day. Katie had screamed her way through the Red Brick General Store because she wanted something, Lily didn't know what and didn't care. She could be so stubborn, especially compared to the boys. Lily's mother-in-law called it ego strength. "I've never seen a baby with such a clear sense of herself." Katie was willful in a way that continually surprised Lily. Jack said it was a stage—"Call it 'hell' and give it a time frame."

When they'd reached the checkout at the market, Lily had perched Katie on the high counter, and the baby had screamed in fear, grabbing Lily's hair as Lily rifled through her purse for her wallet. "Goddammit, Kate," she yelled, and the baby had cried even harder. She couldn't believe that she had just heard this "noted" psychologist say that unless you were out there discovering a cure for cancer there was no more important job than staying home with your kids.

Except for the cashier, the store was filled with men. They were on their way to work and they stood behind her in line with doughnuts and rolls stacked on top of sixteen-ounce coffees. None of them looked as though he was on his way to cure cancer. She hadn't thought about what she looked like to them, not then. She was too busy worrying about whether she had the $1.13 to pay for the eggs and whether there was going to be enough time for her to cook them, let them cool, and make them into a salad all before ten-thirty, when she would need to leave the house.

Now she wondered if there was some way for those people in the General Store to be contacted, unofficially subpoenaed. There were any number of people in town who had, over the past few weeks, seen Katie in the post office or the dry cleaner or the liquor store, seen her arch her back and swing out her arms and legs at the inception of a tantrum. And there were any number of people around town who had witnessed Lily respond to the six-teen-month-old with all the control of a child herself.

"Okay, let me get this straight." Mrs. Thoms stood up from her seat at the kitchen table and walked over to the empty space where Lily had roughly indicated she usually kept the high chair. She pulled her skirt down from the hem with a slight wig-gle. "Are you in the habit of leaving your baby alone at meal-time?"

"Look," Lily began, but she caught herself, swallowed some air, and walked to the cabinet where she kept the coffee mugs. Taped to the inside of the door were the instructions for the Heimlich maneuver, the same ones that had been posted in every restaurant she'd worked in since the mid-'80s.

"I know about choking," she said, gripping the white wooden knob of the cabinet. "I've taken infant and child first aid and CPR twice now, enough times to know that I don't ever want to have to use it. Meals are social times. I don't even leave my older children when they're eating. I left the room for a minute, and when I did—"

Lily stopped. She had told this story so many times now—to people in white coats in hospitals, to friends over the phone, to the mothers in the burn unit, who jumped each time hot coffee splashed down from the mouth of the vending machine—and always when she told it she was far away from this room, from the moment of the story, and more important, from the point of it. Up until this minute, the point had been Katie's injuries, Katie's prognosis, Katie's recovery. Now the point was Lily.

"Was the water boiling when you left the room?"

"I really don't know." Lily was standing on the threshold of the kitchen, leaning against the doorframe.

"How much water was in the pot?"

"I don't know. The pot was small. A quart, maybe less."

"How long were you out of view?" Mrs. Thoms grabbed her clipboard from the table. "How long was she out of your sight?"

"I just ran upstairs."

"A few seconds?"

Lily stared. The accident had happened at the end of a long week. It was hot. She was tired. And she was pissed. Pissed at Katie for whining so much, pissed at herself for yelling so much. Pissed that some woman was getting on the radio throwing down a moral gauntlet, telling other women what they should and should not be doing with their lives, when no one ever told men they had to choose between fathering their children and furthering their careers. Most women who worked had to. It wasn't a matter of learning to make do with less or working for the extras, as this expert kept insisting.

Katie had banged on her empty tray a few times when Lily left the kitchen. Lily paused at the top of the stairs and listened. The baby wasn't crying, she was only mad. If Lily could be granted two, three, five minutes in which to function in a different realm, she'd return to the kitchen a better mother. Everything would be okay.

The number. Lily reached the top of the stairs and realized that she'd probably heard the phone number of the radio station repeated twenty times this morning, but she couldn't remember it. She cursed herself out loud and ran down the stairs to the front hall closet for the phone book. Katie was quiet now, so Lily ran back upstairs without looking into the kitchen.

She picked up her nightgown from the floor by her bed and began rehearsing what she would say. She slid her hand between the mattress and the box spring and tucked in the top sheet. It was unnatural for one person to stay home all day and only care for the home and the children, and for the other to be gone all day from those children and do nothing but work in the world outside the home. Hadn't we evolved beyond that, yet? She pulled the sheet taut on Jack's side of the bed. She wasn't the kind of person who wanted her thoughts broadcast all over the greater Boston area, was she? She pulled up the spread and placed her grandmother's doll with the magic wand on top of the pillows. God, who the hell did she think she was?

"And you think she pulled the chair along the counter—like hand over hand—until she reached the pot on this front burner?" Mrs. Thoms pointed with the eraser end of her pencil.

Lily nodded. She'd seen the high chair skate across the tile floor in a game the boys sometimes played.

"Was the pot handle in or out?"

"I always try to remember to turn my pot handles to the back of the stove." Lily paused. "I'm not sure, though."

Mrs. Thoms's pencil moved rapidly across her paper now, deboning this mess, Lily thought, into tidy piles of right and wrong.

"Did she scream immediately?"

Lily nodded. She had never been able to distinguish among the various types of cries in any of her newborns, but as they got older it was easy to pick out pain from frustration or anger or injustice. And this cry was unlike any she had ever heard. It was, itself, a kind of siren. As Lily ran down the stairs and neared the kitchen, she involuntarily screamed, matching Katie's volume, as if to staunch the pain. She alternated between "Oh my God!" and "It's all right, baby, it's okay!"

Katie's face was red and tight, not from crying, but from exertion. She was frantically trying to push herself out of the chair. Lily ran to her, crunching bits of eggshell underfoot. The floor near the high chair was wet. When Lily finally reached the baby and gripped the sides of the high chair tray, she saw that it was filled with steaming water. The small white plastic tray had buckled slightly at one corner, probably where the pot had landed and rested for a moment. Katie was kicking her legs furiously and screaming, "MamaMamaMama."

Working counter to her every instinct, Lily moved slowly. She slid the high chair tray away from the baby. As she began to turn with the tray to place it on the counter, some of the boiling water that had collected in the trough around the edges splashed onto Lily's shorts, and she jumped. Struggling to unhook the strap around Katie's waist, she saw that the baby's bare legs were dripping wet. The front of her right leg below the knee and the tops of both feet, even her little round toes, were bright red, as if from a bad sunburn. She whipped Katie from the high chair and headed for the sink, kicking the dry, hot pan that lay on the floor and sending the two remaining eggs rolling out across the uneven tile floor.

The sink was full of breakfast dishes. Lily smacked the faucet to cold with her elbow, and with one hand began tossing the knives and glasses up onto the counter. A juice glass glided across the large puddle that had formed on the Formica and smashed onto the floor. Lily only barely registered the crash above the sound of Katie's screaming.

"Why didn't you call 911?" Mrs. Thoms asked.

"I wasn't really sure what had happened at first. Katie was trying to get out of the chair, and as I went to her I saw the water, the hot water on the tray, underfoot, on her feet. I filled the sink with cold water and then I put her legs in it."

"And then?"

"I knew the best thing was the cold water. As it turns out, I probably saved her the skin graft, keeping her in that water for as long as I did." As far as Lily knew, this effort with the cold water was about as beneficial for Katie as the late-night hospital-room visit from her mother-in-law's young priest. It was hard to tell a story in which your every action was the wrong one. So Lily had allowed herself this one embellished instance of good mothering.

"Didn't you call your husband, a neighbor?" Mrs. Thoms glanced out the window then, as if remembering their "isolation."

"Jack was at work. The company's in Government Center. It would have taken him forty-five minutes to get here."

Jack had asked her the same question in the emergency room. Why hadn't she called him first? The five minutes she had forced herself to force Katie to remain in the cold water had seemed an eternity. "It's almost over, honey, almost over now," she kept repeating to the baby. Some part of her really thought that this immersion in cold water would be enough. Encircling the baby with one arm, Lily dipped her free hand into the water and traced the rest of Katie's body, checking for any other places where she might have been scalded. Not her scalp, her forehead, not her face, thank God, not the almond-shaped eyes she'd inherited from Lily, nor Lily's mother's blunt nose, nor Jack's bowed lips. All these people had remained intact in Katie. She had not melted the skin on her hands, as had the little boy from Lowell whom they would soon meet at the Shriners. Katie's little white hands with the tiny squares of nail were still perfect, as were her round arms and chest and belly. Not even the tops of her thighs had been burned, having been shielded by the high chair tray.

"You didn't call anyone?" Mrs. Thoms asked, seeming to have just noticed the antique phone mounted on the wall directly below the real one.

"I called a friend who has a little boy in Greg's nursery school class. She was going to explain my absence at the picnic and take Greg home to her house if I wasn't back from the emergency room by twelve-thirty."

"Didn't you want someone to come with you?" Mrs. Thoms stared directly at Lily. "I'm not one hundred percent sure I understand your . . . reasoning."

Lily massaged her temples. There could be no pill-taking, not even aspirin, in front of this woman. "I didn't know how bad it was. We live seven minutes from the hospital. I just wanted to get her there. The doctor at the Shriners told us it takes forty-eight hours to assess a thermal burn. Even the doctor in the emergency room classified them then as first-degree burns. I didn't know, I just didn't know."

Before leaving for the hospital, Lily had grabbed a couple of dish towels and thrown them into the cool water in the sink and tried to wrap one each around the baby's legs. Katie was alternately crying and moaning now. As Lily ran to the car, the baby clutched at her bare arms, her hair, her sweaty tank top. Lily couldn't possibly put Katie in her car seat, in the back, where she couldn't see her, couldn't touch her. So she tried to lay her down in the front. But the bucket seat wasn't wide enough, and Lily had ended up holding her somewhere between her lap and the console that housed the emergency brake. She had thought about that, about how dangerous it was to be driving that way, about how something worse than had already happened might happen. She had even thought some keen-eyed policeman might stop her, give her a ticket for breaking the child restraint law, for endangering her daughter, for being a bad mother.

Mrs. Thoms slowly flipped through some of her papers on the table. Lily watched her and wondered if this business with the car seat was going to come up. She opened and closed the silverware drawer a few times. There was an unopened package of napkins left from Katie's first birthday party. The boys had picked out the paper goods—bears in pink tutus. That's what girls like, they'd said. Maybe Lily could make a little party for Katie when she came home from the hospital, just family and cake and ice cream.

"Little ones can be hard to handle, can't they?" Mrs. Thoms said. "Would you say that Katie is a difficult child for you to handle?"

"She's spirited," Lily said.

"What kind of discipline do you use with your children? Your boys seem to be quite . . . calm, but with a spirited child, say?"

"She's only sixteen months old," Lily said.

Mrs. Thoms wrote this down and smiled. "I really have only one more question for you." She looked up at Lily. "Why do you think this happened?"

Lily knew why it had happened. Of course, there had been abuse. Not the kind the caseworker had in mind. No, Lily had not abused the body of her child, but rather the gift of her. Conceiving this third child had been self-indulgent. She'd wanted once more to possess for nine months the thrill of a double life, a dual existence. She'd wanted another chance to transcend her solitary self. At thirty-six, certain possibilities had already boiled out. She would never apprentice in a kitchen in Lyons. She would never be a hot "young" chef. She would never own a restaurant with a three-star rating. But she could have three children. Three children were an accomplishment, as well as a means of slowing down time. Even if she was no longer young, she could remain the mother of young children.

She'd hungered to sate a wholly personal desire, but babies, and certainly children, should never be intended as the complete source of their mothers' private nourishment. And the postpartum depression that loosed itself in Lily after Katie's birth was nothing more than a minute-to-minute reminder of the proper order of things. Babies suckled their mothers to survive, not the other way round.

And so with the advent of this planned but unexpected baby, Lily bobbed and weaved through her days, obsessively scouting escape. Two newspapers were delivered to the house on weekdays and three on Sundays. Lily left them unfolded on tables, counters, and beds. On her way out the door, she'd grab sections to lay down in the front seat of the car, to scan while stopped at a red light or stuck in traffic. She asked Jack to bring home his professional journals from work. A year's worth of *Food Arts* lay on top of her nightstand, in a sloping pile high enough to block her view down the hallway when she was lying in bed. When it was just she and Katie, as it often was now, the radio would be on, news and talk, in the kitchen and the car. She'd even brought a little transistor down to the laundry room. She suspected that all this had less to do with being connected to the world at large and more to do with separating the world of adults from that of babies.

Lily had known it was abuse from the moment the nurse in the emergency room held Katie's leg under the overhead spot. "The dermis has but so many layers," the resident who first saw them said. Lily thought she might vomit as the doctor poured bottle after bottle of cool saline solution over the burns. She remembered how perfect that milky baby skin had looked and smelled when Katie had first been handed to her, just one flight up, in that very building only the year before. Lily knew why the accident had happened. She was being punished for having abused the gift that was her daughter.

"I asked you why you thought this happened," Mrs. Thoms said, somewhat impatiently now.

"Accidents happen," Lily said. "It was an accident."

"Mum, Mum," Greg yelled and banged on the screen door. "I've got to go, Mum, bad. Daddy said to go outside, but I didn't want to."

Mrs. Thoms walked to the back door and swung it open for him with a grand gesture. "When you gotta go, you gotta go."

Greg ignored her and ran through the kitchen.

"Do you need me to turn the light on?" Lily said, half running with him down the hall.

"No," he said, from behind the closed door. "The whole time you were gone I could do it myself."

"Okay. Call me if you need me." Lily walked back into the kitchen slowly.

"So," Mrs. Thoms said, repositioning herself at the table. "You're saying that you think the burns were the result of an accident. Nothing could have been done to prevent it."

"I didn't say that."

"Mum, I'm done and I can't snap," Greg called from the bathroom.

Lily walked toward the hallway, and with the length of the whole kitchen between her and Mrs. Thoms, she turned. "Had I realized that she was capable of pulling herself along in the high chair like that, I never would have placed it where I did."

"Well, frankly, I think it's a bit more complicated than that."

"Mum, I said I couldn't snap." Greg stomped up to Lily. He was struggling to connect the two sides of his waistband.

Lily sank down and snapped his shorts. "Please don't talk to me that way," she said, picking him up and holding him close.

"Do you think parenting classes might help?" Mrs. Thoms asked.

Greg struggled to get down, and then he ran across the kitchen and out the door into the backyard. Before the screen door could slam shut, Lily heard him yell to his brother and his father, "That lady wants Mum to get parents' glasses."

Lily walked up close to Mrs. Thoms now, close enough to notice for the first time the slightest flaw on her perfect face, scarred-over bite marks at the outside edge of one eye. She wanted to say, "I'm a good mother." Instead she said, "My oldest child is seven. In seven years we've only been to the emergency room twice. You can check the records at Lincoln."

"We check the records of a number of area hospitals. Some parents shop around," Mrs. Thoms said, tapping the eraser end of her pencil on the top of her files.

# Lily

Jack wiped his feet slowly on the welcome mat and then pulled the screen door closed behind him. Lily knew he'd want to wash his hands next, so she slid out of his way as he started for the sink. She walked to the corner nearest the back door, behind the kitchen table, and pressed her cheek against the cool wall. From this angle, she could see Mrs. Thoms and the boys outside, but couldn't be seen by them. This corner was where the boys always hid, snorting and slapping each other, when they wanted to scare her as she came in from the yard. Mrs. Thoms was showing them something she'd pulled from her enormous pocketbook.

Jack was making coffee, shaking the open can over the filter, as he always did, without measuring. Lily stuck her finger into the dry soil of the African violet in the center of the table. No one had been watering anything around here.

"You did a good job on the house," she said, looking over at him. His hair was lighter from the time he'd already spent outdoors this spring. He was tan too, that pale melon color he got at the start of each summer, when he was patient enough to take the sun slowly. Except for a softening around his cheekbones and jaw, he looked about the way he had when she'd first met him at twenty-three, "like the beach," she'd said, blue eyes, sandy hair, and skin the warm color of the sky just after the fireball has set. "Really," she said. "Everything looks great."

His back was to her, and he nodded slightly, so slightly that Lily wondered if he hadn't just noticed a nick in the Formica. It was his turn now, and she waited.

He blew a ladybug from the counter into his palm and followed it as it crawled up toward his wristwatch.

"Don't you want to know how it went?" she asked finally.

He looked at her, at the ladybug, at the hissing coffeemaker, then back at her.

"I think we're okay, basically. I mean, it seems like an exercise in humiliation. And maybe that's it." Lily turned and looked out the back door. The boys were laughing, at least Greg was, loudly. "Well, they don't sound too traumatized," she said.

Jack walked to the cupboard and pulled down one mug.

"I thought maybe we could have a little party for Katie when she comes home in a few days. I thought that the boys and I would decorate, and then you could stop and get a cake from Angelo. I'll call him. Maybe your mother would come?" Lily said.

"I think we should have Father Paul talk to her."

"To Mrs. Thoms? You mean your mother's priest?" Lily had taken to referring to him, silently, as Monsignor Miracle. He was a nice enough guy, and intelligent, actually, she thought, for a priest, but Jack's mother bowed and scraped around him, and ever since the "healing" incident, it struck Lily that she was lobbying to have him canonized. "He doesn't even know us," Lily said.

"He knows the family."

"He knows your mother."

"He knows Katie," Jack said.

Lily laughed. " 'The suffering of the innocents.' That's actually what he said when he first saw her."

"So?"

"Nothing." Lily looked down at the soil trapped under her fingernail. "Wouldn't it make us look more guilty to come up with a priest at this point?"

"There aren't degrees of guilt, Lillian," Jack said. "It's not like a burn." His back was to her again, and he was bracing his palms against the countertop as if he were trying to bench-press the entire kitchen.

"Why are you doing this to me?" she said.

"What, what am I doing?"

"What is it, exactly, you think I'm guilty of?"

"I don't know." As he spoke, Lily watched his shoulder blades rhythmically poke the flat cotton of his shirt. "I'm trying to figure that out."

"Why don't you fucking ask me? Why don't you talk to me?" She was eager now to bring his consecrated fury to the surface.

"That would only confuse things. Your voice confuses me. It gets in the way of my trying to figure out who you are and why what happened . . . how you allowed that to happen." He said all this slowly, with a kind of remote beneficence as if he were narrating an Old Testament story for an untutored modern audience.

"It's not yours to figure out," Lily said. "It was an accident. It just happened."

"You know what amazes me most about this whole thing?" Jack said. "Your lack of remorse."

She jumped up from the kitchen table. This guilt was *hers*, generated solely by *her* actions or inactions, one of her few wholly personal possessions. How dare he name it and define it, serve it up to her as his own creation.

She pushed her chair into the table hard.

"Cut it out," he said, stepping away from the sink toward her.

She slammed the chair again, and he lunged for the African violet, too late to catch it as it slid off the edge of the table.

Shards of painted pottery and clods of dry soil littered the tile floor.

"We're thirsty," Ben said, announcing himself before he'd reached the back door.

"I think we're just about through," Mrs. Thoms said, stepping into the kitchen. "Jesus."

"Mummy, what did you do?" Greg said, moving toward her, crunching bits of the broken flower pot under his sneakers.

Mrs. Thoms held out a protective arm and pulled him back toward her.

"Don't cry, Mum." He broke free of the caseworker and ran to his mother, hugging her around the hips.

"What's happening?" Ben said. He was barely inside the kitchen, his fingers still on the handle of the screen door.

Lily wiped her eyes with the back of one hand and used the other to stroke Greg's head.

She looked over at Ben. His cheeks were reddening, and his small hand was balled up into a fist by his side. "Mom, what did you do?" he said, opening and shutting the wood-framed screen door, softly at first, so that it sounded like the distant beating of birds' wings. "I'm not going. I'm not going with her," he said, as he slammed the old door, again and again.

"Who?" Mrs. Thoms asked. She turned toward him and knelt down. As she waited for a response, she looked back toward Lily, who was now slowly making her way across the hazardous floor, Greg still clinging to her leg.

"Who wants to take you away?" Mrs. Thoms asked, reaching out to touch Ben.

"You do," he said, finally letting go of the door and backing up against the screen. "You do, you bitch," he added in a quieter voice.

"Benjamin!" Jack yelled.

"It's all right," Mrs. Thoms said. She stood up and began to move away.

"No one's taking you anywhere, honey," Lily said, cradling his face. "No one's going anywhere."

"You said Katie was okay. I heard you say that to Daddy, yesterday, that if it wasn't for her"—he tilted his chin toward Mrs. Thoms—"Katie might be home sooner. Katie's just a baby. She didn't do anything wrong. She doesn't know better."

"Nobody said she did anything wrong," Jack said.

"That's not really a hospital, is it?" Ben said.

"Of course it is," Lily said.

"Well, then why can't we go up there? Why aren't we allowed in?"

"Oh, Ben, honey." He was crying now, hard and loud. Lily sat down and pulled both her sons to her.

"But I liked that flower, Mum." Greg looked down at the uprooted African violet and started to cry too, now. "And we'll never be able to glue it together. Look. It's wrecked."

Mrs. Thoms laughed nervously. "Really, you'd think it exploded."

"I was wiping down the table and went to move the plant. You know how things just skim across a wet surface," Jack said, looking her hard in the eyes.

Mrs. Thoms pulled down her skirt and picked up her bag. "Well, whatever, be careful cleaning it up. Those sharp pieces could go right through a sneaker sole." She looked at her watch. "I was just about to wrap things up anyway. Since Katie's scheduled to be discharged in the next few days, you should be hearing something soon." She turned and ran her eyes the length of the kitchen floor again.

Jack walked over and shook hands goodbye, but Lily remained in her chair, holding Ben and Greg. Mrs. Thoms nodded to her, and Lily nodded back. Only after the screen door had slammed shut did she feel the tiny ceramic shard in her ankle and notice the thin but steady stream of blood running down into her sandal.

# Jack

Visiting hours were long over. The fathers were gone. At night, the hospital was a female ghetto. Jack watched from his spot in a corner of the visitors' lounge as mothers and grandmothers, the occasional selfless female friend, quietly walked down the hall to the bathroom, clutching their toothbrushes and overnight bags. The Sox were on TV somewhere in this building, he was sure. If he, rather than Lily, had been the one to do the nine-night tour of duty here, he would have known where to watch the game. When the caseworker left this morning, the boys had begged Lily not to go back to the Shriners, and she had finally agreed to let Jack stay over with Katie in the hospital.

The lounge was noisy. Jack assumed the six women sitting in the center of the room were all here for the same eleven-year-old Cambodian boy whose face had been burned by splattering grease in his uncle's restaurant. They were breaking the rules, staying past eight. They spoke, it seemed to Jack, in spurts, all at once on top of each other. Then there would be a lull and one would resume some needlework and another would fold and refold the paper coffee cup she had ripped open into one long strip. The mother of the boy had twice now shuffled up to Jack and handed him a picture of her son "before." "See how smooth his face . . . perfect." While her relatives exclaimed again and again over something, she sat hunched in her molded seat, staring out toward the hallway. Jack wondered what kind of drugs they'd given her to take the edge off the guilt. Kids in a restaurant kitchen, what a shitty idea.

He'd worked in a family-run restaurant when he was in college. It was a steak place, and on weekends the owner's wife would come in wearing a cocktail dress, hair all sprayed stiff. She'd spend the dinner rush half standing, half sitting on a bar stool just inside the order window, drinking White Russians and smoking Winstons. The kids, a girl and a boy, would watch TV in the lounge until it filled up, then they'd come into the kitchen to "help." Jack liked to tease them, forcing them to race around his spitting Fryolator as if it were a tetherball. He never let his own kids into one of his kitchens except after hours. Wet heat, dry heat, knives—not to mention guttermouths—kitchens were no place for children. He wondered what horrors that Cambodian mother had endured bringing her son to this country, only to allow him to be permanently disfigured by a takeout dinner.

Every once in a while one of the women would look over at him and he would smile, then look back at his book, *The Selected Works of Edgar Allen Poe*. He'd spent a couple of nights since the accident at his mother's house—going to get the boys, staying for dinner, and then collapsing in one of the small bedrooms upstairs—and he'd found the book one morning at three o'clock after a bad dream. He'd climbed out of bed to switch on the whole-house fan in the attic. His mother had lined the hot wood steps leading up with all the old Modern Library editions. He squinted his eyes against the light from the bare bulb in the atticway, and the gold-embossed men with their flaming torches began running up the right side of the staircase.

Those Modern Library editions were what his parents had

read when he was a kid. After dinner, they'd station themselves at either end of the living room. Jack's father would be on the couch, his mother in the Harvard chair, each with a reading lamp and an ashtray pulled from where it looked best to where it was useful. The phone, the Rolling Stones, Laura Nyro, none of this seemed to distract them. They would read until it was late. His mother couldn't go to sleep, she said, in a house where teenagers where still awake and roaming. Jack would brush his teeth upstairs and hear the percolator, the clacking spoons, the box of Lorna Doones. His father would invariably read a passage aloud to his mother, some nugget, one she had probably underlined when she read the book herself the week before. "Just like in Dorset's class," he'd say, referring to a course they'd each taken twenty years before. Then she'd murmur agreement, only to ask him a few minutes later what he really meant by that.

Katie's accident had made him think more about his father than he had in the three years since he'd died of a heart attack. A group of cyclists had found him in his car off to the side of Route 2 outside Leominster. After losing his father, Katie's burn and all that went with it was the next worst thing that had ever happened to him.

The night he found the book he had dreamed about his father, and now every two or three nights he had that same dream, a nightmare, really. In the dream his father would call him on the phone. Jack would be ecstatic to hear his voice, that mellow pulse of consonants against air, like the rhythmic brush of the jazz drummers his father had so admired. The fact that he was dead and talking on the phone, they both agreed, was pretty damn funny. They'd hang up, planning to meet later. Then Jack would find himself at work. He'd pick up the phone to place an order, but no matter what number he dialed, his father was always on the other end. At first it was okay. Jack had so much to tell him, everything he'd missed. But as the dream progressed, his father would begin to question him, his choices, his actions. With each additional phone call, his father would get nastier, taunting him, then harassing him, something he had never done to Jack in real life. The last phone call before he woke up was always the same, it was always a vague but violent threat to the kids.

Jack marked his place in the book with the business card of a beef purveyor he no longer used. The overhead lights in the hallway connecting the lounge with the burn unit had been dimmed, and what looked to him like running lights had been switched on at ankle height. He'd seen only one familiar nurse tonight. Wendy, he thought her name was, the one who'd brought them dinner that first awful night after Katie was admitted.

He toed the large metal circle on the wall that activated the double doors leading into the unit. Before going in, he stared down at the stack of blue paper gowns and the box of latex gloves. They didn't expect him to sleep in these things, did they? Lily hadn't mentioned that, or maybe she had. He was doing his best to ignore her. Just now he didn't give a fuck what she thought was funny or amazing or outrageous. He couldn't stand for her to broker his perceptions anymore. Her slant on reality, her particular interpretation of daily life, was fine, it even turned him on sometimes—when life was regular. But this business with Katie, this hospital, the social worker—it just was what it was, and to hear her mull or analyze or rationalize or hypothesize, even slightly, sparked small fires all along the lining of his gut.

"Jack." Father Paul stepped out from behind Katie's privacy curtain. He quickly held up his gloved hand and smiled. "No, no, everything's fine."

"Christ, you scared me." Jack ran his fingers through his hair. "Everything okay? I was just down . . ." He motioned toward the lounge.

"Sox on?"

"No TV in there." At least Paul still liked baseball. Father Paul, Paul Cooney, the younger brother of a high school friend.

No particular interest in religion that Jack had known about. In fact, he'd been a little wild. Jack vaguely remembered a night down the Cape when Paul had passed out under a lifeguard chair. Maybe not.

"How'd it go today?" Paul asked, pushing open the doors into the hallway where they could talk above a whisper.

Jack shrugged. "They mostly talked to Lily. She says she thinks we're okay. It's crazy, a bad dream."

One of the nurses walked by and patted Jack on the shoulder. "Father," she said, nodding to Paul.

"I hope my mother didn't fly you down here. She's been known to be a little . . . obsessive?"

"Your mother's a gem."

"You mean compared to the other wackos who attend Mass on a regular basis, right?"

Paul laughed. "These go in a special garbage can?" he said, looking down at his gown and gloves.

"Probably." Jack watched as Father Paul ripped the paper smock from over his black shirt and clerical collar. He balled up the gown in one hand as if he were doing a grip exercise. "Want to get a beer?"

Jack looked at his watch. "Catch the last few innings? Sure."


Longfellow's was almost empty. Jack ordered a pint and a shot for each of them. He wondered if he should have left the hospital without telling anyone where he was going. Lily had never left, at least that's what she said.

Paul reached his long skinny arm down the bar and grabbed a side-salad bowl filled with pretzels. "The bishop's actually gotten a few calls about Kate."

"From DSS? You shitting me?"

"No, from people who think her healing was . . . from people who want the bishop to know about the unusual nature of her recovery."

"Yes!" Jack tapped a victory beat on the edge of the bar. Cooper had just doubled. When it was clear that he was safe, Jack looked away from the TV toward Paul. "What do you mean? What people?"

"Some people from St. Stephen's—somebody's barber, a nurse from the unit."

"Yeah?" Jack said. He saw that one of the waitresses was staring at Paul. From the back, all in black, he looked like any other yuppie in this town.

Father Paul blushed. "This is a little embarrassing."

"What? Being here?" Jack asked.

"No, Jack, what I'm trying to tell you. Your wife must have told you that I visited Kate two nights in a row, right around the time the doctors were telling you she'd need a skin graft, remember? She had a fever. Anyway, I did a laying on of hands, I mean, your wife said it was okay, left me alone with Kate to pray, for me to pray for her . . . and you know . . ."

Dr. Wheeler had explained to Jack and Lily at the outset that the difference between second- and third-degree burns was that second-degree burns healed. "Infection can actually convert a classification," she'd said one evening as Lily sat cradling Katie through a tangle of IV lines. The fever was still high. They were pumping her with antibiotics and checking her diaper every hour. Her urine output was low because her fluid loss had been "significant." As Wheeler talked, Jack doodled on the back of one of Lily's magazines, interchangeable cats and dogs. Occasionally he'd hold them up for Katie, whose eyes were at half-mast from the morphine.

"What we're hoping for is that there's enough underlying tissue for healing to take place." Wheeler was leaning against Katie's crib. The lapel of her lab coat was a jumble of clip-on angels. "You saw when I removed the dressings how the eschar, the burned tissue, was, in places, just beginning to separate. We need to debride it, and by that I mean clean it—get rid of all the slough—so that only the granulating wound is left. The challenge is to get rid of all that necrotic tissue," she said, grimacing. "If we don't, then the healthy skin will get infected. Right now, the wound is looking dirty." Jack had not been able to listen the next evening when things were no better and Wheeler tactfully began describing the process of an autograft.

Lily called him the next morning at work to say there'd been a turnaround. Wheeler explained that there were obviously these islands of epithelium in these deep granulating wounds, enough for some significant healing to begin. "Children's bodies are amazingly regenerative," she said. Jack's mother had used the word "miraculous," but Jack hadn't thought she meant it literally. It was a saying, an expression, a sixty-five-year-old's version of "awesome," or "radical," words he wished had never made it east of the Rockies.

"So, are people going to start camping out on my front lawn or yours?" He reached for a handful of pretzels.

Paul laughed and ran his thumb around the edge of his still-full shot glass. "I hope not. This kind of healing, it's really all about love, you know. I just dropped by tonight to see how Kate was doing. I figured I'd bump into you or your wife, and I thought I might warn you that you might be getting a call from the diocese."

"The same guy who handles exorcisms?" Jack looked at Paul and laughed. "Sorry. It's just a little weird. I guess it's just one of those Cathoholic things I can't quite get into."

"Cathoholic?" Paul sipped his beer. "It's really just an extension of . . ."

He stopped, and Jack relaxed, relieved not to have to hear him use the word "love" again. He never knew what priests were after when they used that word. How could a childless priest who supposedly didn't participate in flesh-and-blood love possibly understand the magnitude of what he was preaching? It seemed to him that priests were these ritual intermediaries, just like the host and the wine. What did he need a priest for when he had God? And what did he need communion for when he had Benjamin, Greg, and Katie?

"Some people are, you know, more open to the possibilities of the Spirit than others," Paul said. "I understand that."

Christ. Jack looked up to see the Sox make their last out for the eighth. Paul wasn't even watching.

"So, will this be good for your career?" Jack said. If the bishop was into this now, Jack wondered if he would make a call for them to the state. "Has a Mrs. Thoms gotten in touch with you, from DSS?"

Paul shook his head.

"If you can think of anything good to say about us . . ." Jack patted the breast pocket of his shirt. It was empty. "I must have her number at home."

"You mean this caseworker? Except for my brief chat with your wife the other night, I really don't know Lily. Did Father Burke marry you? At St. Stephen's? Maybe you'd like to give him a call."

Son of a bitch. Jack shook his head and finished the last of his Jack Daniel's. He chose not to tell Father Paul that he and Lily had been married in the bar of the Eagle Mountain Inn in New Hampshire, where Lily was working then. They'd planned for the ceremony to be held in the field behind the restaurant, with a view of Mount Washington ten miles away. Rain on your wedding day is good luck, everyone repeated as they were herded into the dark cocktail lounge with its tartan-plaid carpet and rum-barrel stools. They'd been married by a local justice, which had satisfied no one, including the justice herself. Jack had spent the first few minutes of his married life apologizing to the woman for the fact that the ice machine had let loose a few hundred cubes just as she began her brief remarks.

They'd wanted a priest and a rabbi. Father Burke had smiled

and said that was fine, just as long as he was the one who performed the actual marriage vows. Lily had found only one rabbi who would, by his presence, condone this intermarriage, and he was a therapist who could "deal with being a team player" as long as they consented to twelve sessions of prenuptial counseling at sixty-five dollars a session.

None of the children had been baptized. The boys had been circumcised by the doctor who delivered them, and some weeks after each birth, Jack would buy half a dozen bottles of sparkling wine, smoke a turkey, bake a "Welcome" cake, and invite some friends and family. After the turkey and before the cake, he and Lily would stand holding the crying newborn in front of their crumbling fireplace and take turns, she explaining the meaning behind the names—Benjamin for her father, Boris; Gregory for her mother, Gloria; Katherine for Jack's father, Kevin—he making a toast that his mother would refer to later as "that lovely prayer of yours." Jack wondered if Katie's nonstatus as a Catholic would interfere with Father Paul's being dubbed a miracle worker. He hoped so.

"I'd better be heading back," Jack said.

Paul reached for his wallet, and Jack waved him away.

As he walked back to the Shriners, Jack wondered what his mother would make of all Paul's brown-nosing. Maybe she already knew. His father would have called it typical, and dismissed it, but his mother's relationship with God and the Church was far more layered. On their way to confession one Friday afternoon years ago when he was a boy, his mother had pulled the car over and told Jack that her greatest transgression that week was against herself, her true nature, and did he think that was really the sort of thing that Father Phillips could possibly fathom, well-meaning soul that he was. She had, by that point, stopped telling her children what to believe, and instead had subverted her natural inclination to instruct into a voracious scrutiny of her own faith. Jack's two older sisters alternately called her a hypocrite and a head case. And on a given Thursday night, these questions of soul would flare dramatically, raising him above the flat plain of seventh-grade life. "The challenge, always, is to transcend this," she would say, slapping the surface of her skin, with one hand, while the other held open a copy of Heschel's *Man's Quest for God.* Pressing the spine of the book flat to the kitchen table, she would read to whoever would listen. " 'As a tree torn from the soil, as a river separated from its source, the human soul wanes when detached from what is greater than itself. . . . Unless we aspire to the utmost, we shrink to inferiority. . . . The self is not the hub' "—she would look straight at Jack, who somehow liked hanging around for these exhortations— " 'but the spoke of the revolving wheel.' "

Things were different in the houses of his friends. Their mothers said their rosaries while their nails dried. They decorated their dens with side-by-side pictures of the Pope and JFK. They probably thought Thomas Merton was a guy who lived two blocks over and worked for the MBTA. His parents had only one picture in their den, a rip-off of Ben Shahn's peace dove.

Around the time he was twelve, his mother showed him that there could be breathing room in one's relationship with God. And by the time he was fifteen and smoking pot and driving around Boston with friends in "borrowed" cars, he had come to depend on the presence in his household of a Catholicism that at times stood apart from, and even in opposition to, the Church. It was license to misbehave without being dubbed wicked, to walk the high wire, knowing there was a safety net. Above all, his mother believed deeply in an ever-loving and forgiving God. Jack knew now, only after having his own children, that what he believed in was not so much his mother's God, but his mother.

# Jack

Jack manipulated Barney's purple paw to feed Katie a piece of jellied toast from her breakfast tray. At mealtime the nurses tried to arrange the children in a semicircle in the middle of the ward. Three were in high chairs, five in regular chairs with hospital trays rolled up to them. Some remained in their beds, with the curtains pulled open so they could see the others if they wanted to. Many of the children who were up and eating had already been grafted at least once, and most multiple times. A few of them had graduated to this little semicircle of their peers after months spent in isolation in the hyperbaric chambers down the hall. For them, sitting out here on the ward was like being at a party.

Jack couldn't look at some of these kids. Exploding furnaces, faulty wiring, kerosene heaters, caustic chemicals, sizzling grease, scalding water—that's how Lily referred to the other children, categorizing them by the agents of their destruction. That was Lily, not satisfied unless she had the inside story. Jack was happier not knowing the "how" of it. He classified these kids in only the most general ways—worsening, improving; bedridden, ambulatory; disfigured, scarred.

Only about two-thirds of the kids spoke English, so Jack had Barney nibble a few Cheerios, sip from a couple of straws, wipe his always-open mouth on a hospital gown, collapse on an empty stretcher, and burp.

"Can I talk to you?"

Jack looked up from his place on the gurney. The cold hand with all the bracelets belonged to Linda, the hospital social worker.

She nodded in the direction of Katie's bed. Jack looked over at Katie, who was still eating, laughing now at an older boy balancing a spoon across the bridge of his nose.

He followed Linda into Katie's "room" and looked at his watch. He'd missed so much work during the last week. Lily was supposed to have been here at eight-thirty this morning.

"There seems to be a bit of a snag," Linda said, shielding herself behind the rocking chair.

Jack hated this woman. Her concern was so global it was ludicrous.

"The investigator in your case, the caseworker who went out to your house, has petitioned for an Order of Care and Protection, and the judge has granted it."

"What? What are you talking about—"

"It's an OTC, an Order of Temporary Custody. It's a seventy-two-hour hold, during which time DSS gathers more information about the case. It's rather unorthodox, since your daughter is still hospitalized, but my guess is that there's been some question as to when she'd be medically ready for discharge. DSS has a certain window of opportunity—"

"They came to my house. I let this woman come into my house—" He looked down at Katie's little sneakers, lined up neatly beneath the crib. He picked them up and held them to his chest.

"I know this must be very hard for you . . . difficult to understand . . ." Linda stood, swaying slightly from side to side, and batting at the back of the rocker as it rolled into her again and again. "The state seems to feel—"

"No," Jack said. "The state doesn't *feel* a fucking thing."

Linda swayed some more. "DSS, from what I gather, has reason to believe that your daughter may be at risk at home. They have an obligation . . ."

Jack thought back to what Ben had said in the kitchen yesterday—that this place wasn't really a hospital.

"There'll be something called a seventy-two-hour hearing, at which point the judge will appoint an attorney for you, but between you, me, and the wall," she said quietly, "I strongly suggest that you get yourself a lawyer now, today."

"Really?" Jack said. He slid his fingers inside Katie's sneakers, barely past the second knuckle. "I thought you told us that would look bad." He slammed the soles of the sneakers together. A two-week-old pebble dribbled out of the treads. "I asked you that last week, when this whole thing started, remember?"

"It's a completely different ball of wax now. There could be the potential here for a criminal charge against your wife." Linda ran her hands down two of the spindles at the back of the rocking chair and set her bracelets jingling. "Based on what's in their file now, they could possibly hand that over to the county prosecutor's office. Your wife could be arrested. If they wanted, they could make a case, possibly, for removing your other children as well. You need to defend yourself. Actually, you need to defend your wife. This whole thing has snowballed."

Jack nodded at the hospital social worker and looked over at the things in Katie's crib—her blanket, the stuffed penguin his mother had brought, the old tan bear from home, the one the boys called Tedda—he'd have to leave them behind. He'd walk slowly out to the center of the ward where the children were still eating, release her from the high chair, as if he were just hugging her, and walk off the ward.

He slid open the privacy curtain and moved past Linda. One

of the nurses had already taken Katie out of her high chair. Jack scooped her up off the floor, careful not to disturb the splint on her right foot. "Come on, Katydid," he breathed into her ear.

"Boon, boon," she yelled as he began to walk toward the double doors carrying her.

"It's okay, hon, Mumma's waiting for us."

"Boon!" she screamed. "Boon!"

"I think this is what she's after," Linda said, touching him through his paper smock and handing Katie a partly deflated Mylar balloon that said "Get Well Soon or Else." "Trust me," Linda said. "You'll only make things worse if you leave, please."

Jack looked around, beyond Katie's sticky cheek, the dying balloon, Linda's nest of black-and-gray curls. Nobody noticed that this was happening. Nurses were talking on the phone, clearing trays, a kid was screaming in Spanish, carts were squeaking, toilets were flushing. No one knew he was losing his baby girl. He could feel the blood pulsing in his fingers as he stroked Katie's bare arms. Care and Protection. That was his job. How could she be safer with anyone else? How could this be happening?

"You're my girl," he whispered as he placed Katie on the floor in the center of the ward. "No one's going to take away my girl."

He turned to the social worker. "Is there something in writing?" he said.

"You'll be served a summons."

"I'd like to show my wife something in writing."

# Jack

Lunch for 18. That's what it said on the chalkboard by the phone. Wilted greens with goat cheese, loin of tuna in rosemary sauce, new potatoes, strawberry tartlets for dessert. Cyn, his assistant, was separating the eggs for the crème anglaise when he walked in at ten twenty-seven. He waved and walked past her to his locker at the back of the kitchen. He pulled his golf shirt up over his head and slipped into his whites.

"How's the tuna look?" he yelled to her, fingering a pair of checked pants through their dry-cleaning bag. Fucking nubby pants. He'd wait until noon, when he'd be on view, to change out of his khakis.

"Sushi it's not," she said.

He could see her now, maneuvering the half-empty flat of eggs back into the walk-in.

"Don't know what I'd do without you, kiddo," he said.

She kicked the walk-in door shut with one industrial-weight black boot. "What?"

"Were you sweating?" He pulled the knotty fabric buttons of his jacket through three of the four buttonholes.

"It's the board, you know? The board's having lunch," she said.

"Six for lunch, sure, you could do that, no problemo—"

"Eighteen, Jack. It's eighteen, Jesus Christ—"

"Gotcha," he said, and shut his locker door. "I love to see you squirm."

"You're a real cocksucker, you know that?" She laughed. From around the corner he heard her slam the saucepan down on the range. "What are you doing back there anyway, your nails? We got a case of rocket lettuce to wash, asparagus to trim. We got to do up the tuna sauce, hull and slice these berries. Ask me about these fucking berries."

"Hey, Cyn," Jack said, walking over to the pen-gouged conference table that served as his desk. "Mind over matter."

She held up her hand, "I know, I know, 'You don't mind and I don't matter.' "


It had taken him a long time to get out of the hospital. Lily had cried in the middle of the ward when he told her about the seventy-two-hour hold. She had wept so openly and so loudly that several of the other mothers ran over, assuming, of course, that Katie's medical condition had worsened.

Later, when they were in the play therapy room, Lily had looked out the window and said, "God's punishing us, for something." Jack watched Katie and one of the volunteers as they shoved a spotted dog down the chimney of a Little Tykes cottage. Jack had seen the woman before, accepted the challenge of looking at her straight on. The majority of the volunteers had been childhood burn patients. Many were scarred, some had been grafted, Jack guessed. But for this young woman, scar and skin graft were the only messages of her face. Wherever the patchwork needed to be slack enough to allow for movement, around the jaw and lips, the transplanted skin hung in flaps, reminding Jack of a homemade puppet. Each time the plastic dog came flying out the front door of the plastic house, Katie laughed, as if perfectly surprised and wholly delighted. And every time the woman perched the dog back up on the chimney Katie smiled at her, as if she were perfectly familiar and wholly beautiful.

"Why . . ." Lily began again, looking over at Jack. "Why is God punishing us?"

God, Jack thought about saying to his wife, you mean the God who didn't allow Katie to die, the God who saved her at the last minute from having to undergo a skin graft? Instead he walked up beside her at the window and in a low voice said, "If in fact there is a God, Lillian, it seems painfully clear to me that it is Katie who is being punished."

"We've got to be in this together," she said sharply, as if commanding him.

Cyn backed far enough away from the stove to make eye contact with Jack, just as Jack's call went through to his brother-in-law in Chicago. She turned toward the range when she heard his voice crack.

David hollered hello into the phone three times, before Jack could get out a weak "Hey." It was stupid to call David. David did real estate law. Jack knew David would waste no time telling him he couldn't help him and asking, incredulously, didn't he or anyone in that whole enormous family of his know one goddamn attorney out there. And he'd end the call asking Jack if they needed money. Just say the word.

"Yeah, hey, buddy, it's Jack."

"Everybody okay? Katie?"

"Jesus, man, we've, ah, ah . . ." Jack sat down on his desk, on top of menus and memos and pens and pencils. A bulging can of pitted black olives that had to go back to Monarch rolled to the floor. "We've got a huge problem here. It's all fucked up. All fucked up."

Jack could hear that he'd been taken off the speakerphone. He pictured his brother-in-law nuzzling the receiver with the aid of one of those executive phone perches. Maybe he even had a headset. As he told David the story, he realized that Lily had related almost nothing to him, not about DSS, not even about the initial attending's report.

"You do understand that I can't represent you."

"Of course," Jack said. "I just need a name, a good name. Someone who can make this unhappen."

"Shit. What did the two of you say to these people? I don't understand. How did it get this far? This is crazy."

There was a beeping on the line.

"I'm going to have to take this call. You need someone who does family law. I've got to think, okay? . . . Private counsel does-n't usually . . . You're going to be hard pressed to find an attor-ney familiar with this territory. I mean, we're talking about the wasteland of court-appointed attorneys here—this social agency stuff."

"The guy you clerked for out here . . . I thought maybe he might know a lawyer. . . ."

"I'll get you a name. You're at work?"

"Yeah." Jack gave him the number.

"I'll call you back around three your time. And tell my sister to call me. I want to know exactly what she told this caseworker. The interview should have been . . . she should have talked to me about this before."

"Lily's—"

"Jack, look, you're going to have to be prepared to come up with some money here. This kind of thing could get quite expen-sive."

"I hear you."

"Garni?" Jack said, walking over to Cyn's prep table with a few bunches of fresh rosemary.

"Garnish? Fuck the garnish. We've got no sauce, no veggie, no—"

"Okay, okay."

"The chicken stock is in the walk-in, under the tray of leftover Indian pudding—a no-go in the summer, Jack."

He saluted and marched around the corner. When he pulled down on the handle of the walk-in he could smell it, smell what a fuck-off he'd been lately, even before the accident. From where he stood on the threshold of the refrigerator he could see an uncovered stockpot filled with some kind of chowder that had obviously broken down, a four-quart bowl of asparagus and walnut risotto (he hadn't done a risotto since before Memorial Day, he didn't think), and a loosely wrapped package of lamb shanks that should have been frozen a week ago. He kicked aside a crate of runny yellow peppers and checked the thermostat. All he needed now was a visit by the Health Department, that and a case of corporate food poisoning.

Where had he been for the past few months? Fucking the dog? He had no secret vice he'd squirreled away work time to pursue. On the contrary, before the accident he'd been coming in earlier and staying later. But he hadn't been working harder. He'd spent almost no time planning his menus for the summer. Living simultaneously in the present and a few weeks ahead of yourself was the executive chef's chief function, catering to the diner's immediate desire all the while planning for the secret pleasures of his future. To hump like that in two directions you had to jot down "shad roe" on the slim calendar you should have been carrying around in your back pocket all the time. You had to consider it a loss to have missed the short season for fiddlehead ferns or soft-shell crabs. To satiate others' desires you had to register desire yourself. You had to care deeply about what was ripe, juicy, firm to the touch, full and sweet and ready to pluck from the soil or the sea. Somewhere along the way, his sensuality had boiled out. And now he was left with a job he didn't particularly like and that barely engaged him.

"Did you find it?" Cyn yelled. "If you talk and work it might help. Talk and work, work and talk."

Jack finally emerged with the chicken stock and slid the pot onto the heat. Some of the liquid sloshed over into the flame, causing a brief sizzle and a flare.

"When are they going to let Katie come home?" Cyn said, reaching up to turn down the boom box on the shelf above her station.

"Let's do tabouleh instead of spuds. It'll be quicker."

"Tillson loves potatoes."

"Fuck him. We're doing a breakfast tomorrow. He'll get potatoes twice tomorrow." Jack pulled the box of asparagus toward him with a spatula. "Shit, then, we'll need tomatoes. Do we have tomatoes?"

Cyn turned and glared at him.

"Sorry. I'm off my game, way off." With the flat of his knife, he tamped a bunch of asparagus into line. "Katie," he finally said. "They're keeping her . . . a few more days, at least."

"I'm sorry, Jack. Lily must be so upset."

He kept the tip of his knife on the cutting board and brought down the wide part of the blade into the bundle of asparagus spears. A few ends rolled onto the floor.

"You're still not talking to her?" Cyn was behind him now, whisking her custard on the stove.

He lined up some more asparagus. "I never said we weren't talking."

"Well, you haven't exactly— Shit, this is curdling."

Jack grabbed the dish towel slung over his apron strings and pulled the crème anglaise off the heat.

"Look at that, right there, scrambled yolk, all balled up . . ."

Jack took the whisk from her hand and beat the custard with force.

"That's it?" she said. "All you're doing is breaking the lumps into pieces. That's not exactly fixing the problem."

Jack plunged his index finger into the hot yellow mixture. "Look. See anything? I defy you to find a lump. Set this up in an ice bath before you go any further."

"I thought you were like going to do something, you know, something chemical," Cyn said, returning with a mixing bowl filled with ice.

"Your pie shells cool?"

"They're frozen."

"Better get them out." He trimmed the last of the asparagus, then grabbed the flat of strawberries from Cyn's bench and began slicing off the green tops.

Cyn came back around the corner with a tray of individual tart shells.

"It's a mess," Jack said, beginning to slice some of the berries into little fans, their pointed ends still attached. "The state's holding Katie in protective custody. Seems the caseworker didn't have a very good time at our house yesterday."

"God, Jack. I'm sorry. I figured, you know . . . I heard you on the phone before . . . I figured something bad was going on." She arranged the shells in neat rows along the butcher block. "You know, if there's anything I can do . . ."

Jack smiled at her. "Hey, you've got a fucking earring in your nose. You don't know your earlobe from your nostril, and you're going to help me." He wiped the red berry juice off his fingers and looked over at her. "Thanks, hon."

Cyn began ladling the warm custard into the shells. "You've got to talk to her, Jack."

"I don't have anything to say." He pulled out the garbage pail from under his bench and scraped in the green stems with the back of his knife.

"This must be awful for her." Cyn reached over and popped a couple of strawberries into her mouth.

"I feel awful for Katie, and at the end of every day, when I'm done feeling bad for Katie—it's an amazing thing—but I don't have any sympathy left over for Lily. I'm plumb out." He slid the stainless-steel bowl of sliced berries over to Cyn and pulled open a crate of lettuce. He watched for a moment as she began arranging the berries in concentric circles on each tart. She looked up and he nodded.

"How are the boys doing?"

"I'm trying to keep them busy."

"Yeah, but how do they seem?"

Jack plucked at the heads of lettuce, piling the gritty leaves into a colander. "Fine. They're fine. You know, they'll be okay."

"What are you telling them?"

When the colander was full of greens and reds, Jack carried it over to the small vegetable sink and began washing the lettuce gently under cold water, leaf by leaf. They'd had a small sink like this at their shop, and until each of the boys was about three months old, they had bathed them there, dish towels rolled along one stainless-steel edge to protect their floppy necks, and one clean white apron laid out on the counter for bundling and drying. When he left the hospital this morning, they hadn't discussed what they would tell Ben and Greg. Nothing. They didn't need to tell them anything.

"This is hard for them, too." Cyn dumped a jar of jelly into a pot on the range.

"My mother's spoiling them rotten." Jack spread out two dish towels and piled on the wet lettuce.

"It probably isn't helping that their parents are at each other's throats. I'm only speaking from experience—as a former kid."

This was something Lily never did in the kitchen, not when they were working. Of course they talked, but not like this. Cyn used talk. She needed conversation to distract herself from the work, the physical work, the tedium that cooking in quantity could engender. She hadn't yet learned, maybe wouldn't ever learn, that the repetition of the task could become a kind of mantra, loosing your thoughts. He always had his best ideas when he was deep into it, peeling fifty pounds of potatoes or shredding twenty pounds of cheese.

Jack was grateful that he'd gone into the restaurant business before the advent of the celebrity chef and this new generation of foodies. Cooking was manual labor. Cooks were servants. That had never bothered him, and for Lily it had been a kind of antidote to her childhood. She had told him once that she hadn't felt real until the day she first walked into a restaurant kitchen.

"Sushi it's not," Jack said, reaching into the plastic-lined box of tuna. "Fish." He fondled the thick flesh until he got Cyn to laugh. "Fish," he said again, bringing the raw stuff to his lips. "Fish." He kissed it, and she laughed even harder.

# Lily

"Mama." Katie laughed a low, muffled laugh, her thumb deep inside her mouth, as Lily reached over and licked the tiniest speck of tomato sauce from her eyelid. One of the other mothers had ordered pizza for the children at lunch. The nurses encouraged the parents to bring in food, anything at all. Weight loss was inevitable with burns. The children simply needed calories.

"Who loves you?" Lily said as she lay next to Katie in the crib. The metal cage surrounding the mattress could be made to give way in all the right places, allowing parents to comfort their children, comfort themselves.

"Mama," Katie answered, her thumb still a big wet impediment in her mouth. "Mama."

Lily twirled a curl of Katie's black hair around one finger, stroked her full belly with the back of her hand, put her nose in the soft, warm hollow of flesh at her neck. She could not stop touching her. During those first few days when Lily thought Katie might die she had caught herself synchronizing her breathing with Katie's. It was a reflex—like opening her own mouth while spooning food into the baby's. In the throes of that medical crisis, Lily had recognized in herself an almost atavistic desire to heal Katie by pulling her back inside, so that the pain might be borne on Lily's own nerve endings, the regeneration of the skin born of her own sturdier system. And now that the threat of being separated from Katie had reemerged, so had the urge to assume her, body and soul, up into that waiting space.

Katie was almost asleep. Lily pulled the baby's free thumb up to her own lips, and a spasm of a smile caught at the edge of Katie's mouth. There was no other truth but this.

Lily walked to the pay phone in the hall. She reached into her purse for some change and for a fragment of a Xanax. She'd made a mess of the last two pills by trying to cut them with the side of her Subaru key.

Ben answered the phone at her mother-in-law's house. His mouth was full. "We knew it would be you, Mom. We're eating lunch."

"You are?" Lily said, the words coming out through her nose as she felt herself beginning to cry.

"Did you know that Nana makes red soup?" Greg had picked up on another extension.

Lily shook her head just the way he did when he responded in the negative to a question over the phone. "No, honey, I didn't."

"She didn't make it. It's from a can," Ben said. "Mom, did you know that there was a kind of clam chowder that was red?"

"No, me, me! I want to say it! I'm telling her. Mum," Greg continued, "Nana calls this soup Mummy's soup because, you know what, Mum, you know what it's called?"

"What, sweetie? What's it called?"

"Manhattan Clam Chowder," Ben jumped in.

"I'm saying it! I'm saying it, Ben! Mum, you know what it's called?"

"No, sweetie. What? What's the red soup called?"

"Manhattan Clam Chowder."

"Really?" Lily said. She craned her neck and dried her eyes on the shoulder of her blouse.

"Manhattan's another word for New York City. Did you know that, Mum?" Greg said.

"Everyone knows that," Ben said.

"So, Mum," Greg continued, unscathed, "that means you like it better than the white kind—"

"New England Clam Chowder," Ben said officially.

"'Cause that's where you're from."

"Actually—" Lily began.

"Lil?" her mother-in-law asked cautiously.

"Is everybody still on?" Lily heard one click, some breathing, and finally a slam.

"Are they off, Fran?"

"Don't cry, honey. Oh, Lily. She's going to be okay."

"Jack hasn't called you yet, has he?"

"No."

"That caseworker got a judge to grant this Order of Protection. They race to do these things before the hospital discharges. The Department of Social Services actually takes custody while they determine—"

"Oh my God, Lillian." Lily could hear her mother-in-law pulling out a chair. "How can this be happening to you? How can this be happening? You poor lamb."

"God, Franny. You won't let them take my baby away. . . ." Lily was sobbing hard.

"Who's there with you? Is someone there with you? Is Jack there? Lily, where's Jack?"

There was a long silence, while Lily swallowed hard and looked for a tissue or a napkin or something in her pocketbook. "I didn't do anything wrong, Franny." Lily blew her nose loudly. "You know that, don't you? Of all people, you know that."

"Of course I do. Did you call your brother? I imagine you need to get a lawyer. Did you call David?"

"No. Jack said he would. He hasn't called me since he left here. That was before ten. He found out first. He's at work. He went to work."

"You want me to come down there? I'm coming down there right now."

"I don't want the boys to get scared. I don't think . . . I don't look very good right now . . . ," Lily said.

"Could that, that friend of yours, glory be, what's her name? You know the one, the one with the house with the peeling paint and the dog, the dog with the skin problem."

Lily laughed. She was still crying, but she laughed. "Julia, Julia Cozzi."

"Could she take them this afternoon? I'll call her. Those kids are forever calling down here to see if they can help me out."

Lily appreciated the way her mother-in-law referred to her and Jack's friends as "kids." "I'm sorry to put you through this," Lily said. "I'm so sorry."

Lily hung up the phone and shoved the shredding Dunkin' Donuts napkin she'd used to dry her eyes into the pocket of her shorts. She wished there were someone else to call. Jack was the person she usually called when she was in trouble. Years ago, before they were married, she had called him from a pay phone in the subway. She'd just come from a dismal interview for a job as a pastry chef at a new restaurant. Above the echoes in the leaking station, she told Jack that the celebrity restaurateur had asked her what the hell he was supposed to do with a Barnard girl in his kitchen.

"Where are you?" Jack said.

"Astor Place."

"Who are you?"

"What?" she said, already somewhat saved by the sound of his voice and the intensity of his attention.

"You're Lily Sterne, the Greatest Chef in All the World," he roared as if anticipating competition from an oncoming train.

"Right." She laughed.

"There's nothing you can't do, Lily. I'm serious. There's no limit to who you can be. How come I know that, and you don't? You're going to let some third-rate actor tell you about your profession? Why would you do that?"

"You mean when I could be listening to you, instead?" she said, wondering how sad it must be for everyone else in the world to live without this.

Jack had told her about the prospective custody this morning, delivering the bad news as if it were not news at all, not to him, but rather the preordained result of her freely chosen failings as a human being. He had not held her hand or even taken her aside. She was in this, and maybe everything else, alone. For the first time, Lily wondered whether he had said something about her to the caseworker, something strange, something that in some way implicated her, something to punish her, never envisioning how it would mushroom. Maybe he'd set her up with the Commonwealth of Massachusetts? The Xanax wasn't working.

Lily stretched on a pair of gloves and unfolded a gown. Katie's room was cool, and she pulled the cotton blanket up over the baby's skimpy hospital gown. Last night at home, she'd slept in Katie's hot little room. She'd become used to the noises on the burn unit and had forgotten about the house sounds, the creaking floorboards and the scraping of the pines against the upstairs windows. At two, she'd wandered in and turned on the old metal fan on top of Katie's dresser. She lay down by the crib, covering herself with a worn receiving blanket and wedging her head into the soft black crotch of Katie's panda bear. When Greg found her there sometime after seven in the morning he said that he'd asked Daddy almost every night about sleeping in Katie's crib, but Daddy had always said no, because he was a big boy, and it was great to be big.

The unit was almost quiet now. Except for the youngest

babies, most of the children tended, after a few days, to fall into similar schedules. During nap time the stereo din of *Sesame Street* gave way to the warring plaints of soap operas.

The nurse rocking little Pearl was watching *One Life to Live*. "Poor thing just had a catheter put in," she said as Lily walked over.

Lily reached out with a gloved hand and stroked the baby's toes. This baby probably didn't even know what skin-to-skin touch felt like. Pearl had been there for three months, since she was about ten weeks old. Somebody, Lily hadn't heard who, had plunged her headfirst into a pot of boiling water. Lily had been told that she'd never grow hair or eyelashes or eyebrows. Her eyelids were scarred, but her lips were smooth and rosy and wet, just as a baby's lips should be. Her hands were still bandaged. Those had been burned, too. Perhaps Pearl had instinctively reached out to the sides of the pot.

"Will it hurt her if I stroke her head?" Lily said, reaching out to touch Pearl's rippled head. The nurse was familiar to her, but wasn't one of the ones she knew by name, who'd treated Katie.

The nurse was looking up at the TV. "And we're supposed to believe that this guy's straight? Look at him."

Lily laughed. "I think she might be sleeping."

"This one likes to catnap, big on catnaps."

"Sounds good to me," Lily said.

"Really. The kids get sent home and the mothers wind up sick as dogs."

"What's going to happen to her? I mean, when she gets discharged?" Lily said.

"Who? Our little Pearl of the Sea here? God, I don't know. But any mother who does something like this, if you ask me, ought to be fried in oil. Some things you shouldn't get a second chance for, ever, you know?"

Lily nodded.

"Too bad that she's a girl. No hair on a boy wouldn't be as bad.

And her face . . ." The nurse sighed and rubbed the baby's back while she looked up at the TV.

"I'd be happy to hold her, if you need a break."

The nurse looked directly at Lily now for the first time. She nodded to herself as if she had just recognized something. "You've got your own rocking to do, don't you?"

Lily let her smile fall slightly as she stepped back out of the room. Everyone knew. She couldn't be trusted.

# Lily

Jack was already seated in Eleanor Snow's office when Lily arrived at five-thirty. He turned and stared out the window as she took the leather armchair beside him.

"I've a meeting at seven in Concord, so we'll keep this brief," Snow said in a manner that struck Lily as more military than businesslike.

"Let me quickly reiterate what I've told your husband." The lawyer smoothed out the skirt of her seersucker suit as she perched on the edge of her desk. "I want to be perfectly up-front with you from the start. In my practice, my knowledge of and involvement with DSS is tangential. For the most part, my clients tend to be involved in custody battles with former spouses, rather than with the Department of Social Services. I told your husband over the phone this afternoon that the Juvenile Court judge hearing this case will appoint counsel for you, should you not engage a private attorney, quite possibly counsel for each of you. That representation is free. Counsel will also be appointed for your child."

Lily looked around the office—white oriental carpet, rosewood desk, leather chairs, a view from the twenty-third floor.

This hour with Eleanor Snow, who was now telling them she
didn't especially practice the kind of law in which they were
ensnared, was likely to cost close to a day's pay for Jack. The
medical expenses were covered. The Shriners wouldn't be charging them; that was the principle behind all their children's hospitals. She and Jack had no savings. On the contrary, they owed
close to $24,000 in credit card debt they'd incurred when the
gourmet shop had started to fail. "The Angel of Debt," Jack had
joked one day, dropping the Visa bill onto the prep counter. But
that was over $10,000 ago, back when they could joke, when it
still seemed possible to turn it all around. Legal fees would bury
them for good. One more reason for Lily to feel guilty.

"It's my understanding that the state is very much on the
defensive right now about their record in a number of abuse
cases." Snow moved behind her desk and flipped the top page of
a yellow legal pad. "I'm of course referring to the infant in
Methuen . . ."

Lily remembered switching off the radio in the kitchen the
evening the story broke about the six-month-old who died of
injuries when her mother's boyfriend raped her.

"The little girl had been treated at a hospital for burns on the
buttocks only weeks before," Snow continued. "Treated and
released. Last winter there was the three-year-old in Worcester
who froze to death when his mother left him sleeping in her
locked car overnight while she worked the third shift. After his
death a number of the mother's neighbors and coworkers came
forward claiming they had repeatedly called the police about the
mother's treatment of the child, but DSS had never followed up.
Both cases received large amounts of media attention, and a hue
and cry has gone up, as well it should, for a total overhaul of the
department."

The lawyer lowered her gray head to look for something on
her desk. "Okay, so that's the political climate in which you find
yourselves right now, just so you understand." She fingered her

silver helmet of a hairdo and finally pulled out a Post-it note from beneath a stack of papers.

Lily understood that these news items, which months ago she'd considered tragic yet distant, lamentable but as unconnected to her life as a famine in sub-Saharan Africa or a civil war in Eastern Europe, had quickly married into her family of troubles. These public deaths were, in some way, responsible for her own private life being offered up in sacrifice to this government agency. They couldn't afford not to hire Eleanor Snow or someone like her.

"The judge granted the Order of Care and Protection based on allegations made by the investigator, the caseworker, Mrs. . . . Thoms, right? You're to have a preliminary hearing within seventy-two hours. The burden of proof is on DSS. Unfortunately, it's my understanding that this is a fairly low burden. . . . The hospital social worker? Now what's her name? She has no real influence here, but she did give me . . ."

Lily watched as the lawyer retracted her long tanned neck, forcing her light blue half-glasses to slide to the tip of her nose. She looked over the tops of them at her notepad.

"Linda Polowitz," Lily said.

"Good," the lawyer said without looking up. "This Polowitz on the hospital staff did fax me—she must like you—reports by the two doctors there who were assigned to Katie's case. Their reports to DSS were inconclusive in determining abuse."

The lawyer rolled her chair back from the desk and stretched out her legs. "They're going to run a skeletal series on your daughter, x-rays, to check for past fractures. You'll want to prepare her for that. And if they haven't yet taken photographs, most likely they will. Try to be on hand for as much of this as you can. Your presence at the hospital"—the lawyer swung her eyes up over the tops of her glasses and looked at Lily—"is important now for myriad reasons." Snow pulled off her glasses abruptly and while deeply massaging her closed eyes continued to talk.

"Apparently, while no one claims to have seen a line of immersion anywhere on your daughter's body, the investigator found enough to confirm the suspicions of the emergency room physician, who was the reporter, the one who filed the 51A. I don't yet have the caseworker's report, which would be . . ." She scissored her pen between her second and third fingers. "Of course." She thrust forward her lips disparagingly. "Form 51B."

Lily thought that maybe she had been wrong about the lawyer and her Army-issue interpersonal skills. What she had first discerned in Eleanor Snow as a hot-potato Brahmin accent she realized now might be the inflected voice of an ex-smoker. This woman, whose calf muscles were probably as taut as the catgut on her tennis racquet, seemed more approachable when Lily pictured her drinking her way through a soft pack of Newports.

"I am wondering"— Lily cleared her throat and slid forward in her seat, her bare legs noisily unsticking themselves from the leather upholstery—"why we're on the defensive here?" She crossed her ankles and tugged on her shorts. When she left home this morning to go to the hospital, it had never occurred to her that she would be sitting in an attorney's office on Federal Street that evening. "I was hoping you could find a way to, if not erase this whole thing, at least put a halt to it—something procedural done wrong from the beginning. . . . I mean, there's no reason this should be happening to us."

Instead of responding, the lawyer looked up over her glasses at Jack.

"This is something you've already discussed?" Lily said, annoyed.

"Your daughter sustained some very serious injuries, Mrs. Keliher." Snow bowed her head toward a curling piece of fax paper on her desk and quoted. " 'Partial- and full-thickness burns, categorized as both second- and third-degree burns.' " The attorney looked up at Lily now. "I did a little research prior to our meeting this evening. It is my understanding that burns such as these in a child as young as yours when the skin is still thin can be fatal. DSS would have cause for suspicion based on the injuries alone. Your claim that there were no witnesses, coupled with the fact that the account of your daughter's accident is seemingly incompatible with her age and her developmental characteristics, her strength and dexterity, lay a solid foundation for a real case against you. And perhaps, most significantly, what you claim are accidental splash burns on your daughter's legs can be nearly impossible to distinguish from burns caused by the deliberate throwing of boiling water." The lawyer slid her glasses back along the bony ridge of her nose. "A judge has heard these allegations and declared your daughter to be in imminent danger. This is quite serious, Mrs. Keliher."

"Has my husband told you the story? Did he tell you how the accident happened?"

The lawyer nodded.

"I wasn't even in the room."

"Nobody can corroborate that," the lawyer said.

"Why do I need corroboration? I've been taking care of kids for thousands of hours. My oldest is seven . . ."

"I was given to understand that until fairly recently, you and your husband shared the child-care responsibilities. You've mostly reared your children, with him, in full view . . . you had some kind of a retail business?"

"Gourmet shop," Jack said softly.

"Are you playing devil's advocate here?" Lily asked.

"Your husband is very concerned, Mrs. . . . . Sterne," the lawyer said, correcting herself.

"My husband is in the room. Maybe he'd like to tell me exactly what his concerns are?" Lily pulled her purse from the floor up onto her lap, as if for protection. "Did you voice these concerns to Mrs. Thoms?" she said, turning to him.

Jack had his arms folded across his pin-striped shirt. For the first time Lily noticed he was wearing a blazer.

"Did you say something to that doctor at Lincoln?" she asked.

"I asked a question," he said, running his fingers through his curly hair. "When you were at the pay phone, checking on the boys, I asked a nurse what temperature water has to be to burn skin."

"So?"

"And then I told her that I'd worked in a lot of kitchens. I'd seen some burns before, but I'd never seen anything this bad, not even when an old Garland blew up on a guy. She asked me if you worked. I said you were a professionally trained chef, too. And she said something like, this seemed pretty careless, at best, leaving a child unattended near a stove. She said that sometimes they got these mothers in with these borderline IQs, women who might make that kind of mistake, but someone educated . . ."

"So, if I had a borderline IQ, I'd be in the clear?" Lily shook her head. "What did you say then?"

"You came back into the room, and then the doctor walked back in with the prescription."

"You didn't say anything?"

"Well, she had a point," Jack said, almost under his breath.

"You think I would burn a child, our child?" Lily said, looking down at the rug. "How could you think that of me—"

"Not on purpose."

"So what are you saying?"

"Maybe you were careless? I mean, you know, you walk around at home, practically talking out loud, never about what's going on at the moment—"

"I've got three people's schedules, no, four, other than my own to keep track of. The desires of four other people to remember at all times—their likes and dislikes and comings and goings. I'm going to talk to myself. I have to keep it all straight."

"Will you at least admit that you're preoccupied much of the time?"

The lawyer took off her glasses and balanced them on top of

the steeple she had formed with her long, intertwined fingers.

Lily looked at her. Strangely, she was not embarrassed for Eleanor Snow to have heard all this. She was unconcerned with the picture being painted of her here, not because she was confident in her sense of self, but because there was simply no space in her conscious mind for the safekeeping of any more regret. She stared now at the lawyer, hoping to convey at least this much.

After a long silence, the lawyer shifted her body in her chair and said, "What you are undergoing is extremely stressful. Your private life, your family life, has been invaded, exposed. That's got to be trying on a marriage." She slid open the center drawer of her desk and began jotting something down on a notepad. "I happen to know a first-rate marriage counselor."

"My wife already has a therapist," Jack said quietly.

Lily rolled her eyes at him and then said, "I had a kind of a postpartum depression after the birth of our daughter. I went to a psychologist for a while." This statement, like everything else central to her life right now, did not represent the whole and unabridged truth, which was about as unwieldy as thirty-seven years of life. Lily had been going to one headshrinker or another on and off for years, and even that statement obscured a view of her past she had once considered as integral to her identity as a birthmark. She'd met her first shrink while in restraints in an assessment room at Bellevue when she was sixteen.

"Were you on any medication?" the lawyer asked, taking notes now.

"Zoloft, an antidepressant."

"She stopped nursing to take it," Jack said.

"Katie was seven months old. I nursed her for seven months," Lily explained. She turned in her seat toward Jack. "I wasn't careless enough to take drugs while I was breast-feeding."

"Could this be a problem?" Jack said.

"When did you go off the medication?" the lawyer asked.

"April," Lily said.

"Are you still under a doctor's care?"

Jack looked over at Lily.

"We had agreed that I should stop at the beginning of June. It just wasn't something we could afford any longer."

Lily had been going to Lucy Balsaam for two months when Jack asked her if she saw an end in sight. "No," she said. "That's exactly the problem." After about six months, Jack agreed that Lucy—or Dinsey, as he renamed her when she began prescribing the drugs, in an imitation of the way Greg mispronounced the creator of so much Technicolor fantasy—was helping her, that she seemed happier. After about nine months, he asked if she always had something to talk about each Tuesday night, or did she sometimes have to dream things up, the way he used to invent suitable sins while waiting for his turn in the confessional. A few weeks later he wondered aloud if, when she stopped, they might be as disciplined about saving money as they were about paying Dinsey's bill each month. "It's nothing, what she's charging," Lily said. "I'm near the bottom of her sliding scale." "Still," he said, "over time it adds up, could add up to a vacation, or part of one child's first week in college."

Lily had sought out Lucy Balsaam a few months after Katie's birth because she knew enough to know that everything was all wrong. She had found herself rolled up to the very edge of her life and she sensed that the drop was steep. The baby was to have been her hedge. She'd been counting on the arrival of a new baby to compensate for the loss of their business, and it hadn't, it couldn't. What kind of mother was joyless in the face of new life? Only the very worst kind.

In the end, she'd given up Lucy, not because Jack wanted her to, but because over time, Lucy had helped to roll her away from the edge and toward the flat, broad plain of her life. "I'm taking up couch space," she said to Lucy one day. "Someone else probably needs this time slot." Lucy had told her that her door was always open, something Lily had thought about more than once in the last twelve days.

"Could my therapist be asked to disclose information about me?" Lily asked. She was thinking now of all the treatment notes Lucy had been required to send to the insurance company, which continually threatened to deny even 50 percent coverage for the sessions. She and Lucy had written the appeals together, always citing "Ms. Sterne's need to be able to function in the capacity of mother to three young children."

"You left on good terms? All paid up? She agreed you were done?" Snow asked.

"Yes," Lily said. What Lucy had told her was that she understood the financial pressures they were under.

"Rather than letting them dig for information through your insurance company, why don't we ask this doctor to write a letter on your behalf, to be put in your file? I'm going to try to get letters from your employers, coworkers—"

"But that's for Jack. I mean, I'm the one who needs the—"

"Friends," the lawyer said. "Anyone with an impressive letterhead."

"Most of my friends are other mothers."

"Certainly through the business you had before you have the names of some people who'd be willing to write on your behalf? Husbands of friends? Couples you socialize with?"

Lily nodded.

"Teachers, sitters. Did you ever have the kids in any kind of day care?"

"No," Jack said.

"What about when you were both working?"

Jack shook his head. "We were pretty strapped."

"What did you do with the children all day?"

"There were only our sons, then," Lily said. "And we'd bring them with us. One of us would open up. The other would follow later on with the kids. Sometimes my mother-in-law would come by and take them home for a nap, or we'd take turns. We had a small carpeted area in a window seat with toys and books, a playpen when they were little. When we had to do a big party my mother-in-law would watch them, or sometimes we'd get a high school kid to baby-sit."

"They'd be inside all day?" the lawyer asked.

"They were inside as much as any other kids living year-round in New England." Lily infrequently told people that she and Jack had worked together and had shared most of the child care. Women, especially, were incredulous or jealous or both, as if Jack and Lily had gotten away with something. Everyone always brightened when she got to the part about having to sell the store.

"We weren't taking a whole lot home," Jack added. "Baby-sitting's expensive."

"No one ever complained about the children? Any problems with the Health Department? Any previous problems with DSS? What about school?"

"When Ben started public school, the bus would stop at the corner, in front of the store," Lily said.

"You kept them home until then? Until kindergarten?"

"No," Jack said. "No, they both went to nursery school."

"What about the summer, this summer? Are they in any kind of rec program, summer camp? Will they be visiting relatives?"

"Why?" Lily asked.

"One of the things the state looks for is the degree to which the children are at risk because they're unknown quantities in the community."

"What are you talking about?" Jack said.

"Caseworkers have a risk scale. Infants are at the top. They're not in school. No bus drivers or friends or teachers to keep tabs on them. And they can't talk. The nonverbal child, according to the state, is most at risk for abuse. As children get older and start

school, neighbors, store owners, teachers are all considered ame-
liorating factors—that, along with the hope that since they can
talk, they'll report instances of abuse." The lawyer frowned. "If
you have a child showing up for the town-run camp program
every morning at eight-thirty, someone is going to notice if he's
unkempt or hungry, or bruised."

Lily twisted the thick strap of her purse into a knot and started to cry at the thought of Ben arriving somewhere as unforgiv-
ing as the town park without the scent and sustenance of her
home.

"Lillian," the lawyer said tentatively after a while. "Is there
anything else? I should know everything, no matter how small it
may seem at the moment."

Lily raised one hip off the chair and reached into the pocket
of her shorts for a Kleenex, which she knew she didn't have. A
hand touched her outstretched leg. Jack was offering his handkerchief. "Thank you," she said.

He nodded.

She tried to catch his eye now for a cue as to how to proceed,
but he was back to looking out the window. She waited for a
moment for him to mention the semester she'd spent at Payne
Whitney. But the moment passed.

"Okay, then—" The lawyer stood up.

"Worst case?" Jack said.

"We want to get this resolved prior to Katie's release from the
Shriners. I'm going to try to get this seventy-two-hour hearing
moved up." Snow rested her elbows on her desk and flipped a
page of her engagement calendar.

Lily saw a picture of a firecracker fly by.

"We're coming into a four-day weekend," the lawyer murmured to herself. "The reality here is that I'm not an overloaded
public defender. I've got the time and resources to make this happen."

"What happens at this hearing?" Jack asked.

"The judge will want to identify Katie. DSS will have a few people there, their own attorney. They'll try to back up the allegations, and we'll basically come in with our letters of reference. You have a private pediatrician you've had for years. He knows your family. You are a known quantity in the community. . . . Why don't I make a copy of the summons?"

Lily hadn't yet seen the actual order. Jack had been served at work.

The lawyer screwed up her face. "Well, we'll get it changed," she said, still staring at the summons on her desk.

"What?" Jack asked.

"The date." She shook her head. "Unbelievable." They don't have you down for a seventy-two-hour. They have you down for a prelim."

"What's that mean?"

"It means some poor scribe hit the wrong box with his pen. I'll straighten it out. What else? They got your last name spelled wrong, but at least they spelled it that way twice." She looked up at each of them. "So we're prepared, call everyone who's going to write for you tonight and have the letters faxed here."

The air was close and still when they stepped out of the air-conditioned lobby onto Federal Street.

"Where's the van?" Lily said.

"Cyn's borrowing it. She had to go pick up a bureau in Charlestown or something."

"Oh. How are you getting to your mother's?"

"She's going to meet me." He gestured toward a bar halfway down the block.

"Oh. Well, are we straight about who we're each calling, the letters and references?"

"I am," he said.

"Good," she said. "I'm in a lot around the corner. I would have been late otherwise."

"Tell Katie I love her," he said, starting to turn.

"Tell the boys . . ."

He had his back to her. As he broke into a trot, he reached his arm up into the air and waved.

# Lily

"' . . . past the moon and his mama and papa sleeping tight into the light of the night kitchen . . .' " Fran was sitting cross-legged on the linoleum in the middle of a group of children when Lily got back to the hospital. Lily plucked at her rubber gloves and leaned against the wall, unnoticed.

"Look at this poor little guy. Not only does he fly from his bed, he somersaults out of his clothes."

The little girl who'd burned both her hands and forearms when her brother's homemade bomb exploded slid on the bottom of her hospital gown and toed the edge of the book. "Where does he have no clothes on?"

"What's this big round thing outside his window, and all these little white things?" Fran asked, lifting the book up high, so all the children could see.

"Moon and stars," the children called out, echoing one another until all seven had had their say.

"Do you ever look up at the moon and stars at night, when you're at home? Sometimes it looks big and round like this, and sometimes . . ."

"Sometimes there's no moon," one of the older boys said.

Fran nodded. "Sometimes we can't see the moon and some-times it only wants to show the tiniest sliver of itself, right? And what do the stars look like to you when you see them?"

Lily looked at the group of children. Some of them were young enough and had been in the hospital long enough to have forgotten about moons and stars, except as illustrations in books.

"You know what they look like to me," Fran continued, "they look like eyes, zillions of bright little eyes. If we were at home right now it would almost be time to go to the window or go out-side and say 'Starlight, starbright, first star I see tonight, wish I may, wish I might, have the wish I wish tonight.' "

"I'd wish for all the Power Rangers, red, blue, green, white, but not pink and yellow, 'cause they're girls," one four-year-old boy said.

The other children were quiet, either so young that they were confused by the notion of a wish, or older and skeptical that good things could happen to them as inexplicably as the bad.

Fran opened the book again. " 'Where the bakers who bake till the dawn so we can have cake in the morn mixed Mickey in batter . . .' Do you think you'd like to fly through the night in a bowl full of batter?"

Her mother-in-law read to children the same way she talked to adults, digressing again and again from the story, rolling the kernel of the original tale up and over and through a million sen-sory observations until the listener found herself fuller and rounder, her capacity for response deepened to accommodate an empathy Fran expected. "Maybe if it was chocolate," Fran said as a discussion of favorite flavors ensued. In an attempt to be heard, the louder children moved closer to the book and to Fran. When she began reading again, one child was on her back and three others had tunneled up under her arms.

Lily's parents had both read to her a lot when she was child. On Friday afternoons, her mother would come home after teach-ing her last class with a warm challah and two briefcases—one filled just with picture books from the neighborhood library. When Lily was older, already a reader herself, her father began reading to her. "The *real King Arthur*," he would say, unearthing a volume from his own ancient childhood, the real *Robin Hood*, the real *Treasure Island*. Until she'd had her own children, Lily had thought, uncharitably, that her parents' energy for reading to her and David, their singular enthusiasm for that one parent/child activity, had merely been a ploy to make their own lives easier down the line. Those late weekend afternoons when her parents would have taken over the dining-room table with books and papers would go much smoother if the two children would only engage in the same quiet activity. But when Ben was old enough to be read to, she realized that of all the duties required in caretaking and all the millions of little interactions, reading offered both structure and intimacy. It was something they could do together removed from the relentless quality of domestic life, it picked up where nursing had left off, a way to be together both inside and beyond the life of mother and child.

For her mother to put aside the monograph, the first edition, the doctoral candidate's dissertation, the latest issue of *Russian Studies* in order to read to her was an enormous victory. It was Lily's grandmother, her mother's mother, Shayna, who did all the cooking and washing, the wiping and hand-holding. She used to laugh that she was fat, that she had rolls and rolls of time, all for Lily. Lily felt logy from all that time. She loved her grandmother deeply, but she was quite old by the time Lily was born. Lily couldn't remember a time when she hadn't been aware of the need to be careful with Shayna. The stewardship of that much older generation had required a constant vigilance, which called for an abridgment of her self.

Her mother had abdicated what she considered to be the tiresome job of being a daughter and the time-consuming one of being a mother. Not knowing any better, Lily had spent her whole youth expecting her mother to reclaim her role. She was

always waiting for her mother—to be done with her work, the
last class of the second semester, the final edit, the return from
the conference in Ann Arbor or from the sabbatical in
Leningrad. Her mother had been forty when she was born and
her father forty-seven. They were a fully established team by
then, both romantically and professionally. From the time Lily
was old enough to master subtraction, she'd been figuring and
refiguring how many years until their retirement, until they
stopped this obsessive reading and writing and started to live like
everyone else.

They had died, each of them rather suddenly, eighteen
months apart, almost as if they had planned it, one more collab-
oration. Now, thirteen years after her mother's death, Lily had
been made to realize by her therapist that she had not been
robbed of some idyllic last trimester with her parents. They
never would have put aside their file cabinets to make room for
a Portacrib, never would have moved to the Cape or bought a car
or traveled somewhere normal. "People tend not to do abrupt
about-faces, not at sixty-five and not when they're relatively
happy with their lives," Lucy said. Lily had argued for a couple
of sessions that they weren't happy, that they had died before
they'd learned to be happy. They were exclusive, negative and
judgmental, cynical and sarcastic. They graded everything from
their students' papers to their children's spouses and career
choices, Lily had said.

"Who wasn't happy?" Lucy had asked her.

The first time her parents had met Jack was at the end of Lily's
apprenticeship at the Wiscasset Way. Lily had filled the last
breakfast order, changed into a fresh pair of whites, and stepped
out onto the back porch of the hotel, where her parents were
drinking coffee. "He's very 'other,' " her mother said in her typ-
ically definitive way, clearly audible above the sound of the
pounding surf. When they noticed Lily approaching, her mother slid into a zipping Russian and her father stood up from his

chair, as he always did, even at home, whenever anyone entered the room.

"Doesn't quite possess your drive, does he?" her father had said rhetorically, a few weeks before the wedding. It was a year after her mother had died. He probably already suspected he was sick. They were talking about money. They had to talk about money. There wasn't much, a little for her, a little for David. Maybe down the line, in the future, she'd want to make a change. That was what the money was for. "I'm giving it to you, not to you and Jack, is that clear? Sit on it if you want. Just know it's there in case you ever need an out. There's nothing worse in this life than being without options." The money was all gone now. They'd used half to start up their business and the other half as a down payment on their house.

"My parents worked so hard," she had told Lucy guiltily. "They never relaxed. They were always working. Even when they were with us, they were always working, the two of them."

"Who wasn't happy?" Lucy asked again.

Watching Fran now, with all these little children around her, Lily longed for her mother, not because she would have been able to descend upon this nightmare and right it, not even because she would have been a shoulder to cry on, no, Lily had Fran for those things. Fran could enter a house where someone was dying or about to be born and seamlessly set about cooking and cleaning and tending. Fran eased the way in other people's lives. Fran was a mother's mother. Lily longed for her own mother right now merely to be reminded, however briefly, that she had been a child once, that she'd been cherished. She would have paid a huge sum for one instant of experiencing either of her parents with her children, for that glimpse she knew adults were occasionally allowed of what might have been true about their childhoods.

"Again, again," the boy on Fran's back was yelling in her ear. "Read it again."

As Fran reached for a new book, Katie noticed Lily and held her hands up toward her mother. She should already have been walking on her healing feet. Lily and Jack had been told to encourage weight-bearing and not to carry her around. The tops of both feet had been burned, but the right foot was more severely affected, since all the toes were involved. In the end, the damage to the skin between her knee and her ankle on the right leg would be cosmetic—no muscle had been involved, nothing to impede function permanently. Lily beckoned to Katie, and Katie shook her head. Lily beckoned again, exaggeratedly this time, as if she were summoning her daughter to emigrate from one continent to another. Katie smiled now and began to crawl toward Lily, pulling herself along on her palms and her elbows, dragging her stomach along the dirty linoleum, her bandaged right leg safely in the air. Lily could barely watch this poor imitation of a skill Katie had mastered nearly a year before.

"Are you my tired girl?" Lily said, carefully picking her up, wrapping her ratty, unraveling white blanket around her own neck. Before the accident any mention of sleep was always met with hysterics. Now, Katie laid her head on her mother's shoulder and stroked her mother's cheek with the fringe of the blanket. Lily lowered the lights in Katie's room and sank down into the rocker with her. The baby rolled her body into Lily's, sucked rhythmically on her thumb, and ran the unbandaged part of her left leg up and down Lily's bare arm.

Now that she had the docile child she'd longed for two weeks ago, she felt sick. She had read in one of the many cola-stained parenting pamphlets scattered about the waiting rooms a short article about the effects on development of severe illness and injury. The piece cited cases of famous people who had suffered physical trials as children and had emerged transformed. Several mentions were made of children having been fundamentally altered by the trauma experienced by a brother or sister.

It frightened Lily to think that the scalding water had tamed and tempered Katie. Before the accident, Lily had wanted Katie to knuckle under, be a good girl, be quiet, reasonable; and then Lily had thrown up her hands, turned her back, and it had happened. Had Katie been older, Lily thought, she might consciously have made a connection between the two. That she was so young meant only that Lily would never know for sure what conclusions the child had drawn.

Left alone once in her mother's office at the university for what seemed like a long time, Lily had devised a game of crisscrossing the room in the rolling armchair. She pushed off from desk drawers and walls, closing her eyes as she spun across the gray linoleum, trying to anticipate the moment of contact. She grabbed onto the doorknob and pushed hard against the frosted office door and the chair sailed into a tower of metal file cabinets, causing the bottom corner drawer to fly open. And there she was, in her red tartan-plaid dress, staring up from the bottom bin, just on top of David's picture. Shayna had dressed them up back in the fall and taken them downtown to Best & Co.

The framed photographs lay at the top of an uneven pile. Underneath was the silhouette David had made of himself in art class, Lily's Mother's Day card, a macaroni necklace, and the cat ashtray she'd made just that past winter, one ear now chipped off. Lily reached in carefully. There was something with Hebrew letters on it, David's sixth-grade report card, a sachet Lily had sewn in Brownies, and somebody's baby picture with a pile of gummed-up paper clips stuck to it. Lily plucked out the cat ashtray and stuffed it into her raincoat pocket. She took David's silhouette and taped it to the front of her mother's desk. She reshuffled everything so that her mother would know she'd been there. When she shut the drawer she saw that it was clearly labeled HOME.

She climbed up onto the windowsill in the office and rested her cheek against the cool damp glass. The campus was nearly empty on a Sunday morning. She calculated. Five more years until she was a teenager. Nine until she got to leave home and go to a place like this. Maybe only twelve until she was married and a mother. Twelve more years until everything could be set right. "My kids will love me," she said aloud, letting her lips graze the black casement on the window. "When I'm a mother, my kids will love me more than anything in the world."

"God forgive me," Lily said aloud as she stroked Katie's smooth round arms. "I'm sorry, little girl, so sorry," she said, looking into her dark eyes, while Katie massaged Lily's cheek with the dusty fringe of her blanket. "Mama loves you so much, so much." Lily pulled Katie's head to her lips, and the baby allowed herself to be held too close, to be smelled and kissed and very nearly inhaled. "More than anything in the world."

When Lily stopped just outside the ward to strip off her gown, she found her mother-in-law neatly folding a stack of rubber gloves.

"If I leave three dollars . . . I think that should cover it," she said, looking up nervously at Lily and then reaching into her jeans pocket for some crumpled bills. "Water balloons," she said. "Won't the boys just love these. I'm running out of . . . ideas, distractions, you know. They need to be distracted."

Lily nodded. "I don't think you need to leave money."

"Oh, I want to." She jammed the gloves into her purple fanny pack and looked up at Lily. "How did it go? You know, I asked Bobby McEvoy—you know the McEvoys. Bobby was a classmate of Jean's or Erin's. Anyway, he's a partner at Fiske and Dolan. He didn't know her, but he knew of her, Eleanor Snow. He had heard of her."

"Good things?" Lily asked.

" 'Thorough' is what he said."

Lily shrugged.

"Have you had your supper?" Fran asked. "There's an Indian

restaurant somewhere in this neighborhood. What's her name . . . Kiley." Fran waved her hand in what would have been the direction of her next-door neighbor's house had they been standing in Fran's kitchen. "She raves about it. Wouldn't you love to try that?"

"We've got all these calls to make. Apparently we need a stack of letters at the ready."

"Oh, Jack's with you? Here? I didn't see him. I thought . . ."

"No, he was going to get the boys at Julia's and then go on to your house, I guess."

"Oh," Fran said. "Well, come. We'll have a bite."

Lily shook her head.

"Can I write a letter?" She unhooked the fanny pack from her waist and rooted through it for a pen and some paper. "What can I do? I'll make a list. Let me help call some of these people, at least."

"No, I really have to make these calls myself, but thanks."

"It's a lot of B.S., you know." Fran spread her sneakered feet apart in a combative stance. "The whole thing. I decided on my way down here. Now that you have a lawyer, they'll back right down. I'm committed to not worrying about this. By next week, it'll be nothing more than a reason to write a letter to the commissioner of DSS, which I fully intend to do, whoever he is. I'd love nothing more than to expose the kind of hurtful ineptitude . . ."

"Actually, Fran, there is something. I hate to put you in this position . . . just talk to Jack for me. . . . You know, he's angry at me . . ."

"Oh, Lily, I don't think he's angry at you, per se." Fran tilted her head to one side. "He's—"

"He's not talking to me. I mean, he holds me responsible, you know, and, of course, I mean, he's right, I was . . . I am responsible."

"For an accident?"

"He's disappointed in me. I've disappointed him deeply. I guess . . ."

Fran's fanny pack had slid from her shoulder where she'd slung it down into the crook of her arm, and she let it swing there as she shook her head. "What kind of crap is that? He never learned that in my house. 'Disappointed in you'—come on. I never said that to any of my children. It's not a concept I . . ."

"Well, you know what I mean. You know what he means. I hope he's at least talking—to you. Telling you . . ."

"It's been crazy for him, running down here, the boys, work. He's worried about work, I think. We have talked about that."

Lily nodded. Fran twisted the bracelet of her Swiss Army watch. It had been her husband's and she'd worn it on and off since he died. Greg called it "Nana's clock." Lately she seemed to always have it on. Fran didn't want to hear anything bad about Jack or their marriage. It was, Lily knew now, the reason she hadn't told her mother-in-law about going to a therapist, because if she were to tell the whole tale, she would have to say something less than positive about their marriage.

"Tell him I love him," Lily said.

Fran stepped in toward her and took Lily's hand in her own and said, "You can't worry about that now. Now, all that matters is Katie. Will you be all right? Do you need anything? Want me to bring something up to you before I head home?"

Lily shook her head, allowed herself to be pecked on the cheek, and watched as Fran walked slowly, head down, toward the elevator.

# Lily

Lily was slow to realize that she had been tricked. She and Katie had been in the playroom building walls out of cardboard blocks when Linda gently kneaded her shoulder and asked her to come to her office. Just for a minute. She held up a finger and motioned for Lily to follow, as if Lily were deaf. It was four-thirty when she left the playroom, telling Katie that she should keep on building, as high as she could go, Mama would be right back.

"These are warning signs," Linda said, handing Lily two photocopied forms from the file drawer in her desk. She motioned for Lily to sit, then stood behind her, leaning over the back of her chair, pencil in hand, pointing to each item on the first sheet.

"Things to look for post-trauma, not just with the injured child, but with other family members, especially the siblings."

Later, Lily would remember looking past the checklist and the No. 2 pencil, out to the hallway, where a policeman was walking, noisily, the leather and metal around his hips creaking and clanking. She'd remember because it always frightened her to see a cop in a hospital, a doubling up of misfortune.

Linda looked repeatedly at her watch as she talked to Lily.

"Sleeplessness, bed-wetting, regressive behavior of any kind,

103

aggressive behavior, lethargy, lack of interest in peers . . ."

"Thank you," Lily said finally, inching toward the edge of her chair. "This will be helpful when we're back home, all together." She started for the door.

"Wait," Linda said. "We haven't talked about you, though, have we?" Linda slid into a seat on the client side of the desk.

"I'll be fine once we're all back home."

Linda nodded vigorously as if attempting to reel in Lily's insincerity for inspection.

"You know, I did tell Katie I'd be right back . . . I hate—"

"Often parents are the ones who suffer these symptoms most severely. I'm sure I don't need to tell you how traumatic it is to have a child injured in this way."

*In this way.* Lily thought about that for a moment, wondering if Linda was baiting her. Everything went into the file. Was she hoping for her to spill her guts, or was she picking a fight to see what might reveal itself?

"At the risk of sounding rude," Lily said, "we did hire a lawyer, and it would be, I guess, inappropriate for me to talk about any of this with you." She turned to leave the room, and Linda jumped up from her chair and began to follow her. As they walked back down the hall toward the playroom, Linda squeezed Lily's arm and said, "Coffee?"

Lily ignored her, and a few steps later the social worker again pumped Lily's bare upper arm. "Katie's being released," she said.

"When?" Lily stopped in front of the doors to the rest rooms. The drinking fountain between the doors was stuck in the on position, and she could hear the trickle of water gurgling down the drain.

"Now." Linda looked up at the clock in the hall.

It was ten minutes of five.

"I mean, by now she's been released to the custody of DSS." Linda stepped in closer to Lily, too close. She had crossed a boundary, touching Lily as she spoke, breathing these words directly up Lily's nostrils. Lily's ears began to buzz. She could hear Linda's voice, but more clearly she could hear the water from the fountain gurgling and choking. She turned her head slowly from Linda toward the open doors of the playroom at the end of the hall. Instinctively she began to run, past the kids in wheelchairs, past the ones propelling themselves along on stretchers or pushing other kids in what looked like wheelbarrows.

The cardboard blocks designed to look like bricks had been piled high, almost beyond the windowsill. Most of the same children and aides who had been there twenty minutes before were still there, humming and talking, whining, clapping plastic against plastic. She heard the tired ring of an overhandled toy telephone as she scanned the skin and hair and bandages that individuated these children all dressed in the same blue dotted gowns. This had happened countless times before, this panic, in stores, at the playground, the pond, running up aisles, through mazes, to the edge of the dark water, knowing she would find her in just one more second, sensing her body nearby . . .

"I recommended that your mother-in-law be made her temporary guardian," Linda said, catching up to her. "They seem to have a wonderful relationship from what I've witnessed. This is extremely unusual . . . this whole case . . . the fact that she was still hospitalized when the initial OTC was granted—"

"Shut up," Lily said quietly. "Just shut the fuck up."

She walked from the playroom down the hall to the left, toward the ward. She got her hands partway into the plastic gloves and pushed open the doors.

"I thought it would be easier," Linda said, following a few paces behind. "I know it *is* easier this way."

Lily looked around Katie's room. The diaper bag was gone, and so was her blanket.

"Why didn't Dr. Wheeler come talk to me? Why didn't she tell us she was going to be released?" Lily stared over at the crib. They hadn't yet stripped the sheets.

"I gather there were some security concerns."

"What?"

"If the doctor had told you today that Katie would be released in the morning . . ."

Lily shook her head. "She's still on antibiotics. Does someone have the medicine? What else? She's supposed to have soaks. Are there prescriptions I'm supposed to fill? There are things that need to be done for my daughter. She has medical needs." Lily was shouting now.

"Mrs. Thoms, your caseworker, saw to all of that. She packed up Katie's belongings. I'm sure that everything she needs was included."

"Was my mother-in-law with her when they took her? Is there anyone she knows with her right now?"

"No. Your mother-in-law will be called. Katie's most likely at Mrs. Thoms's office with her, or on the way. They drive with the police."

"Did my husband know about this, that this was going to happen? I mean, you don't just go around snatching children, right? I mean, you do have to tell the parents?"

"I'm going to call him," Linda said.

Lily reached behind the crib Katie had slept in for almost two weeks and pulled up her pocketbook. "Can I at least go sit with my daughter until my mother-in-law gets there? I told her I'd be right back. She thinks I'm coming. . . . You people have to be fucking kidding."

Lily looked around the room. Her things were everywhere, hairbrush, magazines, newspapers, address book, the notes she'd taken at the lawyer's office yesterday, her suitcase, and a gym bag filled with laundry. She moved quickly around the room with the laundry bag in one hand and piled in everything she'd lived on for the past twelve days.

"DSS will arrange for Katie to meet with her court-appointed counsel. Feel free to call me once you're home." Linda tried to make eye contact. "I'm happy to talk with your attorney. Truly, I'd like to help you out."

Lily ignored her, and looked around the little room one last time.

# Jack

"So let's see, I've got two Dalmatians, two Barneys, a Power Ranger, and a . . . name the planets." Jack's oldest sister, Jean, was standing on a chair in her mother's kitchen.

"Solar system, Mum," Jack's niece Chris said. The six cousins were milling about, waiting to eat.

"Kate the Great gets to pick first," Jean said.

"She got to pick first last night," Greg said.

"I feel like one of those women on QVC." Jack watched as Jean swung her hips and leaned in toward the large standing fan, letting her long hair blow wildly around her.

"Watch out there, Auntie Jean," Jack said casually as he walked by the spindly chair where she was perched and suddenly grabbed her around the waist as if he'd just saved her life. She screamed and the kids all laughed.

"Uncle Jackie, do that again," Erin's little boy, Pete, said.

"Jack," Greg said. "My dad's name is *Jack*."

"Jackie's a girl's name anyway," Chris, the oldest of the cousins, said.

"Mum and Auntie Jean call him Jackie, and so doesn't Nana," Pete said in his defense.

"All right, come on," Jack said. "Soup's on."

"*Soup!*" they all screamed. "We're not having soup."

Jack and Jean helped the kids onto chairs, slid them in, poured milk. Jack buckled Katie into the crusty wooden high chair his mother had used for him and his sisters. He got out the ketchup and swung around, Elvis-style, slamming the refrigerator door shut with his bare foot. The kids laughed and Jack felt successful. His sisters' kids were owed a good time. Jean's and Erin's husbands worked together in a business they'd started over ten years before, managing municipal golf courses around the country. When they weren't traveling, they were busy counting their money. Jack ran into them about six or seven times a year. He doubted their own kids averaged much more than that.

Jack looked at the small city of wine bottles on the counter, the pyramid of unshucked corn, the freshly baked shortcake. For a minute he tried to remember what the occasion was.

"Where's my mother?" Ben asked quietly as Erin placed a hot dog on his paper plate.

"In Nana's room. On the phone, honey."

"Who's she talking to?" Jean mouthed silently to Jack.

"Beats my ass," he said.

"Jaaaaack," Erin admonished.

"She told Mum you're being weird." Jean bent over Katie and began slicing her hot dog into smaller pieces. "Jack, you can't give a one-year-old . . . Look at this," she said to Erin.

Jack noticed that Erin wasn't looking at the food on Katie's tray, but at the bandages on her leg and feet. They looked like finely woven cotton tube socks. They reminded Jack of the shapeless knit caps given to newborns in the hospital.

"Weird. He's always weird," Erin said, turning her attention to salting her son's hot dog. "She asked Mum to talk to you."

"Who?" Jack said, pinching a part of Katie's roll and popping it into his mouth.

"*Lily.* Who do you think?" Jean said.

"Well, Christ, the two of you have a goddamn phobia when it comes to using proper names. Mum does the same thing, like pronouns are going to narrow it down."

"You can be such a dick, you know that," Jean said, placing the pot of macaroni and cheese back on the stove.

"Mum's worried about Lily. She looks awful." Erin walked around the table slicing apple onto each child's plate.

"She's scary thin," Jean said.

"You're just jealous." Jack leaned back in his chair and grabbed the pot from the stove. He scraped up the last of the macaroni and cheese with the metal slotted spoon and shoved it into his mouth.

"So aren't you," Jean said, squeezing the flesh above his belt.

"Cut it out," he said, a bit too harshly.

"I don't get it," Erin whispered as she walked past Jack to get more milk. "I mean, who's going to know if you bring Katie home with you guys tonight? I just don't understand this arrangement."

"Oh, Petunia," Jean said, leaning over her younger daughter. "What happens when we don't drink our milk?" She made a monster face, which Kyla ignored, but Erin's little boy started to cry.

"In the hospital they make you drink all your milk, right, Dad?" Greg said. "'Cause if you don't drink your milk then your burns get badder."

Chris and Ben laughed.

"Maybe you two should go out tonight," Jean said. "Mum'll watch the kids."

"I'll watch the kids," Erin said. "Mum's been through enough."

"Go out to dinner," Jean said, beginning to clear the plates. "Somewhere nice."

"You payin'?" Jack said, starting to wash the pots in the sink.

"To tell you the truth, I'd be happy to if it would improve your mood."

Jack smiled at Jean. "Thanks, but Lily's going to want to be with the kids anyway."

"So what's the deal?" Erin said. "I mean, how much longer is this going to go on?"

"The holiday weekend is screwing everything up," Jack said.

It had been four days since the Order of Care and Protection had been granted and they had yet to have their "seventy-two-hour" hearing. "It seems to be something of a euphemism," Snow had informed him on Thursday evening. She'd spent the better part of the day in Juvenile Court, only to find out that the docket was so backed up—case overload, vacation scheduling, the long Fourth of July weekend—they'd be fortunate to be heard by the middle of the month.

"Lily's talking with the lawyer right now." Jack reached under the sink for some Brillo. "I'll tell you one thing. I'm not spending another night in this house. Mum's got these museum-quality mattresses. It's hot as hell up there, anyway."

"It's hot as hell right in this kitchen," Kyla said.

"Hell's a bad word and an even worse place," Jack said.

"Hell's bells, hell's bells," Greg said, clanking his dirty spoon on the side of his head.

"Where did he hear that?" Jack asked, looking over at Benjamin.

"Nana," Ben said. "She says it a lot."

Jack shrugged. "Cocktails, girls?" he asked his sisters.

"That's another thing." Erin began to pick up the cups from the table. "Mum thinks you're drinking too much."

Jack let out a laugh. "She does not. Christ, she's been matching me glass for glass every night for the past, whatever . . . two weeks."

He turned off the water, wiped his hands on his shorts, and walked into the dining room, where his mother kept the liquor, in the cabinet on the left side of the breakfront. It was always January in his mother's dining room. Ever since he was a boy the room had seemed like a winter forest: the tangled thicket of cherry-wood chair legs, the heavy, pine-colored drapes. The oriental rug lay like a layer of snow on top of the regular carpeting, so thick underfoot he always tripped. The hierarchy of Irish crystal in the china cabinet refracted light into the heart of the dark, overgrown room, reminding him of the morning after a spectacular ice storm.

Rye was what his father had drunk, just one a night, neat. The same bottle of Canadian Club, mostly full, after three years, still stood in the breakfront cupboard at the back, partially hidden by the half gallon of vodka Jack had bought a week ago, the quart of Beefeater, the jug of red he would only have used for cooking, but that his mother said was just fine with dinner.

He liked to drink; so did his mother. They could both drink a lot. Same with drugs. As a teenager his tolerance had always been higher than anyone else's in the car, down in the basement, out by the woods. The only drug he'd ever seen his mother take was aspirin, and when she did, she took at least four, and often six. Nothing less worked on her, she said. When he had smoked cigarettes, he had smoked a lot. He hadn't been able to enjoy just the one after dinner or sex. If he was going to smoke he was going to smoke two packs a day, every day, just as Fran had done, back when she had smoked.

He had always thought that a chef's occupational hazard was eating, but during his first restaurant job he realized that smoking and drinking were the vices of men and women who worked for ten hours at a clip, standing and sweating the whole time. Every night, before the rush, the kitchen would send dinner out to the bartender, and when the tray was returned it would be filled with rum and Cokes, White Russians, or 7-and-7s. He'd met a lot of alcoholics working in restaurants. Some of the nicest people he'd ever worked with were drunks.

He remembered finding the sous-chef of the Colonial asleep in a corner of the dining room one morning when he opened up.

Les was curled in a ball under a blue linen tablecloth, and Jack thought he was dead until he touched him. Les coughed, rolled over, and showed up ten minutes later at his station in fresh whites, hair combed and face washed.

Les had his own set of Henckels. He allowed no one to touch the knives he used to carve apples into swans, watermelons into steamships, turnips, radishes, and carrots into entire blossoming gardens. That morning, Jack watched Les wedge a cigarette between his pale lips, unlock his knife drawer, pull out his tools, pour himself a cup of coffee, and, hands trembling, begin to carve the tops of four pounds of pure white baby mushrooms.

Les was about ten years older than Jack, old then, he had thought, easily thirty-two. Jack wondered why Les had decided to do that to himself, why he always hung out at the Colonial's bar after work instead of going home, why he didn't have a wife, why he had never worked anywhere else but at this second-rate food hall when, clearly, he was an artist. He was good with a knife and even better with an ice pick. For the Thanksgiving buffet he had carved a turkey with its wings spread, doves for a wedding reception, a golfer in full swing for a retirement party.

"Just too boring to do it without a hangover, huh?" Jack had said to him that morning.

Les said nothing. He put down his paring knife, sipped his coffee, and finally lit the Camel that had been dangling limply from his lips.

"Sorry," Jack said. "What do I know?"

"Damn straight," Les said, words and smoke blasting out together.

Jack pulled out the bottle of vodka and placed it on the lace runner in the middle of his mother's dining-room table. Maybe he expected too much from people. He'd heard that more than once from kids who worked for him. Almost everybody was a disappointment to him, except Lily. Lily was the only person, aside from his mother, whose standards exceeded his own. That's what bothered him so much about the accident. She wasn't a careless person. If one of them was going to have something like this happen on their watch, clearly it should have been him. He could be reckless, unmindful, cocksure that harm's way would never cross his way.

She was the safe one. He'd somehow improved his chances, he knew, lengthened his life, by attaching himself to her at a young age. She represented a kind of sobriety and evenness, good fortune itself. She was his hedge against everything that could go wrong in life, even randomness. It was horrible enough that this had happened to his baby, but so much the worse that it had happened when the careful parent was home. Because now she could no longer be trusted with balancing out all that was disappointing in himself and the world.

"At least she returns calls on the weekend."

Lily was standing in the doorway between the living room and the dining room. She was wearing one of his mother's dresses. This was her new thing now. She didn't want to leave Katie, not even for forty minutes to drive home and get some clothes. He hadn't offered to bring clothes back to her. He wasn't getting involved in that again. He hoped to Christ she was at least wearing her own underwear.

"Jean and Erin think we should go out to dinner," he said, raising his eyebrows slightly. He didn't want to argue again about Eleanor Snow's competence.

"God, they live in a dream world," Lily whispered and shoved her hands into the pockets of the dress.

"I told them you wouldn't want to leave Katie."

"Like we have all this extra money."

"Their treat."

"Right. We still owe Jean fifteen hundred dollars for the van. I'm really going to let her buy us dinner. Christ, we're probably going to need to borrow money from all of them now to pay Snow. The court-appointed attorney will be calling your mother, so she can set up a meeting with Katie. Now, Snow thinks we need to just turn the seventy-two-hour hearing, or whatever they're calling it now, into an evidentiary hearing—act like it's a full-blown case . . ."

"Well it is," Jack said, running his thumb along the glass seam at the back of the vodka bottle.

"You know what I mean. She thinks we should go in there with actual character witnesses, not just letters of reference. She wants all of us to undergo psychiatric evaluation—everyone, Katie, the boys. She doesn't think it's good enough now just to have Lucy Balsaam vouch for me, even if I could get hold of her."

Whining. That was her newest means of communication.

"She got the name of the psychiatrist, one of the psychiatrists, I guess, the court uses. She wants to know about the nurses. Do we think any of the nurses from the Shriners might vouch for us."

"How could we ask people who work downtown to drive all the way up to Suffield County Juvenile Court—with little or no notice, be out a day's pay? I'm not going to do that to those women, not after the way they extended themselves for us, for Katie. It's just not fair."

"Fair?" Lily said.

"Are we that up against it that we have to pack a courtroom with—"

"Hey, you're the one who's committed to sticking with Snow. I told you I thought it was a mistake . . . I mean, she gets to the end of the conversation and she has the unmitigated . . . whatever, to tell me, again, how fortunate we are that they appointed Fran as Katie's temporary guardian and that I'm even allowed to be with her without supervision."

"She's just trying to—"

"Backpedal?"

"Well, she didn't expect it to go this way," Jack said. They'd been all through this at least twice before in the last few days.

"We really need to talk about how we're going to pay for this," Lily said, changing the subject only slightly.

"Does it really matter?" Jack leaned into the handle of the vodka bottle.

"What does that mean?"

"It means that her services are not a discretionary purchase."

"Why don't you just say 'dismissed' when you're all done. That way I'd be clear, you know."

"Fuck you," Jack said, under his breath. He picked up the vodka and started to walk toward the kitchen, around the dining-room table so as not to have to pass Lily.

"Oh, good," Erin said, craning her neck around the doorway from the kitchen. "If we race out of here now we can make the six-o'clock down at St. Stephen's. Your kids want to come. Is that okay? You want to come, don't you, Jack? Lily will probably love the peace and quiet, won't you, Lil?"

"Is your mother going?" Lily asked.

"I don't know. Why?"

"Katie," Jack said.

Erin appeared confused.

"Well, we can bring her, no biggie."

Lily sighed and turned, walking through the dining room into the living room.

"Katie can't go if Mum isn't there and she can't stay here with Lily unless Mum stays here. Got it?" Jack said impatiently. He pushed past his sister with the bottle and went into the kitchen.

"You can't possibly expect us to remember all this every minute of every day . . . these arbitrary rules," Erin said.

"Nice, Erin," Jean said, wringing out a facecloth, getting it ready for the next set of saucey lips and sticky hands. The littler kids were out on the back porch and the older ones were skulking about the kitchen with cookies, listening to the grown-ups.

"Make her a drink," Jean said to Jack.

"Before church?" Erin said, incredulous, as she sponged off the kitchen table.

"God drinks," Jean said. "I'm sure of it. Are you going?" she asked Jack as he rooted around in the refrigerator for a lime.

"It would be nice for your boys if you went," Erin said.

Jack ignored her.

"Where is Mum, anyway?" Jean asked.

Erin pushed Jack aside and ran some water from the tap into a Barbie cup for herself.

"If we go to church, I'm not going to St. Stephen's. Let's go to Our Lady," Jack said.

"Down by where that box factory or whatever it is used to be? Have you ever been to that church?" Erin gestured toward him with the empty Barbie cup. "The people who go to that church smell."

"Gross," Chris said, looking up at her aunt from the floor, where she and Ben and Kyla were passing around a box of Teddy Grahams.

"We all smell, somewhere," Jack said.

"He's just like Mum," Jean said, barely able to keep from laughing. She grabbed a highball glass from the cupboard and then swung out her arms in an imitation of their mother. "Why don't we all go down to that wonderful old church on Mechanic Street. It's so, so . . . everyone there is so *real*."

They took up an entire pew at St. Stephen's. His mother had tried to orchestrate the seating, holding back grandchildren so that Jack and Lily would be forced to sit together, but it hadn't worked. Neither had her manipulations in the crumbling driveway as she had attempted to assign passengers to cars. Jack had ended up alone in the Subaru with his boys.

"Mom's going to church? Mom never goes to church. Why's Mom going to church?" Ben had asked him ten times on the way to St. Stephen's.

"There was a church at Katie's hospital, wasn't there, Dad? Nana told me," Greg said.

"Mom's really not supposed to go to church, is she, Dad?" Ben continued.

"She wants us all to be together," Jack had finally said, hoping to shut him up.

"That's why we're moving to Nana's, right, Dad?" Greg asked.

"We're not moving to Nana's," Ben said. "We're just staying there because of all the baths Mom has to give Katie."

Jack had let his mother come up with what she called "the white lie that comforts." And so he and Lily had told the boys that they would be staying with Fran for a while because it was so much work to give Katie three long soaks a day. Neither of the boys had questioned it.

"I know why Mum's coming to church, Dad," Greg said certainly from the backseat. "She wants to be Christmas like us, right?"

"Catholic, you idiot, and we're only half. This is very, very strange," Ben said.

The kneelers were filthy and Jack pulled out his handkerchief to wipe them off. He rested his elbows on the pew in front of him and let his forehead press into his fingertips. He'd attended more Masses the past two weeks than he had in the previous two years. His mother had gone most mornings since Katie's accident, and he'd joined her and the boys once or twice.

"Are we the only continent people here?" he'd whispered to her one morning as they sat down, and his mother had laughed and laughed until tears leaked from the corners of her eyes. But the eleven ancient women scattered throughout the church were so nearly deaf no one had even turned around. A few times at the hospital he'd gone off to get a Coke and had wandered into the chapel. He'd prayed for only one thing these past few weeks. He could be very focused when it was demanded of him, and so for the past three weeks he'd been able to scrape to the side all but

Katie's health each time he knelt down to pray. Petitioning God for recovery, for the cessation of pain, for good health, was about as textbook an entreaty as one could make.

But now, the row full of tapping, tsking, sighing children that stretched all the way from his right thigh to Lily's lap perverted what otherwise might have been a perfectly fine communication with his God. He could only shout over the heads of so much distraction to tell God what he didn't want—to protest, rather than pray. He didn't want his sisters and mother to spend a summer's worth of nights dissecting his marriage amid the roar of fans and the sloshing of jug wine. At least, he didn't want to be called in for testimony or examination while the vivisection was occurring. And he didn't want Lily, in some tranquilized state, to spill her guts in a late-night kitchen-table session.

He looked up past the altar at the martyred Jesus and prayed to be made less angry. He stared at the back of the just barbered head in front of him for distraction. He could tell by the guy's tan, the way it just crept over the top of his collar and out from under his short sleeves, that he was a golfer. He hated golfers.

He looked down at the dirty toes of his nieces peaking out from their sandals, past his sisters' running shoes to his wife's unraveling canvas slip-ons. He hated her for fucking it all up for them.

He whispered to Ben that he had left something in the car, and just as Father Paul said, "All rise," he bent his head and buckled his knee and asked God one more time to forgive him for being so angry. Then he walked quickly down the aisle, through the narthex, into the thunderstorm outside.

"You missed it, you missed it, Dad," Ben yelled as they all raced to get into the car. The parking lot was a sea of families in skimpy summer clothes holding bulletins over their heads and bobbing between starting cars.

"Where's my mother?" Jack said as Lily buckled Katie into the car seat in the back and then got in front, flinging rainwater on him as she finger-tossed her hair.

"She's talking to Paul. It's all right, go. Jean and Erin will wait for her."

"But we have Katie." Jack shook his head and turned off the ignition.

Lily swiveled around, her wet dress squeaking on the vinyl seat, and smiled at the children in the back. Jack looked at them through the rearview mirror.

"Do you realize this is the first time in fourteen days that we've all been together, alone, just our family?" she said.

"That's because Katie was in that hospital with all the burnt kids, right, Mum?" Greg said.

"Dad, you're going to wish you hadn't left when we tell you what you just missed." Ben was standing up, trying to wedge his body between his parents' bucket seats. "Father Paul called Kate to the front, the front of the whole place."

Jack turned and looked at Lily. She was still smiling, hair plastered to her forehead, her lashes dark with water. Runny eye makeup blurred her face slightly, making it seem as if he were looking at her through a scrim. For the first time in weeks, she looked happy. He couldn't imagine why.

"Really?" he said.

"I had your mother take her up. Greg wanted to go, too."

"Yeah, when Nana was already halfway there—so he goes running up the aisle. Dork."

"Benjamin!" Jack yelled.

"Well," Ben said, leaning all the way into the front now, his lanky arms draping the tops of the car seats.

"It was just fine," Lily said. "And when they got up to the front—"

"The *altar*," Jack corrected.

"Whatever. He had your mother and Katie face the congregation, and he said he just wanted to introduce a little girl who had been through a great ordeal. And that prayer and good care from the Shriners staff had healed her and that if people in the church didn't know about the Shriners they should. He explained about the Shriners being free, flying in kids from all over. And then he asked that everyone donate the money they might have spent on fireworks for the Fourth to the Shriners, who would, no doubt, be busy caring for a number of kids injured by fireworks over the weekend."

"He's not supposed to do that, you know. I mean, if people want to pony up for a hospital, he should be telling them to give to Holy Name, or someplace like that. Then he plugged his own little miracle show, right?" Jack said.

"No. Not at all," Lily said.

"What miracle show?" Ben asked.

"Nothing." Jack cracked the window slightly. The glass surrounding the car was opaque from the exhalation of the excited little breaths in the back and the deeper sighs up front.

"Father Paul came and prayed for Katie when she was in the hospital," Jack said.

"Anyway," Lily continued, "after the service—"

"The Mass," Jack said.

"Afterwards, all these people came over to us and kissed us and patted Katie on the head, and blessed her and grabbed my hand. It was more support than I've felt anywhere, ever. And it was genuine, all this concern, all these good wishes. It was incredible, really."

"Roll down your window and see if my mother's making any headway," Jack said.

"Wait a minute," Ben said. "What miracle?"

"Father Paul prayed for Katie and she got better," Jack said, using the back of his hand to clear a spot on the windshield.

Lily turned toward Ben. "When it looked like Katie was going to need a special operation on her burned skin, Father Paul came and prayed for her, and the next day, by coincidence . . . You know what that means, right? The next day it just so happened that she was better and didn't need that operation. But . . . some people . . . want to think he worked a miracle."

Jack laughed. "Not quite that simple. You're flushing the very basis of Christianity down the toilet with that kind of an explanation." Jack turned the engine on again and blasted the defroster.

"If you're Jewish, you don't believe in miracles, right?" Ben said.

"He's got you now," Jack whispered.

"No," Lily said slowly. "There's lots of miracles in Judaism—the Red Sea parting, the oil lasting for eight nights—"

"But those are all old ones," Ben said.

"It's complicated," Lily said. "I guess it has to do with the way that priests and rabbis are different . . . with power—"

"Turtle Power," Greg said absentmindedly from the backseat. Jack looked in the rearview mirror and saw him wrestling two action figures against the mud flap of his booster seat.

"You're such an idiot," Ben said.

"Be nice," Lily said.

"Mine," Katie said, leaning over the side of her car seat and trying to grab one of Greg's X-Men.

"Muuuum," Greg called. Jack could hear the scuffle behind him, the repeated clacking of plastic against seat-belt buckles, the muffled sound of skin getting pushed and hit, slapped a little, maybe even bitten.

"That's enough," he said loudly, still not turning around to look.

"Don't touch her leg, you moron," Ben yelled.

"Oh, God." Lily hopped out of the car and opened the back door. "You're never to touch her leg," she hollered. "Do you understand? Never. What did you do? Goddamnit, what did you do?"

"You should be crying, Greg," Ben said. "That was an evil

thing to do, and you should be crying. Crying and begging God to forgive you."

"Enough," Jack said. He released the tension in the back of his seat, and pushed it all the way down, so that he was now lying on the knees of his children.

Katie and Greg laughed.

"It's not funny, Dad," Ben said, pounding Jack's headrest with his fist. "Not everything's funny."

Jack hated Ben when he was like this. When the boy was angry he could age forty years in a matter of seconds, ascend some mount of righteousness from where he talked down to his father.

"You're right, son," Jack said in his best Dudley Dooright voice. "Not everything is funny. Right now, for instance, even with that thing hanging from your nostril, *you* are not funny."

"That's it," Ben said. "I've had it. I'm sick to death, to death of you." He pulled on the door handle and kicked open the door with his sneaker. Jack watched as he started to run across the wet parking lot.

"Shit," Lily said, looking straight at Jack. She yelled for Ben to come back. She walked to Jack's side of the car. "Nice family scene," she said, gesturing to the entire car. "There's people still here."

Jack waved her away and pushed in the cigarette lighter. Katie was crying now, "Mama, Mama, Mama . . ."

Jack narrowed his eyes through the drizzle and watched Lily follow Ben around the side of St. Stephen's as his mother began to head toward the car, smiling and waving, oblivious to the whole ugly world he lived in. Full up to the eyeballs with some kind of faith and blind as a fucking bat.

# Jack

Jack stopped in front of the biggest Victorian on Fairview. It looked naked compared to the other houses on the street, which were still decorated for the Fourth with flags flapping and red, white, and blue bunting draped over the doors. He'd always wondered who lived in these showplaces, who could afford to heat them in the winter. Shrinks. Yeah, that made sense.

He fingered the black-and-gold "Patient Entrance" sign nailed to the corner of the house. It was a tacky thing to do to a house of that stature, slapping on a hardware-store sign. For Rent, For Sale, Help Wanted, Checks Cashed Here, Brains Washed This Way. Lily was supposed to have seen this Dr. Melick first, then he, then the children. But Katie'd had a follow-up visit with Dr. Wheeler this morning and Lily had insisted on going with Fran to take her.

Jack had called Cyn at seven a.m. from the pay phone at the Lauralee Diner to tell her he'd be late for work. He'd waited out on the front steps for them to open. Each night he slept alone in the house he woke earlier and earlier. Couldn't blame it on noise, not real noise, anyway. As he dialed Cyn's number, he looked around the diner quickly for an excuse.

"Squirrels," he told her, looking at a landscaping crew seated at the counter. The greasy teen closest to him was wearing a Chip 'n Dale T-shirt, maybe Chippendales, he couldn't tell. "Chipmunks or squirrels," he said to Cyn, "got into the attic last night. Christ, they'll do some damage."

"Have a heart," she said. "You know those things? Get a Havahart trap. Promise me you will, Jack."

When he entered Melick's waiting room he could hear the yapping of some little dog from deep within the recesses of the house. A shrink with a little dog. There were no magazines in the waiting room, just books. A cheap shrink. Poetry . . . Robert Frost, Elizabeth Bishop, Dylan Thomas, Robert Lowell, Anne Sexton, great. "Maybe you'll get something out of it," Lily had said as he'd left his mother's last night. "Try," she said. "Try to get something from it." This appointment was an evaluation, not an elective in finding more meaning in his life. How could she not understand that what was being researched here was their ability to care for their child? This guy was going to comb the scene for violence and dysfunction. None of this was about emerging a happier individual.

"Charles Melick." A small, thin man with a beard stepped into the waiting room and nodded, his hands clasped behind his narrow back.

Jack stood and extended his hand.

"Watch your step," the shrink said. A little ball of white fur ran between Jack's legs as he followed Melick down a narrow hallway. The dog barked so loudly it seemed to shake from the force. Melick stepped on the button at the top of the white-noise machine outside the office, gestured for Jack to enter, and then rolled two enormous sliding oak doors closed behind them.

"You know, well perhaps you don't, that what you say to me today will be used in your Order of Temporary Custody hearing?

This, unfortunately, is not a privileged session. It's all for the record."

Jack nodded and looked at his watch. "We all have our jobs to do."

The shrink smiled.

"Lots of Kleenex," Jack said, nodding in the directions of three boxes of varying size.

"Sometimes I work with families."

Jack nodded.

The shrink smiled.

Jack looked at his watch again.

"Are you late for something, another appointment?"

"Just work," Jack said, shifting his weight on the couch he wished he hadn't sat in. He was in the middle, too far to reach either armrest. "I'm just . . . a little impatient to get this rolling."

"By all means," the shrink said, picking up a notebook. "What would you like to tell me?" He crossed his legs.

"Nothing. I mean, there's nothing extraordinary to say. We're mainstream, right in the middle, as far as parents go. We're average good parents. We're fine, maybe better than fine."

The shrink nodded vigorously. "You don't think you should be here, do you?"

"Well, it was our choice, in a way. Our attorney thought it was a good idea."

"You still don't think you should be here?"

"Do you?" Jack said. "Really, I'm sure you've read about us, the case. And now looking at me . . . I mean, I'm not covered with tattoos or a week's worth of facial hair."

The shrink stroked his own beard.

"I don't beat my kids."

"No one has suggested that."

"Good."

"I have read a lot about your family. And from what the caseworker says, there seems to be some tension between you and your wife."

"She never interviewed me. The caseworker never interviewed me," Jack said.

"Someone from DSS did come to the house, though, yes?" Melick nodded as if answering his own question. "She alleges that she heard an argument between you and your wife, and that your wife is . . . Well, why don't you finish the sentence for me?"

"Of course we had an argument." Jack exhaled loudly. "We had someone in our house judging us, watching us. That'll make you snap."

"Do you feel responsible for your wife's behavior?"

"She's a big girl."

Melick put his notebook on the small glass table beside his chair. Jack imagined that the deep blue armchair was equipped with all manner of mechanisms somehow hardwired to the patient couch and capable of evoking uncensored responses from him.

"We only have this one meeting. I have only this chance with you. So, let me be honest about what I know. And, in turn, I hope you will level with me. This is all for your daughter's sake, right? The caseworker who did the home study, the intake, writes that you lied for your wife, that you covered for her." He picked up his notebook. "She says that your wife threw something at you in the kitchen the day she visited."

"A plant, a potted plant, happened to break that day."

"Accidentally?" Melick asked.

"It slid off the kitchen table. Bad timing," Jack said.

"In the caseworker's 51B, she says you covered for your wife. In essence that you lied for her."

"There was nothing to lie about," Jack said slowly. "It was . . . an accident." He felt the first part of the word on his tongue hiss and slip and he was shocked at its assertive finish.

"Has she ever thrown anything at you?" Melick asked.

"I don't know. No." Jack laughed. "A baked potato, once."

"Was it hot?"

"She missed me. It hit the wall and smashed."

"Does she throw things at the children?" Melick asked.

"No."

"Do you think she might throw a pot of boiling water?"

"Fuck, no. . . . Look, you let a twenty-year-old come into our house and play connect the dots . . ."

"Are you afraid of your wife, Jack?"

"Do I look like I am?"

"What do you mean?" Melick asked, putting down his note-book, thoughtfully.

"I outweigh my wife by about eighty pounds."

"Fear is not always physical."

Jack stared at the shrink.

Finally, Melick picked up the notebook again. "Why don't you tell me something about your relationship with your wife."

Sex. If he'd prepped at all for this exam, it had been on this question and this one alone. That's what shrinks always wanted to talk about, wasn't it? Lily had said she didn't talk much about sex with Dinsey. She'd told him that once, but he hadn't completely believed her. She had also told him that when she was sixteen and at Payne Whitney, she'd had these strange erotic dreams. They were from the medication, she was certain. And there was a period in their lives together, sometime before they were married, when she would deliberately arouse him by recounting those old odd dreams.

"You mean sex?" Jack asked.

"If that's significant."

"It's usually a plus when it is." Jack leaned over and pulled up one of his socks.

"On a scale of one to ten, how would you rate your marriage?"

"Right now?"

"Or, before the accident, before all this trouble."

"It was getting easier, I guess. We were adjusting to a pretty major rearrangement."

"How so?"

"We lost our business over a year ago," Jack said.

"So, around the time that your daughter was born, then?"

Jack nodded. He had never linked the two events, certainly not in a causal way. Most days, he blamed the crappy New England economy. People didn't pick up chicken breasts stuffed with sun-dried tomatoes on their way home from work when they weren't working. Execs seemed to have all but quit entertaining at home once their budgets for doing so were eliminated. Sometimes Jack thought of those months when it was becoming more and more clear that they might have to give up the business as months in which Lily was getting larger and larger. But he had never associated any of his children with his wife's pregnancies. If anything, Katie, this third child they had impulsively conceived, had functioned *in utero* as a kind of mascot for their team, which was having an exceptionally bad season.

"When quantitative studies are done of major life stresses, losing one's job is very near the top of the list," Melick said.

"Well, we lost everything."

"How so?"

"Money. We lost a lot of money. No one wanted to buy the business from us. We had problems getting out of our lease. We couldn't even unload the equipment at a decent price. We ended up getting half, less than half, of what it was worth."

"Did you enjoy working with your wife?"

"It's what we'd always done. That's how we met. It's how we know each other. We've always worked together."

"You must miss that, then. You're apart all day now. That's something that takes some time getting used to, no?"

"Well, we're not dependent," Jack said. "We always had our own lives. It's just not what we'd planned. But, hey, that's life, right? I mean, we're lucky. Every fucking day I tell myself how lucky we really are."

Dr. Melick was silent for a while, as if Jack might reveal more than he already had.

"You're angry," he said after a while.

"Isn't everybody?"

"I'm asking about you," Melick said.

Jack rearranged his body on the too-soft sofa.

"I think about this a lot. I spend a lot of time thinking about the money that we lost. And over the past year or so, I finally realized that what bugs me so much is not that we lost out, but that someone somewhere, lots of people, actually, benefited from that loss. Do you know what I mean? The jackass who bought our stuff, our ovens, the mixer, the refrigerated cases, all that, for less, a lot less, than it was worth. The landlord who turned around and rerented the space while we still had to cough up for five of those months. They all rode on our backs, you know? I wouldn't have minded if the money had just burned, burned up, ceased to exist, for us or anyone else."

"Justice," Melick said.

"Yeah, exactly."

"You're concerned with that?"

"Sure."

Melick scribbled in his notebook for what seemed like the first time, Jack couldn't be sure. He hadn't been as vigilant about watching Melick as he'd intended. In fact, he'd lost track of this whole meeting back somewhere a few minutes ago.

"What does that word, 'justice,' mean to you?" Melick asked, still writing.

"I don't know." Jack gripped his earlobe. "Fairness, I guess." All he could think of was stupid sayings from his childhood, "even steven," "just deserts," "fair and square." He remembered his sister Erin actually bringing a ruler to the table once when there was cake to be cut. "I'm not worried that I'm getting ripped off. I mean, I'm not paranoid. That's not what I'm talking about. I hope I'm implying something larger. Cosmic fairness, I guess." He laughed.

"A value system?"

Jack nodded. At least the guy wasn't dim.

"Yes." Melick nodded. "So, then, given that value system, how do you feel about your daughter's accident?"

"I don't think about it," Jack said, realizing after he'd spoken that he was, in fact, telling the truth.

"What happens when you do?"

Last night, when he'd bathed Katie for her third soak of the day in the mixture of water and baby oil, he'd massaged the thickened skin of her feet and toes and leg and thought about what happened to different foods when they were blanched. Greens deepened in color when dropped into boiling water. Spinach wilted and shrank. The skin of poultry toughened and sealed itself. Blanched. His baby's skin had been blanched.

"How do you feel when you think about the accident?" Melick pursued.

"Bad," Jack said. "I feel bad."

The doctor nodded, inclining his slight body forward, almost bowing, as if in empathy. "How do you think your wife feels about the accident?"

"I don't know," Jack replied.

Melick cocked his head.

"I guess she's upset. I mean, I know she's upset. She won't let our daughter out of her sight. She's very clingy to the kids, right now."

"And with you? How is she with you?"

Jack shrugged.

"You're not very interested in how she feels, are you?"

"Not at the moment."

"Do you hold her responsible?"

"It was an accident," Jack said, allowing the word to slide out somewhere toward the end of a sigh.

"Do you trust her around your children?"

"It was an accident," Jack said.

The doctor leaned back in his chair and capped his pen.

"I've seen those bumper stickers. I'm sure you have, too. 'Shit Happens.' "

"Right," Jack answered. "And shit keeps happening."

# Jack

When he got to work at ten-thirty, two messages were scrawled for him on the chalkboard by the phone. At the top was "Call home," and under it was "See Norris." Next to Norris's name was a picture of a firecracker, or at least that's what he thought it was a picture of. Norris wanted lunch today to have a Fourth of July theme? Yesterday had been the holiday. The family had all gathered at Erin's for a barbecue. She'd insisted that they walk in the blazing sun to some field in her town to hear a local fife and drum corps perform. Jack had barely been able to watch as the mostly older men marched around the soccer field in long red coats with wool trousers and knee-high black boots. It was like waiting to witness a heart attack. Katie had cried at the hollow boom of the oversized drums, and Lily had let out an audible shriek when the muskets were fired.

After that there was volleyball. Erin had set up a volleyball court in her backyard. She'd looked up the official measurements. The court was regulation. It had taken her all morning. In fact, it had taken so long that she really hadn't had any time to fuss with the food. Lily begged off the volleyball and headed for the kitchen with Jean. And Jack and his mother and Erin and his brothers-in-law, and what seemed like too many small children, had played ruthless volleyball for two hours in a yard without a single shade tree.

He wondered if Melick had made much of his sunburn. People thought that was reckless behavior these days, getting sunburned. As he picked up the phone to dial Norris's office he rolled his right wrist. It had taken a pretty good beating during the game. Norris's secretary told him to come up. It would only take a minute. Jack had spoken to Norris no more than five or six times in the year or so that he'd worked there. Norris had hired him. He was the only one of the partners to feel very strongly about the importance of a private dining room. He was fat. A great fan of *nouvelle cuisine*, he'd told Jack on the first interview, and Jack had smiled politely. He maintained a wine cellar at the office as well as at home. He'd continue to do the buying, but would leave it to Jack to select the appropriate wines for each meal.

As Jack stepped out onto the seventh floor, he wondered if one of the other partners had finally put a gun to Norris's gut and said that the dining room was an insupportable indulgence. The partners traveled frequently. There were days during the past year when he and Cyn had prepared fairly elegant meals for one or two people, and occasionally the dining room sat empty.

"So, is he shitcanning me, or what?" Jack said, picking up a copy of *Institutional Investor* from Lou's desk. Lou was Norris's secretary, a former caddie from his club. "Is he going on a diet? What's the story here?"

"You got any more of that . . . what's that stuff with the cake and the cream all layered?"

"Layer cake?" Jack said.

"No, no," Lou said. "It's got an Italian name."

"Tiramisu?"

"Yeah. You got any of that left? Cyn brought me some of that last week . . . excellent stuff."

"Jack." Norris waved to him from his office. Jack left the door open behind him after he entered, and Norris made no move to close it. He shoved over a legal pad on his extra-wide windowsill and plunked himself down on top of a cooling vent. People usually closed doors and sat behind desks to fire you, Jack thought.

"Lou faxed me down in Falmouth last week. You're looking for references?"

"Yeah. I wanted to call you myself, to explain the situation, but I didn't want to bother you on vacation."

"I don't give out the Cape number," Norris said, smoothing out a blip on the placket of his starched shirt.

Jack nodded.

"This is a legal proceeding you're involved in?"

"Now. Yes. It is." Jack looked out the window through the morning heat, down to the sidewalk. There were no windows in the kitchen, just stainless steel.

"I didn't act on this last week, wouldn't, in fact, act on it without talking to you first."

Jack nodded again.

"You're being sued? Negligence?"

"No," Jack said. He shifted his weight from one foot to the other. "My daughter had an accident at home, at our house, and somehow, through a series of . . . miscommunications, I guess, the Department of Social Services stepped in and got an Order of Temporary Custody."

"Sounds serious, Jack," Norris said, staring up at him.

"It is. Our attorney suggested we gather some letters of reference, character references to submit to the judge . . . well, actually, now I'm in the position of needing character witnesses to make a brief appearance at a hearing."

Norris raised his eyebrows, as if Jack were telling him of something as foreign and distasteful as eating monkey brains.

"What sort of . . . accident are we talking about here?"

"A pot of boiling water got upended on my daughter's feet and most of one leg," Jack said. "My little girl is almost seventeen months old. She pulled the pot off the stove, onto herself."

"Jesus," Norris said, impressed. "Is she all right?"

"She's okay . . . now."

"Good. Keep me posted."

Jack nodded and turned to leave. He thought about what the shrink had said earlier that morning, about his value system and justice. This would eat at him all day now. Jack turned around at the door and faced Norris.

"The hearing will probably be held at the end of the week. We're looking for as many people who can vouch for us as possible. As my employer—"

Norris had his hand on the cradle of the phone. "I see no point in coupling the group's name with this. . . . We're talking about a legal proceeding here." He looked down again and began to bang the oversized buttons on his telephone.

# Lily

"The bus'll pick him up at Mum's," Jean said to Lily as they stood in Erin's kitchen, trying to celebrate the Fourth of July. Jean let most of a half gallon of Hellmann's glug out of the jar and into a lobster pot filled with macaroni.

"What bus?" Lily said. There had been some talk, over the past few days, now that life was communal and no discussion private, of sending the boys to camp. But it wasn't until five minutes earlier that Lily understood Jean had already registered and paid for Ben to go to the soccer camp run by the Rec Department in Winstead, and for Greg to attend a Y program in Fran's town.

"I put down Mum's address. The bus will get him right there at eight-thirty and drop him off at one. God, how does she stand this kitchen?" Jean said, looking around at the piles of paper that covered nearly all of Erin's green marble counters.

Lily sat very still and stared at the heap of raw ground beef in front of her. "You didn't put your mother's name down as Greg's guardian, or anything, did you?"

"No."

"Well, what about next week? When we're back home?"

Jean was slicing celery, long reckless incisions down the spine of each stalk. "I figured nothing was really definite with that, anyway."

"Well, we should know something tomorrow. We should have a hearing date by tomorrow."

"Can you open this?" Jean said, handing her a jar of pimientos.

"I mean, we'll all be back in our house in a week." Lily whacked the jar lid against Erin's butcher block island.

"So, he won't go anymore, or you'll drive him over." Jean reached over for the pimientos. "Don't sweat the small stuff." She reached into the jar with her fingers and made a face. "Gross. Does anyone really like these?"

Lily thought about telling her to use the tip of a knife.

"If I'm driving Ben to Winstead, then I won't even be there when the bus comes for Greg."

"Mum will."

Lily squeezed her own hand in an attempt to comfort herself. No one seemed to understand what it felt like. Her children were being hacked away from her, first Katie, now the boys, as if she were some kind of strangulating weed from which they needed to be saved. Nothing was the same. There were no rules anymore. No routine, no logic, no gravity. "He's never been on a bus before."

"God," Jean said, breaking apart the big flaps of pimiento with her fingers. "What do you bet that will be his favorite part of the whole day? They love the bus. They all do."

"DSS can use anything, you know," Lily said. "I mean, I would hate for them to use this camp form as proof that I was dumping the kids on your mother."

"Look at these things." Jean lightly fingered the pewter pull on one drawer after another and watched as the drawers gently rolled open. "And not one good spoon in any of them."

Lily listened to the pencils and skewers and rolls of tape being lifted and dropped in disgust.

"I thought you said the lawyer told you to send them to camp. It would make them look well-rounded, or something." Jean laughed. "Extracurricular activities for the college application."

Lily sank her hands into the chopped meat and began forming patties. "What she said was that it would make us look normal, involved. The whole thing is so ludicrous, so unfair. It's medieval. There's nothing twentieth-century about this experience."

"On the contrary, Lil," Jean said, pushing aside the macaroni salad she'd been stirring. "This is where it's all led." She pulled out a stool from under the island and sat down.

"Where what's led?" Lily asked.

"Just another example of the long arm of government."

This was about her life, her children, her very self. It wasn't fodder for stimulating conversation. It wasn't an abstraction. "This isn't a conspiracy," Lily said, although at times during the past few days she had nursed that very idea. "It's random . . . unfortunate. It's like another accident." She didn't really believe this. The notion that blame and guilt could be completely absent in the face of misfortune was attractive, but thoroughly dubious.

Jean smiled and shook her head. "There's no such thing as private life anymore. You guys are the victims of too much social legislation, right? We're all overtaxed and overregulated. You let the federal government in . . ."

Lily placed the full thick patties in layers on a paper plate. "You should see some of these kids, Jean. There's this baby, this infant, at the hospital, who was burned on purpose. If it wasn't for this arm of the government you think is so long and awful, she'd go back to that mother and most likely be killed. Would you want to live in a society that couldn't be bothered with burned babies?"

"Women like that shouldn't be allowed to have babies, but that's beside the point. Why should everybody else be punished because some people aren't up to the task of living in a free society?"

Lily took the last wadded-up bit of ground beef and used it to pick up all the little stray strands of raw burger on the butcher block.

"Everything is being sacrificed to the least common denominator."

Lily grabbed a sponge from the sink. "Everything or everyone?"

"Well, this is a perfect example." Jean upended a brown bag filled with tomatoes onto her part of the counter. "In the girls' school, they've completely eliminated all the gifted and talented programs, while increasing all the remedial ones. Now does that seem right?" She took a dull paring knife and began trying to slice through the thick skin of a tomato.

"You want to grow old in a world where people can't read?" Lily said.

"Well, I certainly don't want to live in a world where the goal is to get everybody to some kind of comfortable mediocre level."

"Maybe none of these kids are being served well, most especially these kids in the middle who get neither remedial or gifted help—what about them?"

"God, you're so like Mum, I swear," Jean murmured. "Don't you want the best for your kids?"

"Doesn't everybody?" Lily said. "I mean, the other kids in the class are somebody's primary concern, too, or they should be."

"Well, exactly my point."

Lily didn't see how it was. "We can't only care about our own kids."

Jean laughed. "Yeah, but if we did, and everybody did really care about their kids, we wouldn't even *need* DSS, would we? And none of this would have happened to you. I'm telling you, Lily, you're paying the price for other people's criminal behavior. Your kids are paying the price."

Lily clasped a Spanish onion firmly against the chopping block and began peeling, careful not to slice off the root end, releasing the vapors that would make her cry. She envied Jean, in a way. She was someone who was prepared, always ready to sort through experience and order it in a way that made sense. Lily's mother had been like that.

In eighth grade, Lily's social studies teacher had asked them to outline a chapter on the Gold Rush. Lily's outline had been longer than the chapter itself. Her mother had bent over the pages at the dining-room table, a long brown cigarette in her left hand and a red pen in her right.

"Lilliput," she said. "It's all about being decisive. What counts, what doesn't. You need to impose a structure, your structure. Give me the book."

Lily handed her the fat yellow text and watched her mother do what she always did with books, open to the copyright page, check the authors' names, the publisher, the date, then guess what they'd been paid for "such idiot's delight."

"Not everything is of equal importance, right?" she said. "An outline is a kind of hierarchy, a pecking order. You've got the crowned heads here with the Roman numerals, and then all the little vassals down here with these lowercase letters." She skimmed down Lily's pages with her pen and began crossing out huge chunks of Lily's work. She shook her head. "Once you get into the swing of it, you'll see it's really kind of fun. It's your chance to better the book, you know."

"I like all those details. That's the interesting stuff," Lily said.

"You need to hit the high points."

"It's mean to get rid of all that stuff. It seems wrong."

"Good God, Lillian, sometimes you scare me."

"I didn't say I couldn't do it. I just don't like to."

"Well, it's work. It's hard." Her mother dragged deeply on her cigarette.

"That's not it. It just feels wrong. I don't like leaving things out."

"That's neurotic," her mother said, flipping through the index at the back of the text.

"How can you be sure you're right? What if everything is the same, and nothing is more important than anything else?"

Her mother stubbed out her cigarette and looked at her. "Where do you come from?"

Lily sliced through the root of the onion, then did the same with another, then another, letting the tears flow in an unbroken stream while Jean walked back and forth to the patio with trays of plates and cups and silverware. She envied Jean her politics and her religion, not the content of them, but the structure they afforded. Had Lily's mother believed in God, she would have made a first-rate zealot. She could have proselytized, become a missionary. She might have saved hundreds, even thousands, of souls.

# Lily

Those days just after Katie was released from the hospital reminded Lily of the weeks right after childbirth. She was living life on an unreal plane, in which time and expectation were loosed from their usual bounds. What had happened in that hospital had been violent, and the only way to overpower the memory was by living wholly in the present.

She was under the spell of an odd kind of elation, as if she were existing in that liminal, manic state after the biopsy and before the diagnosis, desperate now for all that was vital in the universe to make itself present, to insinuate itself within her. She fell in love with Katie again in those days after the accident, before the hearing, just as she had with each of her children in their first days of life. The infatuation was uncontrollable and unpredictable, and she reaped its rewards each time she rounded the corner of her mother-in-law's yard or turned from the sink in her kitchen and saw her little girl standing there close enough to touch.

The hearing was finally set, for Tuesday, the 12th. Until then she did nothing but indulge in her children. She canceled Greg's enrollment in camp, and every morning she and Fran and the kids traveled the forty minutes to Winstead for Ben's soccer. Then she and Greg and Katie accompanied Fran on her errands. Lily brought puppets to the Jiffy Lube on Tuesday. On Wednesday, while Fran was getting her hair cut, Lily seated herself and the kids under the dryers and played astronauts.

In the afternoons they went swimming at the lake in Winstead so that the kids could see their friends. Lily gave innumerable water rides, allowed herself to be squirted and splashed, and never once retreated up the beach. She didn't even bring the newspaper, had not looked at one in weeks. And when the ice cream truck rolled to a stop under the pines at a quarter of four every day, she ran with her kids to line up. Then they'd sit on the bed of brown pine needles dripping grape Popsicle juice down their arms, onto their thighs, no napkins, no worrying about mess, or dinner or money. And all the while Lily would repeat to herself, "I'm a good mother, look. See, I'm doing good." And it built on itself. The more she allowed herself to tumble down into the sweet sticky world of her children, the more fun they had and the happier she was, until it felt as if they were all spinning at the apex of some spectacular high, together in one ecstatic orbit.

"How   nice.   You   have your grandma staying with you." Carole Ellis stepped away from her sons, who were in line for ice cream, and squatted down between Ben and Katie. Katie looked up at her, then fished a handful of vanilla ice cream from the top of her bathing suit.

"Katie looks just like her," Carole said, nodding in the direction of Fran, who was reading in the shade of a nearby maple. Fran's fingers and toes were the only parts of her that were visible beneath her Panama hat and sunglasses and the long shift she'd made from two beach towels.

Lily smiled. "My husband's mother." She barely knew Carole. The sports moms all looked alike to her, relentlessly upbeat and unironic, simply popping open their brightly colored golf

umbrellas along the sidelines when it began to pour during practice, while Lily ran to her car for a couple of sections of the newspaper.

"Great summer," Carole said. "You guys having a great summer?"

The boys nodded. Katie tried to reach the ice cream drips on
her chest with her tongue.

"Hot one," Lily said.

"I love it. Can't get enough of it. Clark just goes nuts when I
turn off the central air and open the windows—but I love it. I
guess that's just how I was raised."

Lily smiled.

Carole seemed at a loss for what might come next in the way
of pleasantries, and just as she was about to reclaim her full
height, she noticed Katie's feet and leg. The new skin was pro-
tected beneath a double thickness of knit bandages. Lily had
been told not to expose the area to the sun for at least a year.

"What a lot of bandages for a little girl. Trying to keep up with
your big brothers?"

"No. She got burned all on her feet and one leg, too," Greg
said, working away at his Fudgsicle.

"Well, if you're out here enjoying the day it must be all better," Carole said.

Lily stood up and brushed the pine needles from the seat of
her bathing suit. "Maybe we'll run into you again. We're here
almost every afternoon."

"She was in the hospital," Greg continued. Ben pinched him,
and Greg swung his small but pointy elbow into his brother's ribs.

Carole looked toward Greg and then up at Lily with raised
eyebrows.

Lily nodded and smiled. "She's fine now."

"She almost died," Greg said.

Lily laughed, and Ben hit Greg on the back of his head. "No
she didn't, you idiot," Ben said.

Greg looked up at his brother, more hurt than mad. "How come you told me that then?" he said, his Fudgsicle dripping down his wrist.

Lily looked over at Carole, feeling the need to explain. "It looked at one point like she was going to need a skin graft."

"You're so stupid. God, I wish you would die," Ben said. He threw his ice cream in the direction of the white pines behind him and ran down toward the water.

"Sorry," Lily said, keeping her eyes on Ben. Blond hair, skinny brown back, fluorescent green-and-purple swim trunks.

"You take care now. And you, little one, you feel all better." Carole walked back toward her own sons, who had gotten to the head of the line and had begun calling to her for more money.

"Go and sit with Nan for a minute." Lily jogged from the picnic area down toward the water. Ben hadn't gone in. He was still her Benjamin, her cautious and obedient firstborn.

"That must have been some rotten ice cream," she said, falling into place beside him as he walked away from the swimming area toward the part of the lake the kids called "the swamp."

"Don't do that," he said, swinging his arm out, as if he might hit her. "Dad does that. I hate it."

"What?" Lily said impatiently.

"Make a joke out of everything. It's not funny."

"Right now, if my dad were here he would noogie your arm and say, 'What's the matter, lost your good humor?'—'cause Good Humor was the kind of ice cream, the brand that we always got in New York . . . from the ice cream truck, anyway." Lily belted her arms around her own waist, fighting the urge to touch him.

"Well, my father didn't die when I was a kid," Ben said, kicking the wet sand as he walked.

"Well, mine didn't either," Lily said.

"He didn't?" Ben stopped for a moment. "But he didn't know me."

"Well, he died before you were born, but I was already grown up and married by then."

"Oh."

"Is there some reason you're thinking about dying?"

"I'm not thinking about that," he said. He could be curt for a seven-year-old.

"Oh," Lily said. She looked back at Fran and the kids. Fran was wiping something off her beach dress. "Did you really think that Katie was going to die?" Lily said after a while.

"I don't know," Ben answered in a pained voice, as if she were removing a splinter that was far deeper than either had expected.

"You're right that some kids do die from burns. Maybe you read that somewhere or heard it on the news. But a lot of your body has to be burned for that to happen."

"I know," he said.

"Good." They had run out of beach. Here the lake was edged with tall grass and lily pads. The soil underfoot was thick and gray and muddy. Greenheads hovered. Lily pressed her feet into the sludge and watched the ground ooze up between her toes. "You know," she said, "you can tell me anything. That's my job. Never be afraid to ask me something or tell me something."

He looked up at her for the first time since they'd been walking. He reached down into the water and tried to pack the dirt into the shape of a ball. The mud dripped through his fingers like raw egg. "That's not true," he said.

"What?" she said, startled. "What's not true?"

"There's some things I can't tell you."

Her instinct was to ask, "Like what?" She belted herself tighter. "I wish you didn't feel that way."

"Well, I do," he said, sounding more like a teenager than a little boy.

Lily stood next to him for a while as he aimed at different lily pads with his unformed mud balls. When he was done, he swished his hands in the silty water and started back toward the swimming area.

"You don't seem very happy," she said.

"You always say that," he said, walking now through the shallowest part of the water.

"I do?"

"You always want everybody to be happy. That doesn't make sense. You can't always be happy," he said.

Lily sighed. "No. I guess you can't," she said.

# Lily

While the kids combat-crawled under the cast-off furniture in Dr. Melick's waiting room, Lily tallied shrinks. This new one would bring the total to six, she thought. First, and always, there would be Dr. Treadwell, who had moved her from Bellevue and checked her into Payne Whitney. He had seen her from the time she was sixteen until the end of her sophomore year at Barnard. During her senior year, she'd gone for three appointments to someone in mental health services, who, she later found out, also worked in the admissions office. Then there was the woman in Poughkeepsie she'd seen two times a week for a little less than two years while she was at the Culinary Institute. Then when they'd lived in New Hampshire there was the social worker she'd gone to at the clinic in Conway. Then she was "clean," as Jack liked to joke, for a long time, until Lucy, so that totaled six, if she counted this new guy. Six shrinks, one more than the number of men she'd slept with in her life.

Fran was tense. She seemed overly concerned with the children's behavior. She pulled Katie down from her standing position on an old armchair and told Ben to please not touch the delicate books. The plan was for the boys to go in together first, then Lily. Fran had said she would walk with the kids up to North Street for ice cream while Lily was "inside." All the way here in the car she'd insisted on referring to Melick as "the counselor," until Greg had finally asked what the name of this camp was.

Lily walked around the waiting room and looked through the poetry, Sylvia Plath, Sharon Olds, and, of course, Robert Bly. Before she'd found Lucy, Lily had walked out of a psychologist's waiting room in Acton. She'd arrived early for her initial visit with the woman, but had been somewhat slow to pick up the inspirational messages of the framed posters that hung on the walls amid the Amish quilts and the collection of antique maple sugar buckets. Just before the hour, she read the caption on one of the framed photos: ". . . and when the man looked back from where he'd come, he saw that all along the way there had been a second set of footprints, in step with his own. . . ." Certain that she was overreacting, she quickly flipped through the magazines on the coffee table. Under a copy of *Arts and Antiques Weekly*, she found a thick volume entitled *Biblical Healing: Scripture Readings for Recovery*.

Katie cried when her brothers were shown into the office by Dr. Melick. Greg looked back once, and Lily reminded him that there would be a trip to the ice cream shop afterward. Before the doctor closed the door to the waiting room, Lily heard Greg ask him if there was going to be a shot.

"He seems nice enough," Fran said, looking out the window into the doctor's backyard. "He's a small man. That's nice for the boys, less threatening."

Lily bit her lip.

"Maybe we should go outside. Go for a walk. There's nothing here for Katie. Did you bring any toys?" Fran slid her fingers beneath her wire-frame glasses and rubbed her watery blue eyes.

Fran was tired. This had all been too much for her.

"Sometimes I think about what would have happened if you hadn't been here, been able and willing to be the one to take Katie . . ." Lily said.

"You need to have a little more faith . . . faith that things will work out," Fran said sharply.

Lily sank down into the sofa and crossed her legs under her long denim skirt. Lucy had said that often. "You need to trust that things in general generally go well. That in the end, all will be fine." There wasn't a single fiber in her body that operated under that assumption. "Glass half empty or half full," Lucy had said. But Lily knew that it was far more complicated than that. You couldn't just shake off an entire belief system, one you'd been raised with, even conceived under. Watch your step, watch your back, don't kid yourself, that's what she'd always heard. Be alert, be aware, don't miss a beat or a glance or a whisper or the faint hint of the distant odor of doom. Get the jump on it, don't let anything take you by surprise, or anyone play you for a fool. The presumption of security, "faith" as Fran called it, was not part of that mind-set. And Lily knew it to be a particularly Jewish mind-set, so much so that it had become a joke, an exaggerated ethnic characteristic. But Lucy Balsaam and Fran Keliher detected it in her as an unfortunate and amendable personality trait, rather than the genetic marker Lily suspected it was. Maybe they were right. Maybe fifty years beyond Auschwitz, a hundred years after the pogroms in czarist Russia, this trait, the suspicion that had kept Jews on their toes farther back than fifteenth-century Spain, back to the time of Ramses II, had produced the desired Darwinian effect, and was now obsolete, even deleterious to survival. "It's holding you back," Lucy had said to her. "Your fear," she had called it. "Your fear is holding you back in life." But her fear was part of her. It was inextricably linked to who she was.

"Do you think this is happening because you're white?" Fran said suddenly. She bent down to trade her car keys for the pile of hardcover books Katie was attempting to stack.

Fran had said just the opposite yesterday after talking on the phone with Katie's court-appointed attorney. The woman explained that while she had been appointed to the case when the judge initially ordered the OTC, she often didn't meet with her clients until the hearing date. After having read the file and talking with Fran, she decided to hold off on the meeting. There were other cases in which the children involved were wholly dependent upon her advocacy. Legal triage, she said. Fran had gotten off the phone and said, "Thank God we all went to college and aren't on food stamps." Jack said, "Thank God Mum has such a high charm factor."

"I've been thinking about it, and I think it might be a kind of reverse discrimination," Fran said, looking out the window of the waiting room. "Which, I think, actually, has a place, you know . . . for the pendulum to swing back to center."

"I don't know," Lily said. "The lawyer told us, last week . . . warned us that the department's hired a lot more caseworkers. They've messed up . . . kids have died, more than a few children have died in the state in the past year." Lily whispered this last part, hating for even an unaware child to be subject to the information.

"Why? Why else would they be pursuing this, pursuing you? I can't, for the life of me, imagine why this hasn't already been dropped." Fran sighed and reached out to stroke Katie's straight dark hair.

Lily thought that Fran was capable of making her feelings known in a strangely ambient way. She had a knack for expressing doubt and displeasure with people so that it only came over you sporadically, like a patchy high after smoking homegrown pot, forcing you to spend longer and longer periods of time doubting your own perception. She could be genuinely disingenuous. Lily tried to determine if this was one of those moments now, if Fran was voicing some involuted displeasure with her.

"If they could do this to you, they could do this to anybody.

And we're paying for this. Our tax dollars are going to pay for this . . . kangaroo court." Fran crouched down next to Katie on the floor and beeped the horn on her imaginary car. "Parents do all kinds of things to get through the day. Three little ones all to yourself. . . . Some of these judges who put their kids in day care all day ought to just try it. Just talking to you, any idiot could see that you are a loving, conscientious mother with nothing to hide."

The great counterclockwise system of Fran's outrage was going to cut a wider and wider path, leveling whatever was structurally unsound in its wake. The fear that the last person she could depend on was about to denounce her whipped about Lily so loudly that she could only barely hear herself say, "It was my fault."

Fran didn't look up from her spot on the faded dhurrie, where she alternately pressed down one heel then the other on the pedals of Katie's pretend car.

"I left her downstairs while I went up to call a radio show, which I never did. I just wasted time up there." From down the hall Lily could hear someone cough or laugh, maybe the shutting of a door, she couldn't tell above the buzz of the white noise machine. "I don't know how long it was. Four, five minutes. No, probably longer."

When Fran finally did look up at her, Lily could see she was pale, her skin papery dry. "I used to tie Jack to a tree when we lived on Broadbridge Avenue. Three kids all under the age of five. I had no choice."

Lily had heard this before, many times. The doorknob to the waiting room turned one way, then the other, and then Lily heard the pounding of a small fist. It was Greg.

"He wants me to be in here and Ben in there. Then we'll switch, he said."

Lily looked at her watch. "How was it?"

Greg shrugged. "Can I drive too?" he asked Fran.

"You'll need to pop the hood first. Engine trouble."

Greg laughed and knelt down on the floor in front of his sister and grandmother.

"Five minutes to contemplate your navel, or whatever. Good grief. Honestly, you should see the look on your face. The cat who swallowed the canary. My sister-in-law, Thea, used to . . ." Fran laughed. "She used to switch on the TV, take the phone off the hook, lock the kids in the house, and run down to Cleveland Circle, have her hair done. Once a week, for years. Honestly. No seat belts. The kids used to roam around the car like it was a playground. When Jean was ten, I used to have her baby-sit for the other two. I mean, we'd go all the way down to Duxbury to visit my brother. Never came home before one. When I was in high school I used to baby-sit for the people next door. Every night of the week those people went out. I'd come over at seven. The girls would be in their nightgowns, and Mrs. Blumenthal would tell me that if they weren't back by eleven-thirty, I should just lock up and go home and she'd pay me the next day. Those kids were five and six, something like that. We were young and dumb and it all worked out fine. I feel terrible for mothers today . . . all this awareness . . . where has it gotten them? Mothering is not a profession. It's a function, a wonderfully important, at times divine, function, but it can't stand up to the quality controls career women want to impose on it or the ego gratification they try to get from it."

Fran continued to work the stiff imaginary pedals, flexing and pointing her ankles with fury. "It's not a profession. It's not comparable to anything else. There's a lot more leeway than . . ." She waved her hand. "Honestly, I wish there was a mirror in this room. You should see yourself. The anguish. I'm really sick of it. Women spend their lives twisted up in knots always trying to see where they went wrong—the unkind word or gesture, the omission, the neglect. Women are the ones who buy all those 'How to' books—the parenting books, the marriage books. All that improvement . . . it's just a form of misogyny. It's all crap. I'm so sick of it."

Lily had seen Fran this angry only once before. It was the winter after her husband had died, and there was a great deal of confusion when it came time to file her tax return. Neither the attorney who had probated the will, nor the accountant, nor Fran herself could find any record of Kevin's having paid his third-quarter taxes. Lily and Jack had come over to help. They were down in Kevin's office in the basement. Twenty-five or thirty Garelick Farms milk crates, each tightly packed with file folders, covered the floor.

"Look at the mess he's left me with," Fran railed. Lily watched her mother-in-law walk in and out of the maze of crates, waiting for Fran to upend everything, heave thirty-two years of paper toward the washer and dryer, the spare fridge, the piles of bent bicycles and broken hockey sticks. But instead, Fran began furiously dialing numbers. She called Kevin's friends, old accounts, public agencies.

As Lily methodically read through the last six months of canceled checks, she listened to Fran work her way up some chain of command at the IRS. "Hi, I'm Fran Keliher and you are . . . ? Oh, it's a pleasure to speak with you, Lawrence, Dave, Kenneth, Roland. Perhaps you can help me. Actually, I'm sure you can help me. You sound like a very helpful fellow. I'm recently widowed . . ." It went on like that for hours as Lily read through the last checks Kevin had written, to the mechanic and the septic service, then all through the checks Fran had written to the funeral home, the cemetery, the supermarket for the deli platters, the hospital for the services they'd rendered to a dead man.

When the last IRS employee had gone home and the dirty basement windows had filled with black, Fran told Jack and Lily to go. She pulled down an old electric typewriter and began clacking away. "I have a list," she said. "Nineteen names and they're all going to hear from me. A fifty-eight-hundred-dollar estimated payment. I'll be damned if I don't get credit for it. Damned. Make yourselves a sandwich before you leave."

Lily thought Fran was having a breakdown and shouldn't be left alone. As they walked past the lit cellar windows on the way to their car, Jack said, "That's her way. Some people have temper tantrums and throw things, my mother chooses to repeat herself, wear you down rather than knock you down."

Three days later they received a letter. It was addressed to all the siblings. She told them how she'd stayed up all night writing nineteen letters, the same letter nineteen times. The nuns who had taught her in school had known something. *Rote learning can reach down into you and ignite awareness. With every letter I wrote to those bean counters, I cursed your father, out loud, for keeping his business records so poorly, for his massive disorganization, his inattention to detail. I thought about the moment I had first laid eyes on him. He was doing a handstand in front of Dunster House, showing off to some girl, and everything, but everything, came tumbling out of his pockets: wallet, keys, coins, pens, chewing gum, comb. And he had the biggest goddamn grin on his red face of anyone I'd ever seen. That was the way Dad was. He'd do a handspring when he felt like it, with no mind to it all tumbling out. Your dad lived a happy life. Keep no secrets, children. Have fun, goddamnit. And leave a mess when you die.*

The letters kept coming for the next several months, one a week, sometimes more. After a while Jack and his sisters stopped calling each other when they received them. Often the letters centered around an anecdote, a memory of Kevin, previously unknown to the children. Many were intimate, but never embarrassingly so, Lily didn't think. As time went on the letters focused more and more on Fran herself, her childhood, her parents, experiences she'd never told to her children, feelings she'd never admitted to anyone. *It's an inhuman burden to be the sole receptacle for memory*, she wrote.

Sometimes Lily would be moved to write back to her, to respond to, or comment on, some of these intimacies. It seemed all wrong to her to receive the letters, as Jack did, without a word of thanks or encouragement. But in the face of so much raw emotion, Lily's letters back struck her as nothing more than an empty act of etiquette. She politely acknowledged receipt of a lifetime of secrets, but never replied by way of sharing any of her own. And then the opportunity came to an end. The letters ceased. Fran emerged somehow fitter, as if certain now that she, too, wouldn't die without having impressed upon her family the importance of who she was.

"Fran," Lily said now softly, hoping to draw her away from Katie and Greg for a moment. "There is something else. DSS figures I have a kind of a history. I saw a therapist over in Holloway for most of a year, not long after Katie was born. I was on some medication for a while. They made some hay out of that, I guess."

Fran smoothed her hands over the bumps her knees made under her white cotton slacks, the way kids leveled off the sand in a pail just before inverting it to make a castle. "How are you now?"

"I've been off the medication since February. It was mostly a postpartum thing, I think."

"And . . . are you still seeing a counselor?"

Lily shook her head.

"You know, you could have told me."

Lily nodded.

"I'm sorry. Sorry that I couldn't have been more help to you. . . . I didn't even . . . When did all this happen? You seemed so good with the baby. So happy to have a girl. Well, I'm not very observant."

Lily laughed, relieved that this hurdle had been passed. "It wasn't a big deal," she lied. "I was embarrassed."

"Jack should have told me. That's what family is for."

"I asked him not to."

"He should have anyway." Fran massaged the corners of her eyes, and both the kids laughed, as if she were making funny faces for their amusement. "Your old Nana looks funny, doesn't she?"

Lily looked at her watch. "This is taking a long time, don't you think?"

Fran got up from the floor and sank down into the chair opposite Lily.

"Nana, you forgot to shut the door," Greg said.

Fran obliged, making a clicking sound with her tongue. "What else?" she said, looking at Lily.

Lily smiled at the kids.

"No, I mean you, hon. What else?"

"Well," Lily said, taking a deep breath. "The other thing that may come up at the hearing is completely irrelevant now, twenty years after the fact." She motioned for Fran to come sit beside her, out of earshot of the children. "When I was sixteen, I spent some time on a psych ward. The police picked me up one day after school dodging cars on the West Side Highway." She couldn't look at Fran as she said this. She cocked her head, hoping, for a moment, to appear somewhat blithe. "Statistically, a very unusual means for a young female to attempt suicide. I couldn't have been very serious about it."

"Oh, God," Fran said. She clutched her small hands together. "What . . . precipitated it?"

"Adolescence," Lily said, incapable, now that she had been "successfully healed," of answering from the perspective of that sixteen-year-old girl. Her grandmother had died in March of her junior year in high school. The doctors told Lily's parents that Lily was suffering from a "psychotic grief reaction." What she remembered now was that she'd been inconsolable. She hadn't thought she could live without Shayna's love and protection.

"So much pain and suffering," Fran said.

"Nothing compared to what your son is putting me through right now." Lily laughed.

"No, really. The girls and I always say how tough you are. Rock-solid. You're rock-solid."

"I just didn't want you to be shocked during the hearing. The judge or whoever might bring it up."

"You didn't feel free to tell me?"

"I was sixteen. It wasn't important. It's not like it was a secret."

"Your past is who you are." Fran stopped. Ben was standing beside them, having appeared without warning.

Lily held out her arms to him and he sat down on the couch next to her.

"I thought maybe you got lost," Dr. Melick said, from the doorway.

Lily looked up at him, confused.

"I sent Benjamin to fetch his brother." He looked down at his watch. "At a half past a freckle, easily."

Greg laughed and Benjamin stared down at the floor.

"Greg, do you like blocks?" Dr. Melick asked.

Greg jumped up from where he had been playing with his sister and jogged over to the doctor. "I'll be right back," he said, pointing his index finger at Lily. "Don't let Katie drive the car while I'm gone. She could crash it."

Lily nodded. After he'd left the room, she tapped Ben's leg. "Were you poking around this big old house?"

He shrugged.

"Did Dr. Melick send you to get Greg a long time ago?"

"Sort of."

Lily looked over at Fran. She wondered if Benjamin had heard their discussion.

At one-thirty it was Lily's turn. The office was at the front of the house. One entire wall of the room was given over to a bay window, with upholstered corduroy seat cushions. Everything in the room was white, except for the well-worn blue armchair where Melick sat. The blocks were just as Greg had left them, and Lily went over to look at what he'd constructed. She could faintly hear her mother-in-law talking to the children in the waiting room, telling them they were going to go on an "adventure walk."

"Train station," Melick said, nodding toward the blocks.

Lily nodded. "He loves trains."

"Your children are delightful," the doctor said.

She knew enough to say thank you.

"You and your husband seem to have done a fine job with them."

That's why I'm here, then. Lily smiled.

"Your attorney mentioned on the phone that part of her preemptory strike had to do with more closely examining your 'history,' attempting to discern whether, in fact, it really was now 'history.' Maybe we could talk a little about that."

Lily wondered how much Snow had told him. "I had something of a postpartum depression following the birth of my last child."

"The child who was burned. And that's the problem for which you sought treatment last year?"

Lily nodded and sat down on the couch opposite his chair. She sank into the gap between the two foam cushions and hesitated for a moment, not knowing which side to slide toward.

"So, the birth of your daughter put you into some kind of tailspin?"

Lily held open her hands and looked down at her palms for a moment before answering. "That was the diagnosis on the insurance form. A whole lot of things happened in our lives at once, and I had trouble . . . processing it all."

"What sorts of things?"

"My husband and I had a food business. We're both chefs. Well, he still is a chef. We had a gourmet shop. It was a huge part of our lives. We invested everything into it, and in the end we just came up empty."

"You lost your professional identity?" Melick said, adjusting himself in the large wing chair.

"That and a lot of money. Not a good combination." She smiled.

Melick raised his eyebrows in seeming agreement. "So, perhaps, it was more of an adjustment disorder?"

"I don't know. My therapist prescribed medication, and it worked. So, it's hard to really say."

"How old was your daughter when you began the medication?"

"Seven months."

"And you stayed on . . . What was prescribed?"

"Zoloft."

"Zoloft," he said aloud as he jotted this in his notebook. "Zoloft was the first medication you tried?"

Lily wanted desperately to confine the discussion to the recent past. There was no reason to expect he was now asking about anything else. "Yes," she said.

"And you continued on the medication until . . . ?"

"April."

Melick poured himself a glass of water from a chrome pitcher on the coffee table between them. He offered some to Lily, and she declined. "I assume you continued in therapy after going off the medication?"

"I just stopped seeing my therapist about a month ago."

"Emerging studies of postpartum depression, of what happens chemically to women after they give birth . . . we're finding that this is not a period of time limited to six weeks, or even, say, six months."

"I've read that, too." Lily had four or five conflicting takes on the intent of the statement. This interview reminded her far too much of the endless variations of a game she used to play with her brother, their own grade-school blend of all the cold war spy shows on TV, *Mission Impossible*, *The Girl from U.N.C.L.E.* The high point of the game was always the attempted coercion of the confession. In the end the good guys remained impenetrable, superhuman in their efforts to retain their secrets in the face of both torture and temptation.

"You're obviously an intelligent, educated woman. Do you think this accident could have something to do with your regaining your . . . equilibrium?"

"Do you know Lucy Balsaam? She practices in Holloway. I was in therapy with her for almost a year. She knows me, inside out. She'd be happy to tell you I'm not a child beater. She seems to be out of the country—"

"You're angry."

"Wouldn't you be if you were in the midst of coping with an accident . . . with a critically injured child, and all of a sudden somebody decided you'd done the injuring and your baby should be taken from you? I'm being unjustly accused of something really horrible."

Melick nodded. "Justice. Funny. That's a word that came up for your husband, as well, different context. You look surprised."

"We're not always on the same wavelength," Lily said.

"Does that bother you?"

"Of course, well, not always. He's my husband, I love him. People can't always see eye to eye."

"You don't like conflict."

"Most people don't," Lily said, crossing her legs beneath her skirt.

Melick nodded. "Toddlers create a lot of conflict. Actually, they are in conflict themselves, almost continually."

Lily nodded. They were back to *The Girl from U.N.C.L.E.* again.

"The need for independence butts up against the fear of separation. . . . Well, I'm sure you know all this. You have two other children who seem to have mostly weathered that transition quite well."

"You are the first person in this whole process who seems to have noticed that. I mean, if I were a child abuser, why wouldn't I have abused my sons? If I am such a rotten mother . . . if I had abused the older two, wouldn't that be apparent?"

"Perhaps."

"Do you have children?" Lily had never asked Lucy a direct personal question. It was against the law, the law of the land of shrinkdom. As the patient, her job was to answer, reflect, at most pose a rhetorical question, which in essence was always a kind of answer in the mind of a shrink.

Melick nodded.

"People don't go around telling you what a good job you're doing raising them, do they?"

"I only have one. And I did tell you right off when you first came in that your children were a delight."

"My children are my on-the-job record, I guess. But in this whole nightmare, no one has given me one ounce of . . . whatever . . . I don't want credit . . . but faith, faith." Lily was staring intently at the condensation on the outside of the water pitcher. As she talked she watched tears of water pool on the glass-topped table. When she finally looked up, she saw Melick writing furiously.

"Would you mind if I made a few suggestions, Mrs. Keliher?"

Lily smiled.

"You know when the women's magazines run these lists of the most stressful life experiences, they go for the most common ones. But I would venture that being investigated by DSS is right up there. You might consider going back into treatment for a while with Dr. Balsaam. This cannot have been easy. I would suggest the same for your husband. But he struck me as being rather . . . resistant."

Lily laughed.

"He could probably use someone to talk to, as well."

Lily inched forward on the deep sofa, sensing that Melick was wrapping things up.

"One other thing," he said, as he tucked his pen into his composition notebook. "Watch the kids."

"Of course," Lily said, standing up.

"Oh, no." Melick held up his hand, laughing. "No, no. I mean, watch them for reactions to all this. It's a very, very scary thing to have a sibling hurt so badly that your daily routine is upended for weeks and weeks. Your older son . . . don't let things percolate too long with him."

# Jack

The hearing room was open. Jack took a seat at the long banquet table in the center and put his copy of the summons in front of him as if it were his place card.

*Care and Protection Summons*
*Trial Court of Massachusetts. District Court Department*
*Docket Number 571195*

Child(ren) Named in Petition:    Katherine Sterne
Kelleher

Name of Petitioner:    Virginia W. Thoms, Department
of Social Services

Name and Address of Guardian, Custodian, or Other Party:
John N. Kellehe and Lilian N Sterne, Checkerbury
Lane, Winstead, Mass.

To the Party named above: A petition has been filed with this court alleging that the child or children named above, being under eighteen years of age and within the jurisdiction of this court, is or are in need of care and protection pursuant to the authority of Massachusetts General Laws, chapter 119, section 24.

You are hereby summoned to appear in this court on the appearance date noted above to show cause why said child or children should not be committed to the custody of the Massachusetts Department of Social Services or other appropriate order made. If the box above labeled "72-hour (emergency)" is checked, the court will also determine at the hearing whether to extend any custody order now in effect.

You have the right to be represented by an attorney. If you are unable to afford an attorney you may be entitled to have the court appoint one for you. If you intend to ask the court to appoint an attorney to represent you, you should contact the court immediately upon receipt of this summons.

The law requires the judge to see ("identify") the child(ren) named in the petition. You are directed to bring the child(ren) named above to the court for identification.

The last quarter of the page was written in both Spanish and Chinese, but the entire document read like a foreign language. In the last two weeks Jack had fingered the paper over and over, an obverse rosary, yielding nothing but a continuous loop of pain. Still, he'd been reluctant to part with it at the entrance to the courthouse when the security guard motioned for him to walk through the metal detector and remove his backpack for x-ray. The summons was his passport, his compass in this hell.

The last time he'd been in a courthouse had been over twenty years ago. His father had driven him down, and they'd met his lawyer, Dunleavy or Donohue or Donnelly, he could no longer remember. Erin had called him "the back-alley litigator," because he was famous among certain groups of high school students for making DWIs disappear. Jack was seventeen. He'd been stopped while driving his grandmother home after his cousin Paul's wedding. Jack's father had vilified the desk sergeant when he came to pick him up. Kevin Keliher never drank to excess and was incapable of believing that his son had. Jack had endured no more than seven minutes in a peeling, dusty courtroom before the whole business had been reduced to a "failure to keep to the right."

"No bleeding afterward, no chance of infection . . . what an operator," Erin had said when he'd come home that day. He'd felt guilty about the arrest and unrelieved by the reduced charge. Jack's father chose to see the whole incident as a victory over the suburban police, who everyone knew were overly fond of beating on teens. It was weeks before Jack could look at his father head-on. He didn't know which humiliation was worse, the fact that he'd fallen so far short of his father's expectations or that his father was, seemingly, so ignorant of the failure.

On the ride over this morning, his mother had called him an ostrich. For over twenty-five minutes, he had listened, with extreme patience, he thought, as Lily and his mother went round and round the minicrisis of Ben's pilfering of Fran's crucifix. Lily had noticed it only that morning, as they were getting ready to leave for the courthouse. The six-inch silver crucifix had been removed from above Fran's dresser and attached, with a good deal of Scotch tape, to the wall above Ben's bed. The way the "discussion" of this crisis unfolded reminded him of one of those manually operated railroad carts. His wife and his mother worked like dogs together to emotionally prime the worry machine, sufficiently launching it so that it ran ahead of all reason, with no reliable means of stopping, other than crashing violently into something or someone.

"Of course," his mother had said to Lily, "you do know that I would never intimate the religious, force it on a child that way? You do know that, don't you?"

Lily, who was in the backseat entertaining Katie with a toy accordion, countered with, "Of course, I don't object to the crucifix," which Jack knew to be an out-and-out lie. "It's the . . . surreption on Ben's part, his desire to have a secret, that bothers me."

The great thing about the worry machine, Jack thought, was that it freed his mother and Lily from the need to be honest. In fact, the worry machine thrived on exaggeration and denial. Jack waited until he had parked the car in the municipal garage across from the courthouse before suggesting that the real issue here was one of stealing. Lily clicked her tongue and shook her head, and his mother launched into this ostrich-in-the-sand riff, keeping it up all the way through the labyrinth of the parking garage until Lily said she was going to faint or throw up or both.

"It's good and cold in here." Eleanor Snow swung her tan attaché case up onto the table in the hearing room and sat down next to Jack. They'd talked daily since they'd met at her office, but he'd seen her only that one time, and now, amid this sea of linoleum and fluorescent lighting, Jack thought she looked smaller and grayer, fallible.

Lily had wanted to dump Snow after it became clear that she wasn't going to be able to move up the hearing date and they would have to abide by the sloppy rules of the initial summons. Jack had disagreed. "We have no possible basis of comparison," he'd said. "I don't know who you think your dream-date defender is."

"That's rich," Lily said. "You're willing to give her the benefit of the doubt, but not me." They were upstairs in his mother's airless bedroom, the mouthpiece of the phone smashed into the white chenille bedspread as Jack repeated what Snow had said the night before and was reiterating now on the other end of the line—that they should utilize this time before the hearing, make it work for them in their attempt to regain custody. They needed these additional ten days to pull together the character witnesses who would present just the right sort of profile of the family. The extra time might give them the opportunity to finally get through to Lucy Balsaam, whose answering-machine message said only that she was away until the end of July and gave the name of a covering therapist.

Lily carried on then, and every other time he got on the phone with Snow. She would walk around his mother's bedroom and pick up a book or a brush or a pair of nail clippers, whatever she could find, and periodically crack it against the dresser or the nightstand or the windowsill. She'd mumble, too, slowly increasing the volume until he was merely moving his lips, and the sounds coming out were all hers, as if he were an actor in a poorly dubbed film. Finally, they'd taken to communicating with Snow separately.

"We'll be starting in about five minutes," Snow said, pressing her thumbs against the metal locks on her briefcase. She looked around the empty room.

"They're outside, on the steps . . . getting a little air," Jack said. He'd left Lily with her head between her legs at the bottom of the steps leading into the courthouse. Fran insisted on staying with her, so he'd been forced to pass Katie over to her.

"Feller?" Snow said.

Jack turned and saw Melick hesitating in the doorway. The shrink walked back out, checked the room number, and then entered, patting himself tenderly on the chest. It was unclear to Jack who was to play host in this situation. He shoved his hands into his pockets, gave a "Hey, how're you doing," and wandered over to inspect the state flag in the corner of the room. The ribbon of Latin around the Indian in the center of the flag was beyond his high school reach: *Ense petit placidam sub libertate quietem.* Peace and quiet?

"You'd better go get them," Snow said suddenly. She looked up at the clock on the wall and then down at her watch. "While you're out there, keep an eye out for Feller."

Dr. Feller was the pediatrician they'd used since Ben was born.

He'd been reluctant to get involved in any way that wasn't completely mandatory. Snow had proved her worth by finally getting him to agree to appear today, even without a subpoena.

Jack was barely out in the hall when Katie wobbled toward him. He clapped his hands and she sped up, grinning broadly at her own accomplishment. Jack's mother followed behind. She was talking animatedly to an older black woman. When they reached him, his mother introduced her as "the baby's lawyer," and Jack began to laugh uncontrollably. He tried to stop, shook his head, bent down to pick up Katie, reminded himself of where they all were. The force of the suppressed laughter caused his eyes to well up. He looked as if he were crying.

"Jack." His mother called his name loudly, as if to take him to task or bring him to his senses, he wasn't sure which. He wanted to say something, apologize to the lawyer, but he didn't dare open his mouth. He had no idea what might come out.

"Jack," his mother said again. He looked up, beyond their little group, farther down the hallway. Lily and Father Paul were approaching, painfully slowly, arm in arm, grieving widow and consoling vicar returning from the cemetery. From sixty feet away Jack could see the sandbagged look on her face, as if she expected nothing, except, perhaps, a piling on of more sadness. That "hit me again" look would only sink them here. Where had Father Paul come from? Jack stopped laughing.

"And this must be Miss Katie herself." Snow looked over the tops of her glasses as Jack sat down with Katie on his lap and everyone else filled in on their side of the table. "I've heard a lot about you," Snow said, extending her pinky to the baby.

"Who called the priest?" Jack whispered to Snow as she made a lame attempt to ingratiate herself with Katie.

"Your wife," Snow whispered back. "It can't hurt. He's a . . . presence, that's all." She shifted her attention back to Katie. "And I've brought a little treat."

Lily shook her head vehemently as Snow pulled a lollipop from her briefcase.

"Maybe when my mother takes her out into the hall. After the judge has gotten a good look at perfection," Jack said.

Lily had obsessed over Katie's appearance for the hearing. She'd bought and returned three dresses before finding one that she thought neither hid nor called attention to the bandages. She'd washed the baby within an inch of her life this morning. She'd even washed Barney, taking it from the crib after Katie was asleep and returning the scented but visibly dulled version to her side before she woke up.

"Impressive stack," Snow said. She pulled a file folder marked "Keliher support letters" from her briefcase and slapped it onto the conference table. "I sent copies ahead to the judge, along with an explanation about the absence of a letter from your wife's therapist."

Lily had tried without success to reach Lucy Balsaam, who, it turned out, was traveling for six weeks throughout Turkey. As far as Jack was concerned, Snow had saved their asses by having arranged for the evaluations by Melick.

"Okay," Snow said, looking at Lily and Fran, then at Jack. "Remember, the burden of proof is on them. Legally, the next step is an enormous one. No judge takes lightly such major interference with parental rights. They need to prove that Katie is still at risk in the home—"

"She never was," Lily said.

Snow ignored her. "Remember what I said—the judge is looking for proactive changes in the situation."

More shoes clicked and squealed across the linoleum. Jack looked behind him to see Mrs. Thoms enter with a middle-aged man and woman. Just behind them, Dr. Svanda strode in. Svanda was the accuser from the ER who'd ignited this whole thing. Snow had also neglected to mention he would be present today.

"Have the baby sit on Lily's lap, don't you think?" Jack's mother whispered to no one in particular.

"Good morning, I'm Judge Pua." A small Malaysian-looking woman headed toward the table, followed by a heavyset woman, the court recorder. As the judge approached, Jack saw that she would be taking the seat at the head of the table, closest to him. He turned to Snow to trade places with her. His mother moved to the second string of chairs, just behind him, with Melick and Father Paul. Jack disliked having Father Paul at his back. He was beginning to acknowledge that he disliked him, wherever he was and whatever he was doing. What motivated the guy? He couldn't trust him when he didn't know what he wanted.

"Did Feller call you?" Snow whispered to Jack.

"I'm going out to look for him," Jack said.

Snow shook her head. "You can't leave now. Shit."

Lily stared at Jack. It was clear that Snow was nervous. She had no business panicking yet, Jack thought.

"Let's ask Paul to call Feller's office," Lily said.

"Paul?" Jack said, confused.

"Father Paul," Lily said.

Snow shook her head.

The judge placed her draped arms up on the table. "All the parties involved, I trust, understand that this is not a trial. It is a hearing. And it is a preliminary hearing, not an evidentiary hearing." She looked around the room and sighed. "This is a closed hearing. All the records will be impounded. We are here today to determine if the Department of Social Services should retain custody while a full investigation is undertaken."

She looked around the room again, somewhat dramatically. The enormous black silk bow at the back of her head scraped loudly against her robes. "I see a lot of people here, too many. I will take a wild guess, now, and assume that the parents are contesting." She looked up again. "A lot of people."

She opened up the folder in front of her. Without looking up she continued, "Will each person present please identify himself. Make sure to clarify your relationship to the child, as well."

When it came time for Katie's court-appointed counsel to identify Katie, the judge stood up and walked over to where Katie was seated in Lily's lap. She was a short round woman, and when she crouched down on the floor in front of Katie, Jack thought she bore a striking resemblance to the egg-shaped people who snapped so soundly into Katie's plastic school bus.

Katie smiled at the judge, and reached out and pulled a fistful of her hair from her bun. The judge inched closer, and allowed herself to be inspected a few moments longer. "Okay, now, Katherine, you want to see what I brought with me today?"

Katie wriggled down off Lily's lap and finally released the judge's hair. Pua made no move to reconstruct her hairdo. Instead, she unzipped the top of her robe, reached inside, and pulled out a tiny plastic cat. It was small enough to have been dispensed from a gumball machine, infinitesimal, bite-sized. Katie stared down at the toy in the judge's palm, hesitating just long enough for Lily to have the presence of mind to pluck it up.

"She still puts everything in her mouth," Jack said, trying to soften the gesture.

Katie banged her fists on Lily's knees and started screaming. Jack tried to hold her. Fran moved to get her Barney from the diaper bag. The judge walked back to her seat at the head of the table. "Now would be a good time for the temporary guardian to please remove the child."

Jack bundled the baby in his arms, her feet pumping madly in the air, occasionally making contact with his shoulder. As he handed Katie to his mother, Snow whispered for her to call Feller.

There was a long silence after they'd left the room. Pua read through some papers in front of her and spent some time simply staring at Lily and Jack. "I am glad to see that . . . Katherine is on the mend. When I granted this emergency custody order . . ."

She raised her eyebrows, as if doing so might broaden her vision. ". . . two weeks ago, the medical condition of this child was foremost in my mind. You had a very seriously . . . wounded child." "Wounded" came out of her mouth, Jack thought, like a low moan. He could have made the same sound if he let himself.

"Second- and third-degree burns on one-twelfth of her body. Dehydration, swelling, infection.

"The reporter, Dr. Svanda from Lincoln Hospital, is here," she said, now reading from the papers in front of her. She began addressing Svanda, but continued to stare at Lily. Lily was sitting in such a way that all Jack could see of her was the rapid flexing of one side of her jaw.

"It just didn't add up," Svanda continued. "She said—"

"The mother?" Pua clarified.

"Yes. The mother said the baby had pulled a big pot off the stove. How? The child, well, you just saw her, she can't be more than three feet tall. No, less. The mother never mentioned anything about her climbing up, nothing like that."

Snow interrupted. "If I may just clarify. My client, Mrs. Sterne, has stated, and I'm sure stated on that day in the hospital, that the child was seated in a high chair at the time of the accident."

Svanda shrugged. Jack watched as the doctor unconsciously gripped the table and tipped back his chair on its two hind legs.

"Is this correct, Mrs. Sterne?"

Lily nodded.

"Do you have that same information?" Pua looked in the general direction of the group from DSS. It seemed to Jack she was still trying to get the players straight.

"She placed the high chair along the same counter with the stove," Mrs. Thoms said enthusiastically.

"Okay?" Pua asked, looking at Svanda. "So what else?"

"The mother struck me as . . . odd. She was quiet, very quiet. Something was off."

Pua looked toward Thoms for corroboration.

Mrs. Thoms read from a paper on the table. "The mother was uncomfortable, seemingly ill at ease in her own home, as if she had something to hide." Jack wished he'd heard that interview, wished he knew exactly how Lily had fucked it up for them.

"She seemed to be someone with a lot of anger," Thoms continued.

"Mrs. Thoms, may I ask you if you are a licensed social worker?"

"No, I'm not," she said, fingering the gold hoop in her ear.

Pua nodded. "But you will be one day, right?"

"I'm in the process of getting my degree, right now."

Jack wondered which one.

"Okay. What other physical, medical findings do you have for us today? What do you know now that you did not know when you petitioned the court?"

"The burns were of varying severity indicating a splash pattern," Mrs. Thoms said, again reading from the papers in front of her.

"X-rays, old fractures?"

"None," Mrs. Thoms said.

"Good. Can we be safe in assuming we're not dealing with a repeat offender here?"

"Well, not exactly," Mrs. Thoms said, opening up a very thick folder that had been in front of one of her supervisors. "It seems that Mrs. Keliher was consistently late in arranging for shots . . . immunizations."

"Are they up to date?" Pua asked.

"The baby is not."

Jesus, Jack thought.

"I assume that one of the men over here is your family pediatrician, Mrs. . . . Is it Sterne or Keliher? Can we clear this up now?" Pua sounded impatient.

Snow whispered to Lily for a moment. "Mrs. Sterne kept her

maiden name after marriage to Mr. Keliher. Dr. Ronald Feller is the child's pediatrician. He is supposed to be here today, as a general character witness, attesting to the competence of these parents, as well as the sound health—"

"And?"

Snow shrugged. "I imagine he got tied up."

"Why is your baby not properly immunized, Mrs. Keliher?"

For the first time, Jack thought something awful might be revealed to him today.

"That must be a mistake. I'm usually—" Lily said.

"A mistake, meaning an oversight on your part, or on the part of DSS, or of your absent pediatrician?"

"I'm pretty sure all my children have had all their immunizations. Katie did have a bad reaction to her first DPT shot, and I decided not to risk—"

"That's the one," Mrs. Thoms called out.

"All your children? How many do you have?" Pua asked, as if Lily were Mother Hubbard.

"We have three."

"First I've heard of it, thank you." The judge looked over at the DSS side of the table. "You have been working for the Department of Social Services for how long?"

Mrs. Thoms whispered to the older woman seated next to her. The attorney for DSS shook his head. "This is my third case without supervision," Mrs. Thoms finally said.

Lily squeezed Jack's thigh under the table.

"What else? What else aside from the burns, themselves, was of concern to you in this case?" The judge seemed to be talking more to herself than to Mrs. Thoms.

"Her emotional instability," Thoms said, almost as if it were a question.

"The baby's?" Pua said. She widened her eyes, as if to swallow the caseworker.

"The mother has a psychiatric history."

Pua tapped the top of her messed-up hair. "Yes, the all-important factor in this case, thank you." She looked down and shuffled through some forms. "Right, mother on medication for depression."

Lily turned toward Jack to pass him a note, and he smelled lemons. Not real ones, but laboratory lemons. She was using his mother's perfume or powder or something. He read the scrawl at the edge of her steno pad: "God, how did we get here?"

Snow shook her head. "My client has not been on medication for some time. Unfortunately the therapist she consulted during the past year is out of the country on vacation. But Dr. Charles Melick, a psychiatrist known to this court, has evaluated each member of the Keliher family, and is here today."

Pua turned to Dr. Melick, who was seated behind Jack and next to Father Paul. "What might you tell us that we don't already know, Doctor?"

Jack watched Melick slowly fold his hands in front of him as if they were detached from his body. Unlike everyone else, he did not consult a stack of papers before speaking. "I found these parents to be conscientious, well informed about the various stages of child development, and loving. There was some issue regarding the family's adjustment to the husband's career change. Apart from that, I found no more dysfunction here than in any other happy family."

The attorney for DSS spoke now for the first time. "I ask that it be duly noted that this psychiatric evaluation was not impartial, but, in fact, was ordered by parents' counsel. That's highly irregular at this juncture." The lawyer for the department seemed to be addressing himself directly to Eleanor Snow. "In fact, it's just not done." He cleared his throat loudly.

"Thank you, Mr. Gallione. It seems that there is, then, nothing new here—"

"Excuse me—"

"Yes, Mr. Gallione? I had assumed you were finished."

"Excuse me, the caseworker involved in this case has uncovered information that is, I believe, crucially important." The DSS attorney seemed excited now.

The judge moved great masses of air with her hands. "Let's have it," she said.

"We've done some research into the mother's medical history. We feel it is important that information previously omitted by the mother be made known. Mainly, that she has a serious history of mental illness, including long-term hospitalization and attempted suicide."

"What's she talking about?" Snow leaned across Jack and stared at Lily for a moment before addressing herself quietly but urgently to Jack. He could see a faint mustache of sweat above her top lip.

"Dr. Melick?" Pua turned toward him.

Melick looked down at his beard. "Neither Mrs. Sterne nor her attorney told me anything of this."

"Excuse me, your honor," Gallione interrupted. "This is precisely what concerns DSS. This pattern of secrecy, on the part of the mother. There well may be other things we just don't know." He shook his head slowly.

"There always are," Pua said.

Everyone was talking now. Eleanor Snow scratched away on her pad while Lily finally filled her in. Lily had convinced Jack that it was unnecessary to divulge the distant past to Snow. Jack knew now that he'd lapsed in his vigilance of her judgment. He'd gone along with the decision, nostalgic for a wife who could actually make the right call. Christ, he was a slow learner.

"Excuse me, clearly, I, too, have just . . ." Snow tapped her pencil rapidly. "If I might just explain that these incidences being referred to regarding Mrs. Sterne's background occurred over twenty years ago."

The judge looked toward Thoms and Gallione for verification.

"Yes," Mrs. Thoms said, "but the nature of mental illness, well, it tends to revisit in times of stress. Mrs. Sterne has already had . . . there have been years of treatment, and this recent, very recent episode where medication was used. There has not been adequate time to obtain the treatment notes for all these years. A full investigation would allow for that. I think the child was lucky this time. If we let this go—"

"Please, Ms. Thoms, no summations," the judge said. "What else? Who haven't we heard from?" The judge looked around with her barn-owl gaze. "The father," she said.

Jack had no idea what to say. Was he supposed to defend his wife's sanity? Was he supposed to defend her mothering? Or was he supposed to tout his own abilities as, as what, a caretaker, a protector?

"Yes, go ahead, Father," the judge said, encouraging Father Paul to speak.

He couldn't fucking believe it.

"Lily asked me to come here today as a . . . I believe what she said was 'a general character witness.' " He smiled and opened his large white hands, then clasped them together, almost clapping them. He shook his head. "I'm fairly well suited to the task. Because I have been asked to bear witness during the past few weeks to her character, and trust me," he smiled broadly, "there is nothing general, nothing common or commonplace about this woman. One only has to have seen her with her daughter, who, as you said, was so critically ill. One only had to bear witness to the two of them together in the hospital. I work a long day in my parish. When I visited little Katie Keliher at the Shriners Burns Institute, it was usually late in the evening. Lily was always there. I don't mean in the building. I mean by her daughter's side. Under the most enormous stress one can imagine, she remained firm in her commitment to her daughter, firm in her belief that a mother's love . . ."

Good Christ. Jack didn't think he could bear it.

"I've known her husband nearly all of my life. I played with him, I've prayed with him . . ."

Jack motioned for Snow to get him to stop, but she seemed mesmerized. Everyone was staring at him, raptly.

"Jack lives his life with a moral code, a set of values, that you'll rarely encounter, frankly, not even among my colleagues."

He got his laugh.

"I just can't imagine anyone better suited to the task of nurturing, guiding, providing for a child."

Judge Pua smiled at him. "Thank you, Father. Okay, okay, what am I looking at here? More time for the Department of Social Services to look into the mother's psychiatric history? That would be the reason, am I right, for continuing the Order of Care and Protection? I am greatly displeased that the mother kept this from her own counsel, from the evaluating psychiatrist. Poor judgment? I don't know. Do the parents not understand the seriousness of all this? I dislike, intensely dislike, this disregard for the truth. So, what to do?

"Let's look at everything else." Pua flipped through the file of support letters Snow had passed to her earlier. "Some fancy letterhead here. Fat stack. What else? Dr. . . . Svanda? Am I right? Okay, you never mentioned seeing a line of immersion, neither did the Shriners doctors." She shuffled all the papers in front of her as she spoke, laying them out in a fan shape. "So, we're left with calling it a splash burn. We need to rule out the deliberate throwing of the water. Well, now this will be difficult." She stared at Mrs. Thoms. "The container . . . a pot . . . not available for measurement. Weight of the child? Never included here. Manual dexterity at this stage of development also omitted from this report. What else? Nearly every name, every spelling, every date, every birthdate in the 51B I now see differs from the information received from the two hospital staffs and the parents. So many inconsistencies, on the part of the professionals involved. The basic intake skills displayed here are absolutely appalling.

"No dry burn mark. High chair, if in fact it was a high chair that was involved, never examined. And it was not until this business of the vaccinations that I even knew there were other children in the home." She lowered her voice, and it seemed to Jack she was talking to herself and that if they wanted to eavesdrop it was of no particular consequence to her.

"If this little one was in imminent danger, then why weren't the others pulled?" She glared at Mrs. Thoms now.

"May I?" Mrs. Thoms's face was bright red and her hands were trembling. "We identified this child, the youngest, as the target of the mother's irrational and aggressive behavior." She read from her notes. "Temperamentally, Katherine is the most difficult, this was acknowledged, more than once, by both parents during the hospital interview."

Pua looked at her and said, "Go easy on the adjectives. They're very costly, very costly. You write that 'the relations between the parents seemed strained, at best, possibly violent. Mother has poor impulse control, inadequate coping skills, low self-esteem, lacks social and emotional contacts outside the family.' Well, given the mother's psychiatric history, that does sound like a recipe for abuse.

"It's a problem. So I'm left with Dr. Melick, who spoke with her for probably, what, only thirty minutes, and a priest who's known the family forever. The priest . . ." Pua turned now to face Father Paul. "Father, you presented a very different picture of the family than the picture DSS has been creating for the past few weeks. This is what happens here. The department identifies a child at risk and then we are all in the position of trying to illuminate the world that child lives in, to get as clear a picture as possible as to the home life she will return to. As Mr. Gallione, himself, said, there are things we just don't know. Day-to-day domestic life defies satisfactory examination. It's the heart of the mystery, as anyone who has cared for young children knows. Am I right, Father, about the heart of the mystery?"

Father Paul smiled.

"Tell me something, Mom, Dad?"

Jack waited for her to ask the question. But she just shrugged.

There was a long silence, after which both Jack and Lily began speaking at once. "We love our children," Jack said.

"It was an accident," Lily added. "I'm a good mother."

"Well, look," the judge said, standing up. "It seems an improbable accident, I'll be honest. A horrible accident. Improbable, but not impossible. Important distinction. As for the other, as far as I know, the Commonwealth of Massachusetts does not remove children from the home of every mother on Prozac, not yet, anyway. Why don't we just dismiss this whole mess. Parental rights are reinstated."

BOOK TWO

# Jack

It hadn't rained in nearly three weeks, not since the end of June. In the suburban county where his mother lived there'd been a ban on watering since the Fourth, but out here, where he and Lily lived, everyone had a well. It was the homeowner's prerogative to let it run dry. As Jack parked the car and got out he saw that the burned-out lawn had spawned a pond, on which floated a sand pail, a couple of waterlogged tennis balls, and an old shampoo bottle. Somebody had arranged the sprinkler so it gave only a pathetic half wave, continually watering the same four feet of turf. Katie's little plastic slide was positioned so that the dumping-out point was directly into the ever deepening mud puddle. A faded Budweiser beach towel and two old dishrags lay like terry-cloth snakes in the grass.

Jack turned off the spigot at the side of the house and watched the last bit of water pulse out of the chrome holes in the sprinkler, then slowly cease to spurt from the twenty-odd rips that ran the length of the hose.

Once the water was off, he could hear them all in the kitchen. He stepped around the deep orange tiger lilies they had planted when they first moved here. The flowers had gone wild, multi-

plied and thickened, their fat green leaves almost completely cam-
ouflaging the house's patchy foundation. Through the back door,
Jack could see that they were all cooking something together.

Lily had the pastry marble out. She was talking in an accent,
imitating someone, Shayna, her grandmother. "Acch, who neets
de oven in Jewlye? A blintz you can cook eet on de top off de
range. Dat's de beauty of de blintz." The kids were laughing and
the boys began a chant of "blintz, blintz, blintz" as if it were a
taunt. And *she* accused *him* of embellishing his childhood.
Nothing drove him crazier than when she did this *Winchell
Mahoney Hour* thing about her grandmother. With each install-
ment the woman seemed less like an actual ancestor and more
like a pop-up peasant from a storybook. She tried too hard, went
over the top. He could hear it in her voice, a kind of desperation
that the kids cleave, no holds barred, to something mythic from
her past, that they love her family—even if for only six minutes—
every bit as much as they embraced everything and everyone
Keliher. He sensed that the kids knew it too, that Ben, at least,
was wise to her need, and so responded as she wished, not want-
ing to hurt her feelings.

He was asking his mother now if brass was like gold. Jack saw
the Sabbath candlesticks on the counter, by the sink. Lily never
cleaned them, and only remembered to light them four or five
Friday nights a year. The phone rang and nobody inside seemed
to notice. Katie was eating blueberries out of the container,
handfuls at a time. The phone rang again, and Lily uttered something he couldn't hear. When it rang a fourth time he pushed
open the back door. "The lights are on but nobody's home," he
said as he walked into the kitchen.

Greg and Katie screamed, "Daddy," and ran toward him. Ben
started to get up and then sat back down again. "Hey, Dad," he
said. "We're making blueberry blintzes."

"What the heck kind of food is that?" he said, forcing a big
oafy expression.

"Jewish food," Greg said, starting to climb up one side of him as if he were a sheer rock wall.

"Isn't this great? All being back together in our house?" Lily said.

"We've been together in our house for a whole week," Ben said.

"Since Tuesday," Lily corrected.

"Can Nana come for dinner?" Greg asked, trying to get a foothold in Jack's groin.

"We've been with her for a month," Ben said.

"So?"

"Nan needs a little rest from us," Jack said, as he swung Greg down to the floor and moved past Lily at the stove.

"Isn't it nice to be just our family?" Lily said enthusiastically.

"You getting anything out of the tap?" Jack asked, as Katie grabbed his hands and tried to attempt the climb her brother had just made.

"What do you mean?" The cast-iron skillet sizzled with grease.

"How long since you three little piggies were out there rolling in the mud? The lawn is flooded and the well's—"

"Shit," Lily said. "Sorry." She put her hand to her mouth. "We got sidetracked."

"Didn't you hear the water running out there?"

"We came in to make Popsicles."

"Yeah, Dad. It's sooooo easy," Greg said. "You take lemonade and you put it in the ice thing with all the little boxes—"

"The ice cube tray," Ben said disparagingly.

"But Mum didn't have like any sticks, so we went into the woods and got sticks and then stuck them in and now there's sticks from the woods in our freezer."

"Wild," Jack said.

"Mum said we're going to eat in the dining room," Greg continued.

"What's with the phone?" Jack asked, looking over on the kitchen counter, where the answering machine flashed 11 in the message number box.

"It's Shabbes. On Shabbes, religious Jews don't answer the phone," Ben began.

"Yeah . . ." Jack said.

Lily laughed. "It hasn't stopped ringing since we walked in at lunchtime. I would have spent all day on the phone if I'd picked it up every time. I thought it was important to let it go—"

"Did it occur to you that it might be an emergency . . . that if it kept ringing off the hook, maybe there was a damn good reason?" Jack said.

The kids got quiet. Only Katie seemed oblivious to the tension in the room. She was back to the blueberries, humming to herself and bouncing the green rejects down on the table.

"What sort of emergency? We're all here," Lily said tentatively.

The phone rang again, and Lily stared at it.

"Well?" Jack said.

Lily made a dramatic, sweeping gesture with her arm, then bowed. The kids laughed, with her, at him. It didn't usually go that way in their household.

Jack grabbed the phone roughly and shouted hello into the mouthpiece.

"Is this the home of Mr. and Mrs. Keliher?" a frail voice on the other end of the line asked.

"Yes," Jack said.

"You ought to be ashamed of yourselves, the both of you."

"Who is this?" Jack demanded. The voice was clearly female and old, but he couldn't connect it with anyone he knew.

"God has designs, grand designs, for . . . perverts like you."

Jack slammed down the phone, but the woman's voice had already imprinted itself in his mind. And for the next few seconds as Lily asked again and again who had called, he felt his pulse speed up and his lips go numb.

"Obscene phone call," he finally whispered to Lily. "A prank or something."

"What did they say?" Lily asked, pulling the skillet off the burner.

"What's obscene, Dad?" Ben asked, as Katie began fingering some raw dough.

"Not nice," Jack said. He pulled a bottle of Absolut from the freezer and poured it into an up glass, one of the two he and Lily had pocketed one winter afternoon years ago from the bar at the Ritz. He carved a curl of lemon peel from a shrunken lemon he'd stowed in the back of the butter compartment for just this purpose, and walked over to the answering machine. Before he pushed "play" he turned to the boys and said, "If we're really eating in the dining room, you'd better start setting up in there."

"Do that funny restaurant talk," Greg said. "You know, that dinner at Lilack's thing."

Lilack's was what Jack had named the restaurant he and Lily thought they might one day own. Stupidly, he had let the kids in on what he now considered the code word for his own failure.

"Please," Greg said, jumping up and down.

"Party of five, at seven with a couple of ankle biters," Jack said.

"What's that, what's that, Dad, ankle biters?" Greg said, convulsing in laughter.

"You know?" Jack said to Ben.

Ben thought for a minute, then shook his head.

"Rug rats," Jack said.

"Babies?" Ben offered.

Jack nodded. "Kids, yeah."

"Ha!" Greg said, slapping his little hand to his bare leg. "Ankle biters!" He stopped for a minute and then looked up at Jack. "I don't get it."

"It's a reference to height, or lack thereof," Jack said, lowering his hand down toward the ground. He walked over to the open shelves where the placemats and napkins were kept, counted out four of each, and handed them to the boys. When they had left the room, he pushed "play." Lily turned from the stove as the messages rewound.

"It's Friday morning, where are you guys? It's Ellen, just calling to see how you're all doing. Call me."

"Burn. Burn . . ."

"Wait, wait, what was that? Play that back," Lily said.

Jack ignored her.

The next message was from Julia Cozzi. "Why didn't you tell me? Oh, I feel so awful . . ."

After that was Mrs. Hines, an old customer of theirs whom they occasionally still catered for. "What can I say? I just opened the *Rooster* . . . is there anything I can do? I know an excellent attorney in town." The *Winstead Rooster* was their town paper. It came out every Friday.

"Stop them," Lily said, walking over to the answering machine.

"No," Jack said. "I want to hear the rest."

"Hi. Jack? I'm a friend of your mother's. I go to her church. I make soft cloth dolls for girls, and I have one I'd love to give to your little burned girl. May I drop it off sometime? My number is . . ."

"Too bad Hitler didn't take you all out . . . you baby boiler . . ." a teenage voice said tentatively.

"That's it, that's enough." Lily moved the platter of blueberry blintzes to the counter. "Let's call the police." She shook her head and slammed the skillet into the sink.

Jack motioned for her to be quiet. He listened to the last five messages. Four were anonymous hate calls, and the last was from Ben's camp counselor. He would need to bring in two dollars next week for a party they were having.

"Don't erase these," he said to Lily as he finished the last of his drink and tucked in his shirt. "I'm going to run up to the General Store and get the *Rooster.*"

"I don't know, maybe we should call the police, much as I . . ."

"Let's see what's in the paper, first." He looked over at Katie, who was now under the kitchen table with a box of markers and Lily's supermarket coupons. "Don't say anything to the kids."

"Can't trust me as far as you can throw me, can you?" Lily said, without turning to look at him.

She should have known better than to push him right now. "Lay off." Jack walked toward the back door.

"I do nothing but." Lily turned around and leaned against the stove.

"*Nothing* is right," he muttered.

"What the fuck does that mean?"

"Water running, phones ringing . . . who's in charge here? I mean, look around. Christ, this room, this whole freaking house, is positively scary. Look, look—" He pointed to Katie, who was now ripping grocery coupons into little pieces and dropping them into her sagging diaper. "She looks like she hasn't been changed in a couple of days." He leaned over and picked her up, instinctively smoothing his hand over the new skin on her leg. "Jesus," he said as he sniffed her bottom.

Lily held out her arms toward Katie, and she lunged for her mother.

"She's just wet," Lily said tersely, trying to pull Katie away from him.

"Mama," Katie cried, and Jack relinquished her.

He turned his back on them and shoved his hands into his pockets, in an attempt to stop himself. He took a few steps toward the door, then came back, leaned across the table, and grabbed one of Lily's blintzes. It was still hot enough to burn his palm. When it hit the window just above the sink, the pastry burst open, smearing the screen with the thick blueberry filling.

Jack didn't go to the General Store, which was less than a mile from their house. Everyone in there knew him, if not by

name, then enough to say hi, ask after the kids. Instead he drove
the five miles to the entrance to the interstate, where there was
an Amoco. Nobody knew anyone there. He pulled out a copy of
the *Winstead Rooster* and leaned against the ice cream case.

News was always in Section A. Jack carefully peeled back the
front page and scissored the inserts, "Horses" and "Summer
Fun," between his legs. Page two was obits, page three was the
police blotter. He looked there first. According to the editors of
the paper, nothing seriously bad ever took place in their town.
Cars collided on wet roads, tools were found to be missing from
unlocked garages, minors sometimes removed car radios, and
disturbances were reported to be under investigation. The police
blotter contained nothing about them and their dealings with
DSS. He knew that the hearing had been officially closed, but he
also knew enough about the legal system now to realize that it
didn't mean a damn thing.

He flipped through the articles about the addition to the
library, the permit being sought for a car wash in town, the problem of overcrowding at the high school. They were on the last
page, eighth column, just above "Blackboard Notes."

> The infant child of Lillian Sterne and John Keliher of
> Checkerberry Lane has been removed from the custody of her
> parents by the Department of Social Services pending an
> investigation of serious burns the child received while under
> the care of the mother. The child was first remanded to the
> custody of the Shriners Hospital in Boston and then to the
> Commonwealth of Massachusetts. The Kelihers have two
> older children who have not, as yet, been removed from the
> Checkerberry Lane home.

Jack thought about driving over to Fred Stowe's house. The
Stowe family owned the paper. Everyone knew the antique house
they lived in on Main Street, and everyone knew that their news

coverage was chronically obsolete by the time the weekly hit the mailboxes. Instead, he walked outside to the pay phone and left a message for Eleanor Snow. The paper usually printed half a page of retractions each week.

He came back inside and grabbed a few more papers. His mother had always done that when any of them was mentioned in the paper. She'd buy five or six copies and carefully cut out the page with their winning run, or field goal, or chorus solo, careful to leave the date at the top clearly visible.

The phone company wanted forty-five dollars to have their number changed to a private one, and it would take five working days for the order to go through. Lily complained that the boys' friends wouldn't be able to call them, and that she'd have to spend most of next week letting people know of the changed number, which she said she felt like doing about as much as she had felt like scraping blueberry off the kitchen window.

When Jack finally unplugged the phone around nine that evening, there were eighteen messages on the tape. After the kids had gone to sleep, he listened to the first two, then turned the volume off. Lily continued to refer to the messages as "evidence," so he didn't erase them. Evidence of what, he wondered, but he wasn't talking to her, so he didn't ask. After she went up to bed, he stayed down in the living room reading.

For the better part of a month he'd lived in the house without Lily, and he'd come to think of the whole of the place as his own, as if she no longer existed. Lily's arrival back in the house felt like an intrusion. He didn't want it to. He had intended to ignore his anger, hoping that if he waited it out it would diminish, and she would painlessly slip back into his life.

He'd been sleeping in the living room since Tuesday night, since they'd all moved back into the house together. On Wednesday morning, Ben had found him on the couch and asked if he had slept there all night. He said he'd fallen asleep watching TV, but after that he had been careful to set the alarm for six and bundle his sheet and pillow back into the linen closet upstairs before the kids woke up.

There was no peace in the house tonight. He could hear the creaking of their bedsprings upstairs as Lily rolled and fumed. The hard shells of flying insects beat against the old metal screens all around the downstairs windows. And the voice on the phone sounded again and again, each time he inhaled: "God has designs, grand designs, for perverts like you."

It was hours after the sun had set, but the temperature was still in the eighties outside, and higher in the house. Both the front door and kitchen door were open for cross-ventilation, as was every single window. Jack shut the doors first and turned the deadbolts. He pushed the kids' easel up against the kitchen door and then slid shut all the first-story windows. Before turning off the lights, he went down to the cellar and grabbed a baseball bat. Then he lay down on the living-room sofa and sweated himself to sleep.

It was still dark out when he woke up to find Ben shaking him roughly with both hands. "Get up, Dad. Get up."

"What?" He reached around to his sore back and felt the knob of the bat.

"Why are you here?"

"Why are you?" Jack said, digging at the crust in the corners of his eyes. Fucking allergies. He put his hand on Ben's shoulder. He was wearing his Red Sox pajamas.

"I heard something," Ben said.

"Me, snoring, probably," Jack said, closing his eyes as Ben reached over to the end of the couch and switched on the floor lamp.

"It's hot down here, Dad."

"It's July."

"The windows are all shut," Ben said.

"Bugs."

"I'm scared," Ben said.

Jack propped himself up on one sweaty elbow and slid as far back into the couch as he could. He patted the cushion and pulled Ben down toward him. "Scared of what, buddy?"

"Bad things," he said.

"We're all scared of bad things," Jack said.

"It's not funny, Dad."

"I'm not trying to be funny, Ben."

"What's a firestorm?" Ben asked after a long interval during which Jack was pretty sure he'd fallen asleep again.

"Hmm?" Jack said, trying to wake himself.

"On the radio, I heard them say there were firestorms somewhere and they were spreading."

"Oh, like forest fires. I guess they're like big fires, huge ones that burn out of control. It happens sometimes out in the West in the summer when it's very windy and it hasn't rained in a while."

"Do people get burned, too?"

"There are these rangers," Jack said, unsure of the information he was disseminating now. "They fight these kinds of fires."

"Can it burn up a whole town?"

"Well, mostly, I think these things happen in wilderness areas." Jack closed his eyes again.

"Never here?"

"It would be unlikely, buddy, improbable."

"But people burn in hell, right?"

"You want me to carry you up to your room? It's been a long time—"

"If you have a cross, then you won't go to hell, right, Dad?"

Jack reached up and swept Ben's damp blond curls off his forehead.

Ben grabbed his hand. "We should go to church, Dad. On Sunday."

"Don't worry about hell, buddy. When you're seven you don't

have to worry about hell, okay? You really want to go to church on Sunday? Maybe you and me will go down to the cathedral in South Boston. It's a beautiful place with enormous stained-glass windows, all blue and red and yellow, just like in Europe."

Ben seemed to relax a bit. He leaned back against Jack, let his hand rest on top of his father's for a minute. "Were you watching the Sox on TV, Dad?" Ben said, glancing at the baseball bat as Jack picked him up off the couch to carry him up to bed.

"Yeah," Jack said.

"Oh," Ben said, as they started up the stairs. "I thought you said at dinner that it was a travel day for them."

Somehow his trying to stretch his legs, which he couldn't do, seemed to cause the doorbell to ring, again and again. He'd forgotten he was on the couch. His shins were butting up against the upholstered arm of the sofa and the cushions were damp with sweat. The bell rang again, and he waited. The kids would get it. It was bright outside, too bright. He looked at his watch on the coffee table. It was eight-thirty. The kids never slept this late. Lily never slept this late. When the bell rang again, Jack wandered into the downstairs bathroom and grabbed a towel and tied it around his waist. It wasn't until he'd already unlocked the door and begun to open it that he remembered about the harassing phone calls, the wackos out there.

"Marnie Dowd." A tall stout woman thrust a ring-filled hand out toward him. "From your mum's church, St. Stephen's."

Jack ran his tongue around his teeth a few times and then said, "Hi."

"I left a message on your answering service. I'm the doll maker. I fixed up one special for your little girl. She's got a bandage on her leg. They say that helps the little ones not to feel so queer about themselves." She handed Jack a grocery bag with something gift-wrapped inside.

Jack nodded and thanked her.

"I'll keep praying for you all," she said, as she carried herself back to her car on her wedge-shaped shoes.

"As in the event of further catastrophe," he said when she was out of earshot. "God bless you," he yelled out disingenuously, giving her a big beefy wave.

Later, when Katie woke up and opened the package, he felt like a real shit. The doll was intricately designed, with dark hair like Katie's, blue eyes, a blue-and-white-striped dress, and Ace bandages on the entire right leg and the top of the left foot. Lily pointed out what had been hand-stitched and where the woman had used a machine. Jack couldn't conceive of spending so much time on a gift for a kid he didn't know. What caused people to do things like that? It was a grand gesture. In general, grand gestures made him uncomfortable. How were you supposed to respond to something like this?

He didn't like to think he was uncharitable. He knew he wasn't, really. As a kid he'd liked to shovel the driveway of the old man who lived at the end of the cul-de-sac. He would get out there on a snowy morning before his mother asked him to. He liked to change the oil in his father's car as a surprise. And every year he worked the dinner to benefit the food banks and soup kitchens of Boston. But none of that measured up to this. He watched as Katie unrolled the doll's bandages. In place of a scar, the woman had sewn in tiny purple hearts.

"What are you going to call her?" Jack said, picking up Katie and kissing her.

"Boo-boo," Katie said.

"Yes, she has a boo-boo. But what are you going to name her?"

Katie squirmed to be put down. "Boo-boo," she said loudly, as if he were deaf.

Over the next few weeks, other gifts arrived. Flowers were sent to Lily with no note attached. Five tickets to a Red Sox game were hand-delivered by an old waiter at Angelo's, a restaurant

Lily had baked for when they'd first opened their shop. Cards
came from old customers, friends of his mother's, aunts, uncles,
the pharmacy in town, and the small print shop they'd used back
when they'd had their store. Katie received a lot of books. Some
were overtly religious, some just thinly veiled "morals."
Members of St. Stephen's sent jewelry, a couple of St.
Christopher's medals, and four crucifixes, all of which Lily quickly hid away.

"One accident isn't enough for these people," Lily said, dangling a tiny golden cross from a chain. "It would be a miracle if
an eighteen-month-old didn't lodge this thing in her trachea."

A box of rosary beads arrived with a note: "Please have your little angel of God radiate her spirit onto these and return them in
the package enclosed. We, too, have sickness in our house and are
praying that you will share your healing with us." Lily had opened
that box while Jack was at work, and had left it on the dining-
room table for him to "handle." Jack waited a few days, then taped
some bubble wrap around the beads and mailed them back.

The hate calls dwindled after the next issue of the *Rooster* was
published. The front-page story and accompanying photo were
of twelve kittens found in the dumpster behind the Purity
Supreme. Two weeks later, the paper reported that the pastor of
the Episcopal church in town had been defrocked for adultery.
Then the calls to Jack and Lily ceased altogether. Either their
neighbors now had bigger and better targets or they'd actually
been influenced by the *Rooster*'s one-sentence retraction stating
that the information regarding the Keliher family had been
incomplete and unintentionally printed in the issue two weeks
prior.

Jack started to leave all the downstairs windows open again.
He'd lie on the couch at night and allow himself to think about
the present, even plan a little. He wished he could take the kids
to the beach for a week, rent a cottage at the Cape, the way his
family had always done. But money was more than tight. Eleanor

Snow's bill had finally arrived: $2,400. He needed to pay back his brother-in-law for soccer camp for Ben. They were trying to scrape together $500 every month to pay down the Visa cash advances from two years ago. And the van. He still hadn't finished repaying Jean's interest-free loan.

He wanted his kids to love summer as much as he had. He wanted them to be happy. He couldn't see how they could be very content hanging around the house with Lily all morning, dutifully trooping off every afternoon to that sinkhole they all called a lake, then back again at five to watch TV. She let them watch too much TV. He hated that, TV in the summertime. They should have been outside on summer evenings playing flashlight tag, looking for Venus. He worried that Lily wasn't enough for the kids. She cared for them, looked after them, intently now, but was she really carving them into vigorous and sociable individuals?

Lily. She'd been making a conscious, almost conscientious effort to touch him lately. When they found themselves crossing paths in the kitchen, she'd place her hands on his hips as she passed. She kissed him goodbye when he let her. And in the evenings, after the kids were in bed, she'd follow him out to the front steps with a glass of wine and force out some amusing anecdote about her day, trying to engage him in some way, as she skimmed his arm, clapped his bent knee, stretched out her own tanned legs.

One night she'd found him in the backyard wandering around and had turned the sprinkler on him. "Let's get naked and get wet," she'd said. He'd shaken his head and walked back into the house. The harder she pushed, of course, the worse it was. It wasn't a matter of a lack of physical attraction, because he could no longer even see her body. Each time he looked in her direction he saw right through her clothes, her skin, her blood and bones. She'd become a vessel of defeat, hers as well as his.

Some weeks after the threatening calls had stopped, he

dreamed he heard a scratching on the screens of the kitchen windows. It was quiet at first, but as it grew louder he knew he'd have to get up from the couch and take a look. In his dream he turned on the fluorescent light in the kitchen, which illuminated him and obscured the source of the noise outside. He knew he needed to turn off the light if he wanted to see who was outside.

In the dream he stood, for what seemed like an eternity, with his hand on the toggle switch, and slowly he felt something beginning to press in on him. He half woke up to find he had an erection and that Lily was lying on top of him. He thought he said, "What are you doing?" But he mustn't have, because she just kept repeating, "It's me, it's me."

He tried not to let himself surface too far above sleep. He was aware enough to know that if he became too conscious, he wouldn't let this happen. He closed his eyes, shut them tight. Her breasts hung down over his face, grazing his eyelids. She'd put on perfume, flowers, vanilla. She brought herself down on him, suddenly, slipping herself over him so quickly he was startled and wondered for a moment if this was going to be violent, a punitive fucking. But she was slow then, rocking back and forth, moving herself all along the shaft of his penis, as if she cared greatly about the result. Her fingers fluttered continuously up and down his sides, then slid down under him, between his buttocks and the down of the sofa. She pulled him to her again and again. He listened to the chittering of the bugs outside, the rattling of a truck somewhere down the road, their wet stomachs coming rhythmically unstuck.

When it was over, he rolled his face to the back of the couch and pulled the sheet up over him. He could feel her standing there for a while, before turning and heading back up the steps to the bedroom. He didn't mention it the next day, and to his amazement, neither did she.

# Lily

"Pink like Piglet," Greg said, reaching over and touching the lighter-colored skin on his sister's leg as they sat in the bathtub together.

Lily poured in the oil she'd been using for six weeks now to soften the new tissue on Katie's leg and feet. She massaged the area with a washcloth to remove the flaking skin. The skin was whole, but not the same. The texture was different, its chemical makeup altered. The melanin was slow to return to the new tissue. Dr. Wheeler had warned them that it could take years.

But Katie *was* healing. Lily and Jack had even received the papers formally dismissing the action against them by DSS. Still, Lily couldn't seem to move on. It was as if the accident, the hospital stay, the hearing were happening again and again, causing everything else to fade into the background. She'd look up and find she was halfway to Fran's house, kids in the backseat of the car, and no memory of having driven there. She had been busy rewriting the end of June. Why had she made egg salad? No one ate egg salad anymore. Why hadn't she taught Katie to learn to tolerate the playpen? Because if she had been in the playpen . . . She'd find herself standing by the washing machine listening to

the water rush into the basin, heart pounding at the remembered
sound of those whirlpool tubs in the hospital where they'd done
the debridement. She could smell the room, the faintest residue
of metals and salts coming across the tip of the tongue. And the
screaming. Screaming that could be heard from anywhere.

"It's   a   storm," Greg said. "A very bad storm, with lots
of waves." He chopped the water with his hands, splashing his
sister.

Katie leaned over and bit him in the meaty part of the shoulder. He looked at her and laughed, and she clamped her teeth
down and growled, "NO."

"Cut the crap," Lily yelled. Father Paul was coming for dinner in twenty minutes, and she'd done nothing to prepare so far
except pick up toys. Jack had been away since Wednesday and
wasn't due back until Monday. The partners were using him and
Cyn for some off-site event, out on Nantucket.

Lily was delinquent in having properly thanked Father Paul
for all he'd done: visiting Katie in the hospital, testifying on their
behalf at the hearing, calling since then three or four times to
check up on them all. She suspected there was a more appropriate means of showing her appreciation, one involving a monetary
donation, but that was out of the question. Besides, she was lonely for adult company. Fran was in Montreal with Erin and Pete.
Jean and her kids were up in Bar Harbor visiting her in-laws.
Julia and Ellen would be gone for the rest of the month. Life in
Winstead seemed to have ebbed away. The lake was at its lowest
level in five years and had taken on a truly pathetic appearance,
as if it had finally become the glorified mud hole Jack always said
it was. There had been so few cars in the lot there this afternoon
that the ice cream truck hadn't even bothered to stop.

Lily drained the bathwater and watched, with towels in hand,
as Greg and Katie slid up and down the porcelain tub on their
round wet bellies.

"We're fish," Greg yelled. "We need water to zist."

Lily nodded. She glanced at her watch on top of the toilet tank. She hadn't even set the table yet. She swooped down on Katie and plucked her from the tub, grasping her under her slippery armpits. "I'm a pelican, a pelican," she said less than enthusiastically. "Pretend I'm a pelican and you're my supper." She gently patted the new skin dry and knelt down to massage in a palmful of lotion. "Good girl, Katie," she said as the child stood perfectly still on the bath mat.

"Good Mumma," Katie mumbled, her thumb in her mouth, her other hand patting Lily lightly on top of her bent head.

The phone rang just as Lily was helping Greg into his pajamas. She felt the vibrations of the ringing bell reverberate somewhere between her chest and her throat. The phone calls had started again on Wednesday afternoon, after Jack had left for Nantucket. It was the same person each time, a woman with a tremulous voice, elderly, Lily thought, unless that was put on. The phone rang again, and Ben yelled from downstairs that he would get it.

"No," she screamed. "No, I've got it." She picked up the phone in her bedroom and said "Yeah" into the mouthpiece in her most threatening voice.

"You ought to be ashamed of yourself," the woman began. "God granted you those three beautiful children, but you've perverted his design, haven't you? You don't deserve them, your children. Your punishment shall be just and swift—"

Lily hung up before she could continue. It never occurred to her to respond. For three days now she had been listening to the woman, often to her entire threatening message, like a child who covers her eyes and believes that no one can see her. If she didn't speak, or even audibly breathe into the receiver, then maybe this woman would not be able to finger Lily's very soul.

Lily chastised herself for not having the strength or the will to stop the caller. Certainly there were things she might do—notify the police, trace the call, change the number. She couldn't simply unplug the phone. Jack would worry. She hadn't told him about the calls. These messages were clearly directed at her, and she was ashamed.

"Why are we always doing this now?" Ben grumbled as they stood by the sideboard in the dining room to light the Shabbes candles. It was far from sundown, but Lily wanted to light the candles before the children went to bed. In the summer, when Lily was a child, her grandmother would stay up until one or two, whenever the flames would die down by themselves. Lily's mother had thought it ridiculous. "I'm not altogether sure God cares if you light them to begin with," she would say. "He's going to care if you blow them out so that you can go to sleep?" Lily loved those summer Shabbats, when she knew for a fact that no matter how long it took her to fall asleep, her grandmother would still be awake, sitting in the living room, "keeping the candles company."

Lily lit the candles and began reciting the blessing. "Baruch ata, Adonai . . ." Greg chimed in on a few of the more memorable syllables. Lily beamed at him and he beamed back.

"You don't even know what you're saying," Ben said, staring at his brother.

"We're thanking God for the light . . . and that can mean lots of different things," Lily said.

"Fire," Ben said, rolling his eyes.

"Good Shabbes," Lily said, bending down to kiss Katie and then Greg. Ben pulled away from her when his turn came. Katie insisted on kissing everyone three times.

"Push them back, Mum," Greg said, staring at the flames. "You know who might, you know . . ."

Lily nodded and nudged the brass candlesticks back slightly toward the wall.

"Great," Ben said as he started to walk out of the room. "Now the whole house will go up."

Lily didn't have the energy to do anything other than ignore him. He'd been acting strangely for the past few weeks, but on Sunday he'd come home downright hostile after camping for the weekend with Jean and Erin and his cousins.

Lily and Paul drank gin and tonics at the kitchen table while the kids ate their dessert. Paul told a story about an old priest he had trained under who was so fat that he'd actually broken a chair one Sunday morning during Mass, simply by sitting down in it. The kids all laughed, even Ben. So he went on with a tale about an altar boy with a gas problem. Benjamin went into paroxysms of laughter. And when it was time for bed, even he agreed to let Paul take them upstairs, as long as he told one more story.

Paul was still upstairs with the kids and Lily was shaving Parmesan into the salad when the phone rang again. She picked it up on the first ring and hollered "Yes?" into the receiver. The adrenaline surged toward her head, making her limbs feel weak.

"Lily?"

It was Jack. The connection was poor. She could hear people talking in the background, and something else, a kind of a white noise, like some New Age music.

He was on a cellular, doing a clambake down on the beach. "Kids behaving for you?"

"Mostly," she said.

"Where are they? It's so quiet."

"Father Paul. I invited him for dinner. He's reading to them upstairs."

"Serves him right. Lily? Are you still there? You wouldn't believe this house."

He had said the same thing the two other times he had called.

"Guy, Guy Waller, actually put in a cart path from the house down to the beach. And he's got golf carts. It's great for us. We can just drive all the stuff down here."

"Good," she said.

"Something wrong?"

She heard Cyn's voice in the background. Maybe Lily should have asked to work this event with Jack. It would have been good for them.

"Oh, yeah," he said. "Before I forget, we're doing a banana ice for dessert at lunch tomorrow. Does the rum go in on the first or second freeze?"

"At the end," she said. "Otherwise the alcohol would keep it from freezing up enough, you know, the consistency." She knew he knew this.

"Good. Thanks. Take care. Love to the kids. Talk to you . . . tomorrow."

When Paul came downstairs, he poured them each some more gin and asked if he could set the table. She dragged the barbecue grill near the outlet by the kitchen door and plugged in the electric starter. The grass was so dry that it was painful to walk on with bare feet. It had been a dry summer, too dry. She looked up at the sky and the darkening haze. She figured it would still be light enough when it was time to put on the halibut.

"Mom?"

Lily jumped and let out a short scream.

Ben laughed.

She hadn't seen or heard him approach, but here he was, right next to her. "God, you scared me, honey."

"Sorry."

"What's wrong?" He was wearing one of Jack's old T-shirts, which covered his legs to below his knees.

"Do I have to go to sleep now?"

Lily bit the inside of her cheek. She wanted to be done with kids for the day. "Are you tired?"

He shook his head.

"Okay. Do you want to go in and watch TV for a while?"

He nodded and walked away as silently as he'd come, entering the house through the front door.

In the few minutes she'd been outside, the edges of the yard where the grass gave way to woods had dropped into darkness. It was muggy and still, too still. She swept the backyard with her eyes again, the swing set, the shed, the soccer goal, the row of white pines.

At around nine she asked Ben to shut off the TV and go up to bed, and she and Paul sat down to dinner. It was quiet as they ate. Paul seemed shy to her now that it was just the two of them. She listened to the sound her fork made as it scraped against the bottom of the wooden salad bowl.

"Your parishioners have been wonderful, sending Katie things. Very thoughtful," she said after a while.

He nodded intently. "This is marvelous." He gestured toward his plate.

"Oh, good, I'm glad," she said, almost surprised to receive a compliment.

"I'm very fortunate to be at St. Stephen's." He nodded again. "It's a warm, caring parish, small enough to feel intimate."

"We did get one really odd—well, it wasn't really a gift, it was a request, I guess. Very strange, to me, anyway. Somebody sent us their rosary beads with a note asking Katie to bless them. I don't know . . . holy hands or something, I guess."

Paul knitted his brow. He reached for some bread and continued to eat.

Lily poured them both more wine. Maybe her cynicism had been too thick. "Butter," she said, getting up from the table.

"Was it somebody from St. Stephen's?" he asked when she came back from the kitchen.

"I think so. The note mentioned a sick family member. I don't know, it just seemed unusual . . . desperate, I guess."

He nodded vigorously, and his straight black hair fell forward into his eyes.

"I mean, given the demographics of your parish, that seemed, to me, kind of out there on the fringe—"

"If you thought you were about to lose the person you

depended upon most in the world, I'm not sure you'd be concerned with how you appeared to others. How far would be too
far to go?" He brushed the hair from his face and looked directly across the table at her.

Lily shifted in the dining-room chair and tucked one leg up
underneath her. She didn't know him well enough to know
whether the question was rhetorical or real. What a strange man.
He'd appeared far more relaxed preaching to a church full of
people and speaking in a courtroom full of animosity than he was
here in her dining room. He could tell fart jokes to the kids one
minute, then advocate the excesses of love to her the next.

"To what lengths would you go to hold on to Jack?" Paul
asked, slicing neatly through the tip of a crisp green bean.

"You mean, if I was dangling from the twelfth floor?" She
laughed and sipped her wine. "I'm sorry if I insulted anybody's
idea of faith. It's just, when someone asks you to have an eighteen-month-old touch their rosary beads so she can transfer her
healing powers . . . that's . . ."

"Irrational?"

"Fantastic," Lily said. "It's like the magical thinking of childhood . . . that someone can touch something and transfer a kind
of power."

"Physical touch can be extraordinary." He crossed his long
thin arms over his black shirt. In the candlelight, the white of his
clerical collar stood out against his Adam's apple like a beacon.

"I don't know. I don't know what I think about that," she lied.
"I know a lot of people do believe in that sort of thing. I mean,
Katie certainly did improve. Just given my background, I can't
really chalk up her improved health to your laying your hands on
her body."

Paul laughed and smiled broadly. "What about physical love?
You of all people, I would think, would appreciate the potency of
skin on skin."

Lily leaned back from the table and pulled her other leg

underneath her so that she was now sitting Indian-style in the
chair. She disliked the way this conversation was going. Was he
obsessed with sex? Of course, people who never had any always
were. She poured more wine and pulled her glass to her chest.

"Lily," he said, leaning over his plate toward the purple candles in the center of the table, "I'm talking about mother love.
The healing touch I was referring to was yours. The power of
mothers to heal through touch, that's the extraordinary
power."

"Oh," she said. "When you said physical—"

"Well, what's more physical than that relationship?"

Lily shrugged.

"What's the matter? You look . . . skeptical. You don't believe
me."

"No. It's just this tendency people have, some people, anyway,
toward idealizing motherhood. I mean, real life's just not like
that."

"And by 'real life,' you mean—"

"Everyday life. My everyday secular life."

He nodded thoughtfully. "Do we need to make the separation? It's all one. It's all sacred."

"For you," she said, stroking the fringes on her napkin.

"For anyone, if they choose to make it so."

She shook her head. "Most people don't make choices. They
just endure. They put one foot in front of the other . . . and if
they're lucky, maybe they get apportioned these . . . scattered
moments of joy, or something." She twisted up her face in an
attempt to mock her own blurry insight.

"You're really pissed off, aren't you?" He pushed his empty
plate to the side.

She laughed. "Coffee?" she said, about to stand up.

"No, no, wait." He patted the table with his long slender fingers. "Tell me."

She stood up, slightly unsteady from the gin and the wine.

"Lily." He stretched his pale uncovered arms across the table. "There is a . . . brokenness . . ."

She felt her face flush, and she looked down under the table for the sandal she'd kicked off. She wasn't about to talk to a priest, even this one, about her marriage. She had no interest in making herself vulnerable before him. "We have dessert." She began to clear the table.

"Sit down for a minute," he said. "I want to do something."

"What?" She laughed nervously. She was no longer able to read the situation or predict what would happen next. And she resented him for it.

"I only want to do this if you'll be comfortable with it. So, be honest."

She looked across at Paul, sure he was about to engage in something so foreign and so lacking in integrity that she would be embarrassed for him.

"Let me pray over you, just for a minute."

"What does that . . . involve?" she said, finally locating her sandal and dragging it toward her with her big toe.

"Your head and your heart," he said. "First I'll lay my hands on your head and pray and then on your heart."

She laughed again. She'd had enough to drink to agree to it. "What should I do? Should I . . ."

Paul walked around the table. Lily sat back down in her chair, cross-legged.

"Close your eyes," he said. "Breathe in slowly through your nose and then out through your mouth a few times. Right. Relax. Think of something."

"What?"

"What's the matter?"

"What do I think of?" He was tall, much taller than Jack, and she could feel him behind her and above her.

"I'd like you to think of a light. Sunlight, firelight, the light of

a candle. Maybe even picture those candles on the server.
They're Sabbath candles, right?"

She nodded. She could feel the heat of his palms above her
hair, but he hadn't touched her yet. She hoped he would get this
over with quickly. Candles, fire, burns. Light was not going to be
a calming image. She'd never successfully meditated, always too
conscious of the process to yield to it. She was capable, though,
of giving herself over thoroughly and entirely. Sometimes when
she cooked, something intricate and potentially excessive, she
could lose herself. And sex, of course; she used to be able to lose
herself in the concentric circles of that building pleasure.

He hadn't touched her head yet, so why were his hands now
hovering over her breasts? This was a mistake, a colossal mistake.
She'd had too much wine—that must be why she was actually
willing his healing priest hands to caress her.

"Okay," he said. "Did you notice anything?" He tapped her
shoulder lightly. "You can open your eyes now, Lily. Some people experience a kind of warmth or heat radiating from the part
of the body I prayed over."

"Something," she said. "I'm not sure what, but I definitely felt
something."

She was relieved when Paul finally left. She stacked the
dishes in the sink and checked the Shabbes candles on the sideboard to make sure they were out. She was appalled at her own
fleeting attraction to Father Paul, a by-product of deprivation,
no doubt. She remembered having left the cover off the grill outside. She'd have to take care of that before locking up and going
to bed. Paul's appeal wasn't physical. It was his faith that was so
enticing. Maybe if you slept with someone who really thought
that all of life was sacred, you'd catch that belief, like a virus, and
you'd believe so, too.

She walked barefoot onto the back steps. A breeze had come

up and the night was turning cooler. The stone stairs had lost all
their warmth from the heat of the day. She looked up at the
clouds pulling themselves across the night sky. Yesterday at the
lake she'd been holding Greg and Katie in the water, one on each
hip, springing up like a jack-in-the-box, again and again, as they
laughed and screamed. And during one of those moments, as she
was bending her knees for the tenth time, pushing off the sandy
bottom of the lake on the balls of her feet, she felt a surge of gratitude that they were still small enough to be held and still young
enough for their mother to be the source of so much happiness.
Maybe that was joy.

She must have dropped the spatula on the grass when she was
done cooking the fish. She reached down now by the barbecue to
get it, and when she stood up, she saw the doll on the grill. The
coals must not have been that hot. It was still recognizable to her
as her doll, the one her grandmother had placed on her own bed
each morning atop the two little crocheted pillows. Glynda, her
grandmother had called her, the good witch, the fairy. Her yellow hair had been all but singed off, and the arm that had held
the wand was dripping down through the slats of the greasy grill.
But parts of the golden brocade dress and the too-blue eyes were
still visible.

She threw the dome-shaped cover over the grill and rolled it
away from the house, thinking the doll might still ignite. She ran
up the back steps and pulled both doors closed behind her. She
couldn't even remember where she'd seen the doll last. After the
accident she'd hidden it somewhere. She'd been worried about
the wand, that Katie would suck on it and choke or poke her eye
out.

She poured herself the last of the wine from dinner and dialed
the number Jack had given her in Nantucket. It was eleven-forty.
The man who answered the phone sounded as if he'd been sleeping. Lily was asked to "kindly hold the wire" while he buzzed the
kitchen. There was a long silence, then a few clicks, and finally

Jack's voice competing with the sounds of clinking glasses and running water.

She told him about the burning doll, and then, as if it were all one story, the phone calls.

"Why didn't you tell me about this before?" he said.

On his end she could hear doors sliding open and shut. He was outside now, she guessed, maybe on a deck. "I was sick of being the bearer of bad news."

"Are the kids okay?"

"What do you mean?" Lily asked too loudly. She broke into a sweat that started at her hairline and seemed to run down the inside of her thighs.

"I don't know," Jack said defensively.

Lily closed the blinds on the kitchen windows. "God," she said. "I'd better go up and make sure."

"I'll call you back," Jack said.

"No," Lily yelled into the phone. "Sorry, I mean, don't hang up. Hold on while I go upstairs."

"Okay," Jack said.

She rested the phone receiver in the dish rack and walked slowly out of the kitchen. She wanted to move quickly, but she could barely get herself across the threshold into the hall. She realized after a few moments that she was holding her breath. By the time she reached the hallway and was about to start up the steps, she was convinced that someone else was in the house. She cursed herself for never having gotten around to covering the two skinny windows that flanked the front door. The metal rods for hanging the long sheers everyone else seemed able to buy were still there from the previous owners. Anybody could have been standing outside with a clear view into this rickety house and the woman inside who wove her way up her own staircase as if she were losing oxygen with each step.

She grabbed onto the molding outside the boys' room and swung her head in, half expecting it to be met with a blunt object. She toed open their closet door from the hall and then jumped into the center of the room. Greg rolled over at the noise, but the top bunk was empty. Lily's heart pounded. Katie was in her crib naked, her diaper tossed onto the floor. Lily moved quickly past the linen closet and down toward her room. The light was on. Benjamin was asleep on top of the bedspread with a flashlight in his hand.

Lily walked downstairs. The house was hers. The walls were once again formidable, the doors true barriers to the outside.

"I'm going to call the police," Jack said when she picked up the phone again. "Cyn thinks I should call the police and that I should come home now. The next ferry isn't until tomorrow morning."

"Well, what do *you* think?" Lily said, angry now that she was no longer frightened.

"A prank. A sicko prank. Bush-league shit—blackened Barbie."

"It wasn't a Barbie. That was Shayna's doll."

"I know," he said. "I was just trying to get you to laugh. I thought a good laugh—"

"Well, I'm not in a big mansion by the ocean with a pile of people all yukking it up."

"Yeah," he said. "Yuk, yuk, yuk. Cyn and I are on our third sinkful of glasses. The rental place out here only takes them back clean. And these people are still out there creating more dirty ones."

"I'd trade with you in a heartbeat," she said.

"I know," he said, his voice soft, almost warm. "It sucks."

"Should I be scared?" she said.

"No. The worst is over," he said confidently.

"You mean you don't hate me anymore." She built a pyramid out of the baguette crumbs on the counter. She'd had too much to drink.

"I mean Katie's burn, the accident, her injury."

"I know," Lily said.

"Would that you really did, darling. Would that you did."

Lily hung up the phone before he could say anything else. She poured herself some Heaven Hill from the bottle she'd bought last Christmas for baking fruitcakes. She left the fatty fish skins to congeal on the plates in the sink. The bread, the biscotti, the dill already wilted—she left it all out on the counter. She didn't bother to shut the silverware drawer or close the cupboards. She walked out of the kitchen and into the hall, never even double-checking the locks on the doors. She was too sad to be scared. As she climbed slowly up the stairs to her bedroom she thought, Whoever wants to get me has to wade through all this first.

It was light out when she woke up, and someone was knocking at the door, not her bedroom door, but the door to the house. Ben was still asleep beside her in the bed. From her bedroom window she could see a police car in the driveway. She pulled on a pair of gym shorts and went downstairs.

She recognized the officer. He was one of the younger policemen in town. He'd come into the shop a few times. She could tell he was trying to place her every time he looked up from his metal-covered notepad.

"Please," she said. "Come in." It seemed wrong to make him stand in the already blazing sun hitting the front steps. As he started to wipe his feet unnecessarily on the doormat, she remembered the kitchen, the mess. The house smelled of fish.

The food out on the counter must have jogged his memory. He pulled out a kitchen chair and said, "Station Break, right?"

She smiled.

"Chefs are always experimenting. That's the difference between a cook and a chef, I'll bet."

Lily asked if he wanted coffee. What she really wanted was to run upstairs and put on a bra and a longer pair of shorts, and depending on why he was here, lock her children in a secret passageway he would never find. She rinsed out last night's coffeepot and filled the canister with cold water.

"Did you report these threatening phone calls when they first started?"

Right. That's why he was here. She combed her fingers through her unbrushed hair. It was dawning on her that she had a hell of a bad headache.

"No," she said. "I mean, I didn't think it would go on. We thought if we ignored it . . . Well, they stopped for a while, three or four weeks."

The cop pushed aside the bottle of balsamic vinegar and the crusty garlic press and opened up his pad. She was glad he was so young. Maybe that accounted for his being unfazed by the state of the kitchen.

"Does the caller use your name when she calls?"

"She knows who we are." Lily swept her thumbs under her eyes. She'd probably never taken off her eye makeup last night. "She refers to an incident—"

"The child abuse thing?" the cop said indifferently.

Lily stared at him for a moment. She wished this were already over. She didn't want the kids to wake up and see a cop in the house.

"We know the story," he said.

"We were mistakenly accused," she said.

He shrugged. She poured him some coffee and pulled away the bowl of day-old green beans in walnut oil from under his nose.

"When your husband called us this morning, he said there had been some incident with this caller last night."

Lily opened the back door and led the policeman into the yard. She pointed toward the grill, but remained on the steps as he walked across the yard.

He looked around the grass for a stick, the grill cover still in his hand. He picked up one of Greg's plastic golf clubs and prodded the doll with it. "Grill rack's shot," he said. After a while he tossed the golf club back onto the grass and replaced the lid on top of the barbecue. "Hear any cars last night, anything? You're up a long driveway here." He followed Lily inside and sat down in front of his coffee.

Lily looked up from pouring herself some coffee and saw Ben standing at the edge of the kitchen.

"Ben, this is Officer . . . Blaise?"

"Blaisedell," he corrected and stuck out his hand.

Ben just stared at him from across the room.

"Everything's okay," Lily said.

"Can I watch TV?" he asked, looking at both Lily and the cop.

She nodded, and he turned silently and went into the living room.

"Sorry. You know, when they just wake up . . ."

"Could I trouble you for some milk?"

"Oh, sorry." Lily looked around the room for a creamer and then just placed the plastic half gallon on the table.

"Where was the doll before?" he asked.

"In the house, in a closet, I think."

"It was definitely a one-of-a-kind type of doll?"

Lily nodded.

"Someone would have had to come into the house, then."

"I think so," Lily said.

"Lost any keys lately? Have any new sitters, cleaning people?"

"No."

"Service people, repairmen?"

Lily shook her head.

"You and your husband estranged?" he said, looking down at his pad.

"No, why?" Lily asked, raising the blinds slightly.

"Oh, sorry," he said. "It's just that he called from . . ."

"Business trip," Lily said.

"Do you have an alarm system?" he said, looking toward the door.

"No."

"Dog?"

"Should I be concerned?" she said, getting annoyed.

The policeman finished his coffee and stood up from the table. "Mostly kids pull this kind of a thing. Could be a teenager putting one over on you on the phone."

"And that's good, if it's a teenager? I mean, that makes it less serious, less of a threat?"

"I was over at a house on Rose Lane yesterday. People got back from vacation and they'd been cleaned out, everything." He shook his head. "Thanks for the coffee. Call if you have any more trouble."

While the kids were eating their cereal, Lily went to the basement and brought up a couple of suitcases. She was sick of waiting, waiting for Jack to come home, for the kids' friends to get back from vacation, for the summer to be over, for the cooler weather, for rain, for enough money to buy an air conditioner, for more threatening phone calls, for something else awful to happen, for Jack to stop hating her. "You guys want to go down to the Cape this weekend?" she called out to the kids from the basement steps.

Ben and Greg screamed and whooped, and Katie started crying, alarmed at the noise.

There was $870 of credit left on one of their Visa cards. Lily would drive them all down to Wellfleet. There had to be a room available in one of those millions of motels along Route 6. They'd bring a beach umbrella, and she'd triple-bandage Katie's leg and feet, maybe even slip Ben's athletic socks over the bandages to be sure.

"What about Dad?" Ben asked, leaning in the doorway of the kitchen. "Will Dad meet us there?"

"Dad's working," Lily said, as if that were explanation enough.

"Well, I know that," Ben said.

"Then why did you ask?" Lily put down the suitcases in the hall.

"When he's done working?" Ben said.

"When he's done working it will be Monday. And on Monday it will be time for him to start working all over again, in Boston. We'll leave him a note."

"We want Daddy," Greg started chanting, happily banging his spoon on the side of the kitchen table. "We want Daddy . . ."

"Da, Da, Da," Katie said, going along with Greg and pounding her fists on the high chair tray.

"Maybe I'll get you all a baby-sitter and go myself," Lily said, lifting Katie out of the high chair.

"How about Nana? Nana can baby-sit. Nana, we want Nana . . ." Greg said.

"Fuck it," Lily said loudly. "I try to do something nice for you . . ." She kicked the old plaid suitcases out of her way and started up the stairs. Katie was crying and yelling, but Lily couldn't tell whether she was saying "Nana" or "Mama."

She threw herself on her bed. She was hot and hungover, and she didn't want to do this job today. Maybe she just couldn't. It was all doing and making and giving when you had kids. It had to come from somewhere, and she was tapped out. Her own parents had regularly taken sabbaticals, from home as well as from the university. She needed a sabbatical.

What would happen if she walked out right now, leaving them behind? What would it feel like to get in the car all by herself? How did people do it when they abandoned their kids? Did they put on a video and slip out the back? Maybe she should just do something completely irresponsible, let the other shoe drop, satisfy the supposition that she was, in fact, a bad mother.

When Ben was one week old she had stared down at him in the bassinet. He was awake, quiet, looking back at her with his blue eyes wide open. And for a moment, somewhere between fatigue and exhaustion, she'd caught this objective glimpse of the two of them, new mother and new baby, and she'd wondered whether she was doing it right. How did she know if she was loving him properly? How much love was enough? During the past seven years she'd thought back to that moment no less than a thousand times. How could she possibly have realized way back then what would develop over time between mother and child, how every day this mad love increased, doubling and tripling, then growing beyond any possible means of quantification? And once in a very rare while, like today, she'd think back to that moment that first week, and she'd acknowledge the particle of raw truth in that novice mother's fear. How much love was enough?

The sitter biked over. Lily hadn't left Katie since the accident. She watched Samantha come up the front walk. At least she was tall. Lily figured that the children would be better off today with a fourteen-year-old who came highly recommended than they would with their agitated mother. She gave Samantha twelve dollars to have a pizza delivered, and she told her she'd be home before it got dark.

When she got to the car, she saw Ben sitting in the front seat. He'd been crying.

"So," she said. "You want to go to the beach?"

# Jack

Jack had never before felt trapped by water, but then he'd never been to Nantucket before with its ferry and its all-controlling ferry schedule. He'd waked up at four after talking to Lily the night before and had not been able to get back to sleep. He'd said something about catching the first ferry back to Hyannis, but Cyn really couldn't manage the Saturday-night dinner by herself.

At five he tiptoed down the stairs of the servants' wing. The towels in this place were so big and thick he could barely tuck one under his arm. Somebody in the Waller household must have shunned the cart path, because there was a narrow but well-worn path down to the beach through the dune grass. He probably should have told Lily to put the kids in the car and come over for the weekend. He could have found a motel room for them somewhere. But everything out here had to be over two hundred dollars a night in August. And besides, she'd never be able to get the car over on a Saturday. Fucking island.

It was light out, even though the sun wouldn't rise for another hour. The Wallers had a "marine info" wall in their kitchen, as if their island lives were really ruled by such natural forces as ebbing tides and waning moons. The tide was low, just coming in

again. Jack hadn't been swimming yet, not in the four days he'd
been here. Work was work. Swimming was personal. He didn't
want Waller to see him enjoying himself in any way. Waller had
the annoying habit of offering Jack drinks and telling him to help
himself to the very food that Jack had just finished preparing, as
if he were another one of his moneyed buddies just over for the
weekend, as if the sweat pooling at the back of his waist was the
product of a round of golf rather than evidence of an afternoon
spent in an airless kitchen. Jack knew he should have insisted on
uniforms for Cyn and himself. "No, not out at the house,"
Waller had said when Jack broached the idea last week. "We're
casual out on the island." Fucking island.

Jack stripped, balled up his shorts, and tossed them against the
dune. He ran through the almost cool air rising off the Atlantic
and dove in. He surfaced for a breath and grunted and gasped. It
was cold, even now in the middle of August. The Gulf Stream.
These people loved to kid themselves. His paternal grandfather
had owned a house in Rockport when he was a kid. And Jack and
his sisters used to sit on the beach there and watch him take his
twenty-minute daily swim. He'd stretch a salt-faded red racer's
swim cap over his bald head and walk into the water with no visible reaction to its always frigid temperature and its often chop-
py surf. Then he'd swim, parallel to the beach, and Jack and Erin
and Jean would jog alongside him. He'd swim just to the jetty,
then turn and come back. At the turn they'd always yell out to
him, neither a cheer nor a snicker but something in between,
something ambivalent, something, Jack realized now, that mirrored his own feelings toward them.

The ocean here was nowhere near as cold as the water off
Cape Ann, but as Jack surfaced again and again, exposing his
naked backside to the warmer air, he felt himself chilled from the
inside out, as if the blood in his veins had been iced and trans-
fused. Jack swam a few long laps parallel to the shore, hoping to
get used to the temperature. He floated on his back facing the

beach and Waller's palace. Gulls swooped down for what had been left behind at last night's clambake. Jack let the water lap at his head, filling his ears. The sound of his own breathing transmuted through the salt water reminded him of the remote, yet ambient sound of a doptone amplifying his children's heartbeats *in utero*. Maybe he should have gone home.

He wrapped himself in the towel and waited for the sunrise. He turned around a couple of times, sensing someone behind him, but it was only the gulls. He tried to pretend for a moment that this was his beach, his house behind him, his escape, his fucking island. Of course, he'd do it differently. He picked up a rock and sketched out a compound in the wet sand. Who didn't want a slice of the Atlantic? Every New Englander did. The compound would consist primarily of a restaurant, his restaurant, then off to the side some cabins, maybe a lodge with a screened-in porch and a place to play basketball. The housing would be for them, the family, nothing fancy. The restaurant would be as open as possible, wide plank floors, timbered walls, logs, with cutouts for windows every few feet. No, that wasn't right. He'd worked at place north of Portland, Oregon, once that looked like that. That wasn't right for here. It bothered him that he didn't have a vision at the ready.

He looked up and realized he'd missed the actual moment the sun had emerged from behind the ocean. It had happened while he was doodling in the sand. The sun was up and barely visible, bleeding into the low clouds. An imperfect sunrise, and he had missed it. He tossed his drawing rock out into the sea.

The land here, Waller's lot, must have cost in the millions. Basting and braising wasn't going to get him a spot on the fucking island. He slipped on his shorts and headed toward the cart path. He wanted to remember to call the police, tell them about the business with the doll. He knew Lily was scared.

It was going to be another hot one. They might even want lunch served inside today. Fucking sit-down lunch just so Waller could clinch some deal. The Wallers' requisite black Lab was heading through the dune grass toward him. He'd have to watch where he stepped. Jack had tried to tell Waller that they needed to vary the settings for the meals. The clambake had been a good idea. The damn dog was probably a crotch sniffer too, just like the master. Jack watched as the dog came galloping toward him. He was so focused on the dog that he didn't realize at first that he had stepped into the covered pit from last night's clambake. Cursing, he jumped onto the cool sand and ran down to the water. The dog followed, darting at him as if it were all a game. Jack sat for a long time at the edge of the water with what little surf there was breaking on him in the front and the dog sniffing at his back. He watched, waiting for the blisters to form and fill. He and Cyn had started that fire at noon yesterday, a little less than twenty hours ago. The pit he'd just walked into could not have been that hot. It wouldn't be a serious burn, he told himself. It hurt like hell, but it wasn't serious.

Cyn had a flowered hatbox filled with vials and creams. None were what he was looking for. "Thank God you didn't forget your extract of primrose, huh?" he said, fingering the strange assortment of supplements and herbs. "Codeine, Demerol, Valium, Extra Strength Tylenol . . . that's the stuff I'm after." He was sitting on the edge of the bathtub with his feet in a shallow pool of cool water.

"That bad, huh?"

He'd made it up from the beach by wrapping each foot in one end of his towel and walking as much as possible on his heels.

"There might be some other pressure points on the body—"

"Believe me, the pain is in my feet," he said.

She squinted at him, as if he were trying to put one over on her. "Nothing is ever that simple, Jack. Pain is complex." She put the top back on her hatbox. "Anyway, I thought you were going home this morning."

"How can I possibly? I need this job, you know. I mean, I have to physically protect them and financially protect them."

"You're joking, right?" she said.

"Why?" he said, confused.

"You're so retro sometimes," she said.

"Well, you know what, Cyn, that's life as a guy."

"What? Being retro?"

He twisted his body from the edge of the tub and looked at her in the mirror above the sink. She was wearing kid's pajamas. For the first time since he'd knocked on her door fifteen minutes ago, he noticed she had Barbies all over her nightshirt. "You don't add up," he said.

"Add up to what? To your stiff idea of who I should be?" she said, starting to leave the room.

"Hey, I'm not that interested," Jack said.

It was the walking back and forth from the kitchen to the deck to set up the omelet station that was the problem. His right foot was worse than his left. After he'd insulted Cyn, who was now slamming stainless-steel bowls against the stainless-steel counter, he'd found some aloe vera gel in a medicine cabinet. He'd slathered the soles of his feet and then put on some thick socks. Each time he stepped he consciously raised his foot without flexing it, as if he were a marionette, his toes on an axis with the front of his knees.

He realized now how carefully he'd been insulated from Katie's physical pain. She was too young to say, "It hurts like . . . it hurts like . . ." Like what? he thought now. He didn't know what it hurt like. It hurt like the devil, as Fran would say.

A few early risers were already on the deck, rattling chairs, looking, Jack thought, too closely shaven, too well rested, too content in their golf shirts and Top-Siders. There was grumbling today, as there had been each morning, about the newspaper delivery. Mercifully, the market was closed, and the cellular phones had been left upstairs.

Egg Beaters. Jack had known enough to bring over a case; of course, that was something that was probably readily available on the fucking island. He'd set up the portable burners so that he could sit on the deck railing and take the pressure off his feet. He flicked some water onto the nonstick sauté pan and watched for it to bead up.

"You're way too pretty to be frowning," one of the many venture capitalists on the deck said loudly to Cyn as she brought out a tray of juice. Jack rolled his eyes as she passed by on her way back to the kitchen, but she didn't choose to return the conspiratorial look.

"What's the story with that one?" the man said, striding over in a way that made even this well-built deck shake. He was tall and fit, his gelled hair combed back over his head. Kind of downtown for a financier in his fifties, Jack thought.

"What can I fix for you this morning, sir?" Jack asked brightly.

"Eggs again, huh? Waller pays you the big money to scramble eggs?"

"I'd be happy to prepare anything you like," Jack said. He was going to charm this guy out of an argument.

"Anything? Well . . ." He exhaled and blew a cloud of mouthwash over a layer of last night's scotch in Jack's general direction. Jack realized slowly that this was the same drunken fool who'd boasted at dinner on Thursday that he never, but never, bought California wine. What was Waller doing, saving the real stuff, the French stuff, for the 30 percent players?

"I thought everyone in this neck of the woods ate finnan haddie?"

Jack smiled.

"Well?"

"I do have some smoked salmon out in the kitchen," Jack said.

"I'm not talking about Jew food," the man said, leaning in toward him. "I'm talking about a proper New England break-fast."

"Jew food?" Jack repeated. The last time he'd heard that expression he'd been eight. He'd gone with his great-aunt Claire to a delicatessen in Brookline, where the shiny golden fish in the case were labeled "whitefish." He'd asked about it, and she'd crinkled her nose. "Who knows," she said. "Jew food."

"You know what I mean, bagels and lox," the man said.

"Oh yeah. Us Jews eat nothing but," Jack said, the pain in his feet fueling his tongue. "Now," he said, gesticulating with his spatula, "you're supposed to say, 'Funny, you don't look . . .' "

The man smiled and shook his head. "Hey, I can spot a mick a mile away."

"If I were you I wouldn't breathe directly over an open flame," Jack said, tapping the sauté pan with his spatula.

"You little shit," the man said. It wasn't his volume that alert-ed the others on the deck but his sudden lunge across the burn-ers for Jack's ear. Jack jumped back into the deck rail, and the youngest and leanest of the money men called off the drunk and suggested to him that they all go into town for breakfast.

"High drama," Cyn said after he'd finally finished breaking down the omelet station and had limped back into the kitchen with everything. "What'd you do? Insult him, too? You've really got a problem, you know that?"

"I was defending your honor. The guy's an ass grabber."

"No, he's a tit rubber."

"He's a pig," Jack said, relieved that Cyn was speaking to him again.

"So, we cook for pigs, we serve pigs, what else is new? Doesn't mean you have to act like a pig."

"I didn't," Jack said.

Waller let out a low whistle to let them know he was coming.

Chop, chop, the king.

He stuck his silver head into the kitchen. "I heard Ambi got a bit ugly this morning."

Jack shrugged.

"There are a couple of mountain bikes in the garage. Help yourself. It's a spectacular ride out through the dunes. Get out of this kitchen. Enjoy yourselves. Have some fun." He pulled his arm over his head and stretched until his back cracked. He was on his way out the door when he slapped his hand to his forehead and turned around. "We'll be a few extra tonight."

"How many?" Jack eased himself into a chair.

"We've got a few neighbors joining us, some of the wives are coming over this afternoon. I'd say twenty-five. Nothing you can't handle. I've been getting a lot of nice feedback on the food, very nice." He stared out the window contemplatively and tapped his lips. "How about something with blueberries for dessert? They grow wild all over the island." He swept his arms out around him, and then sauntered out of the kitchen.

"I'd rather have my left nut cut off right now than go berrying and biking," Jack said after he heard the front door slam.

"Well, I'd love to ride a mountain bike and pick blueberries." Cyn untied her apron and folded it neatly on the counter. "And if it removes me from your presence, all the better. I've decided that you're toxic, like . . . burning rubber. You give off noxious fumes." She pulled her Walkman from a drawer under the center island and left.

At twelve-thirty, Waller called from the club and said they'd all decided to eat there. Jack slid the chicken salad with fresh raspberries and fennel into the refrigerator, along with the julienned vegetables, the aioli, and the focaccia. He poured himself a fist of Absolut and settled down in the "library" to watch the Sox on Waller's big-screen TV. In the middle of the third inning, he called Lily and got some girl who didn't know who he was, even after he identified himself.

"She took the big boy somewhere for the day," she said, before telling Jack she had to go because the baby was crying.

He poured another drink, adding tonic this time. It felt wrong to be inside on a summer day, wrong to be drinking in the middle of the afternoon, even if the vodka had extinguished the worst of the fire on the bottoms of his feet. It felt wrong to be so far from his kids, and even from Lily. He missed Lily. He hadn't seen her since Wednesday and he hadn't talked to her since June.

Since they'd stopped working together, Lily regularly accused him of getting off easy, skipping off to work, leaving it all behind him. But he would much rather put up with shit from his kids than shit from the likes of Ambi or even Waller. It was all wrong to be taking this kind of crap from strangers when he could have been taking it from his family. Watching Greenwell miss a pop-up in the sixth, he decided he hated his life. By the top of the eighth, he understood that it was really his job that he hated, but right now his job felt like his whole fucking life.

He was good and buzzed when he switched over to all tonic and began mixing the marinade for the sea bass. Something "oriental," Waller had told him last week when they'd roughed out the menu for this weekend. "Asian, Pacific Rim," Jack had said, nodding, as if they spoke the same language.

The bass was delivered by a guy in a banged-up Olds who, Jack figured, had spent the postdawn hours out on his fishing boat, the middle of the day behind a fish counter, and the end of the day driving his catch around the island. He wondered what a guy like that could bring in during a year—figuring his year only lasted five or six tourist months, the government could shut down fishing grounds at any time, and he probably didn't own his boat outright. Fishing was like cooking, people romanticized it as a profession, wistfully sighing at the road not taken, as if fishermen and chefs got paid to play. Unlock the equity in your hobby, get paid to fish, get paid to fuss with food.

Jack signed for the fish and handed the guy a Sam Adams from

Waller's refrigerator. The fisherman looked at Jack and then at the beer, as if it were a trick, and Jack noticed that he was young, not underage, he didn't think. Guys who worked outdoors, Jack reasoned, were either young or old. Nobody who spent his life outside six to eight hours a day ever looked middle-aged.

"All right!" the kid said, by way of thanks for the beer. He looked around the kitchen for a moment. "Big enough, huh?"

Jack saw that he was searching for an opener, on the wall, as if he were standing behind a bar.

"You must go to lots of cool places with the Wallers, huh? They travel all over, Japan, Florida, everywhere."

Jack handed him a church key. He saw no point in correcting the boy. He was probably all wrong about his life, as well. The kid had probably never set foot aboard anything other than his green Olds, bobbing up and down these bad roads, a trunkload of fish on ice.

"I could never wear a uniform, though," he said. "You'd never get me in any kind of a get-up."

"Well, we all wear uniforms . . ." Jack began, philosophically.

"Bummer," the kid said. "That's when you know they've really got their hooks into you. See ya."

Jack sliced the scallions and crushed the garlic. "It's like going to graduate school, only free," he'd told his parents when he'd graduated from BC and informed them that he was going to work his way through as many great kitchens as possible. A means to an end, he'd said. The end being working for himself. And now at thirty-eight, he was a bit player in an episode of *Upstairs, Downstairs*.

He'd suffered far worse indignities in past jobs than he had here today. One summer evening when he was working at the Lawn and Racquet Club, he'd been ordered by the manager to carry his ice sculpture of a swan out of the air-conditioned dining room and onto the patio in front of a phalanx of fans, so that the cocktail hour following the member-guest could be "air-cooled." The sculpture had become unrecognizable as a bird in about twenty minutes. That swan had taken him four hours to carve and no one but the dishwasher had really gotten to see it.

He placed a cookie sheet of pine nuts in the just-warm oven. When he'd worked downtown at La Fortuna, he'd been asked to cater a "postoperative party" in the owner's father's private room at Beth Israel. He'd had to use the little bathroom off the old man's room as his base of operation and had smuggled the liquor onto the surgical floor in Depends boxes. There'd been the chef in Sonoma, an ex-marine, who called him "faggothead" every single time he addressed him. All of that was worse than this. But all of that had happened before he was twenty-six. You could put up with almost anything when you were young. The idea of the future hung out there, a giant balm. You could tolerate all kinds of injuries because the rest of your long life offered endless chances for regeneration.

He soaked the skewers for the lamb satés. There was no other explanation. He'd fucked up. He would turn thirty-nine at the end of next month. He was $24,000 in debt on his credit cards, not to mention attorney's fees he owed, and here he was, in service, a fucking domestic without one single glimmer of a plan as to how to turn it all around.

Shrimp toast. Waller insisted on shrimp toast. Jack pulsed the food processor filled with crevettes. It was inexplicable. He'd done well his entire school career, had gotten some scholarship money to go to BC. He'd never been fired or let go. He'd received excellent recommendations from every boss he'd ever worked for. Even the vet up in Maine who'd locked him in the freezer had, in the end, helped him to get the head chef's job at Bellemeade. All signs had pointed toward success, and yet, here he was. It was like a fucking miracle in reverse.

Cyn walked in at five-thirty, sunburned and stoned. She took off her Walkman, and Jack saw a perfect white disk on each beet-red ear. He wasn't even in the mood to tease her. He popped four Tylenol and opened a Coke, covered the bass in a double thickness of foil, and put it in the refrigerator. He wondered what his children would think of him when they grew up. He'd always thought his own father could have done better. He knew he hadn't cared to. He'd done well enough without working too terribly hard, and that had suited him fine. "Dad's missing the motivation gene," Erin had said on more than one occasion. Maybe Jack was, too. He thought of how hard he and Lily had worked in their own business, back when he cared. Bad luck. Bad luck had happened to him, and now he was out here on the edge of the Atlantic waiting for the bad luck to just keep on happening.

His foot began to throb again, and he poured himself a glass of wine from an already opened bottle of Ferrari-Carano. He pared away the thick brown skin from the ginger root and pressed the flesh against the grater. All those days when Katie had been in the hospital, he'd been either too scared or too angry to think of how it felt to be inside her skin. He'd had a million tricks for distancing himself from her. She was little, she was a girl, she had her mother. She was, ultimately, so different from him in every respect that it was impossible to know how she felt. Now his own physical pain shamed him into admitting that he'd abandoned her. Pain was like an artery. Pain could deliver you straight to the heart of just about anything or anyone.

By the time he left, the entire meal was prepared. The bass was on the grill, the shrimp toast and satés were being passed around. The lo mein and the gingered eggplant were done. The coconut halves had been hollowed out, ready for the cold curried soup. Even the crème fraîche for the dessert had been whipped. The last ferry was at nine. He told Cyn he'd give her his last day's pay—there'd only be breakfast to do on Sunday. He didn't ask if she minded or even if she could handle it. He called Waller into the kitchen from outside, where he was busy directing the unfurling of a customized screen cap over the deck. Jack told him about the threatening phone calls and the burning doll. He post-dated the story, rationalizing to himself that the news had just reached him, too, out here on this fucking island.

# Lily

Lily and Ben never made it to the Cape. At the end of the driveway, Ben turned to her and said, "When Daddy's not here, it's like he's dead."

"I know it seems like a long time to you," Lily said, wondering why death was such a recurring theme with this kid. "But you know he's coming back, two more days."

"I practically haven't lived with him all summer," Ben said.

Lily laughed at the exaggeration, realizing too late what a misstep that was. "It's been a hard summer," she offered. "Because of Katie's accident, it hasn't been a regular summer, has it?" She stopped the car at the end of the driveway, unsure where to go.

"Why are we just sitting here?" Ben said impatiently. "Just go, Mom." He kicked the dashboard with his high-tops as he tried to reposition himself in the seat.

"Well," she said slowly. "I don't know where we should go. I'd like to go to the beach. . . . Would you like—"

"There's lots of things you don't know, lots," he said, kicking the dashboard again, this time on purpose.

Lily turned right. They could go to the diner out by the highway. She certainly wasn't going to drive two hours with a kid who

234

seemed on the verge of falling apart. For a moment it seemed that she was the mother of an infant again, at the mercy of his unpredictable needs, scared to put too many miles between themselves and home base. "I'm sorry I got so angry, back at the house, before."

"I didn't care," he said.

"It's been a hard summer for me, too. I thought we could all use a change of scene. My father believed that salt water could cure anything."

"What does *that* mean?" Ben said.

By the time they pulled up in front of the diner, Benjamin's mood had completely overridden whatever need she'd thought she'd had forty minutes before. He walked toward the restaurant without looking at her, head bowed, his long skinny arms bumping into his torso with each step. In the mirrored cake case at the front of the diner, she could see that his eyes were dull and flat. He'd lost all animation. She thought of how Jack used to tell her that she was "gathering" her "darkness" when she felt herself slipping and sliding into depression.

She wasn't hungry, but she ordered pancakes, knowing it would take a long time to eat. When Ben didn't respond to the waitress, she ordered the same for him. As the waitress took the menus she looked at Lily with a mixture of pity and disgust, certain that something was wrong with the boy, but unsure who should bear the blame.

"We could call Dad, if you like," Lily said, sliding down the booth, trying to get out of the way of the sun, which was pouring into the smoky diner. She was hoping that at seven his problems were still easily remedied, that the cause of his increasing sadness was removable, that he could be distracted into happiness, that somehow it wasn't her fault.

"This is really kind of nice, in a way," she said stupidly as the waitress poured her coffee. "Getting to spend the day together, no littles around." "Dates," Ben used to call their outings togeth-er when Greg was an infant and Lily would make a big show of leaving the baby with Jack while the two of them went off together. She knew not to use the word now.

"I hate myself," Ben said suddenly.

Lily reached across the table, and he pulled back into the booth.

"Wait. You're going to hate me, too. So's Dad."

"You're our boy," Lily said, panicked at where this was all heading. "We'll always love you, no matter what."

"Don't say that!" he demanded. "When I tell you . . . I'm going to have to go to, like, some jail for kids. I'm that bad."

"Benjamin, calm down," she said impatiently, his theatrics reminding her unpleasantly of herself. "You are not bad."

He shook his head. "You don't know, Mom. You don't really know me. There's lots of things about me that you don't know. I did that to your doll. I burned that doll you loved so much."

Lily stared at him. Two minutes ago he'd seemed on the verge of tears, but as he told her this his voice grew stronger, clearer, almost proud.

She sipped her coffee, looked out the window. The parking lot was in constant motion. She had no idea how to proceed here. She should have known, should have figured it out. She cursed Jack for sticking her with this all by herself. After a long time she said, "Why?"

He looked up at her with those flat eyes and shrugged.

"That doll was my grandmother's, Shayna's. It was important to me." The desire to smack him coursed through her. She thought back on how frightened she'd been last night in her own house, looking over her shoulder, running from room to room, reduced to a child. She'd wasted the police department's time. More important, they'd attracted public attention to their private life once again when they'd called the police.

"You need to tell me why you did that," she said, cycling back to the fact that something awful had happened while her attention had been elsewhere. While she'd spent her summer picking over her marriage, her son had been buckling and twisting beyond recognition.

The waitress slid the plates from her forearm down onto the table. "Hey, cheer up," she said to Ben as she placed a caddy of syrups between him and Lily. "School don't start for two more weeks yet." She chuckled and winked at Lily.

Ben picked up his fork and started to tear large chunks out of the steaming pancakes.

Lily reached across and squeezed his hand, pressing it to the table. "You need to tell me why you did that."

"Owww," he said. "You're hurting me. Why did you even have kids anyway?" He pushed his plate into hers and ran from the table. Lily took a bite of food and remained in her seat. She could see most of the parking lot from the window. He wasn't outside yet. This was her child, still reluctant to walk two body lengths apart from her at the mall and unwilling to run into the Red Brick General Store by himself for a jug of milk. He wasn't going to run away on her.

The young couple across the aisle stared at her. The waitress came up and asked if she wanted the check. He would come back to the table and cry or apologize, because that's what he did, that was the kind of kid he'd always been, embarrassed to have made a scene. She watched the syrup run down the sides of her pancakes. How had he uncovered the grill? He'd always been scared of fire. He'd been scared to help her light the candles on Greg's last birthday cake, panicked at the warmth of the dripping wax. The grill had still been hot, the cover heavy, unwieldy for someone of his height. Somehow he'd overcome his fear to make his point.

Lily left ten dollars on the table and ran to the vestibule of the diner, half expecting to see Ben pulling at the knob of one of the pinball machines. She walked outside and scanned the parking

lot. Church Hill Road was busy with cars pulling off the highway
for gas and food on a summer Saturday. She turned around and
went back inside. She cracked the door to the men's room. An
elderly man was just coming out. She smiled and he tapped the
men's room sign with his yellow fingernail as he stepped past her.
When he was out of sight, she opened the door again. "Ben, if
you're in there, just tell me, okay?" There was no answer. She
walked back to the entrance of the diner, then to where they'd
been sitting, then back to the parking lot again.

She pushed open the door to the men's room all the way this
time and yelled into the tiled room, "I mean it, Ben. Come out
here right now. This is enough." A man with a ponytail was
standing at the urinal. She looked in the direction of the sinks,
but didn't move.

Benjamin finally emerged from the last stall. "Stay away from
me. I hate you."

The man at the urinal zipped up and stared at her. He was
wearing leather pants and a leather vest with no shirt, a biker. She
looked across the length of dirty blue tile, past the man, now
washing his hands, toward her son. The biker looked first at Ben,
then at Lily. He dried his hands, pulled out a cigarette from his
vest pocket, and lit it.

"Everything okay?" he said to Ben. He nodded in Lily's direction. "You know her?"

"I'm his mother," Lily said.

The man cocked his head and looked at each of them one last
time. Ben said nothing.

"Can't be too careful these days," he said, rubbing his nose
with the same hand that held the cigarette. "Men, women . . . you
got all kinds taking kids . . . molesting them . . . doing God
knows—"

"Everything's fine," Lily said, walking past the man and placing her hands on Benjamin's shoulders.

She guided Ben out of the bathroom, down the steps of the

diner, and into the parking lot. She kept her hands on him, remembering Father Paul's praying over her last night. She could no longer lift Benjamin and she didn't think that she could even hold him tightly enough so he couldn't break free. She doubted that her touch could heal him.

"It's hot," he whined.

"You need to talk to me, Benjamin." She prodded him past their car and around the red and white geraniums planted along the side of the diner, as if the forced march would get him to confess. "We're not leaving this parking lot until you tell me what's going on. You're scaring me," she said, inadvertently. She hadn't meant to reveal herself, hadn't wanted him to hear even one vulnerable breath.

"You're hurting me," he yelled, twisting his shoulders underneath her hands. They were at the back of the restaurant now. Two men who worked in the kitchen were leaning against the dumpster smoking.

"Can I at least sit down?" he said, trying to shake off her hold, one more time.

Lily led him over to the edge of the pavement where it was almost shady. She sat down on the curb and pressed him down beside her.

"I don't know why I did it," he said suddenly. "Sometimes I just do bad things. Lots of people do bad things and they don't know why."

"I've never known you to do anything like this."

"It just happened."

"Did you think about it for a long time before?" Lily asked.

"No," he said, looking right at her. "It was an accident."

She surveyed him, from his skinny brown legs to his black knit shorts to his Bruins T-shirt. He was so familiar and so foreign. "I still don't know why you did it," she said.

"So?" He stood and grabbed a fallen branch a few feet away, at the edge of the woods.

"Don't be fresh."

"I'm not being fresh."

"Well then, why did you do it?"

"Why did you burn Katie?" he said, looking down at the ground, his toe in the crook of the stick.

"Is that what you really think, Benjamin? Or are you just trying to be cruel?"

"It's why Daddy left, right?" he said, almost sympathetically.

"Daddy didn't leave, honey." She wanted to stand up next to him and hug him, but she knew that an embrace would only be comforting to her. "He's just gone for a few days, on a catering job, a big party, you know that. I thought you understood that. I guess there are lots of things I just assumed you understood."

"I'm not stupid," he said.

"God, I know, Benjamin. I know. Do you think I would ever hurt any of you? I'd sooner hurt myself. You're my . . . blessings, my children. What happened with your sister was an accident. I was upstairs. She pulled that pot down herself."

He stepped into the crook of the branch, and it broke easily. He tossed both pieces back toward the woods, and with his hands free he covered his eyes.

Lily moved next to him and stood very close. "You're so sad," she said, starting to cry herself. He lurched one step forward into her chest and heaved a few soundless sobs.

"I'm your mother," she whispered to herself. "Mothers don't hurt their children. They love them, that's their job."

"Mostly," he said.

# Jack

Nantucket Sound was still and dark. Jack limped through the rows of empty seats to the bow of the ferry. The air was cool, the sky was starless, and it seemed to him that he alone was spearheading the crossing, the very first one to feel the bow slice through the wave always just ahead.

If Waller canned him it would be for the best. In fact, he should have canned him months ago. He hadn't been working hard enough. Jack couldn't think of anything more deadening than having a job that demanded so little. He thrived on humping, pressure, performance. In the corporate dining room, he was never expected to outdo himself, only to show up. And the lower the expectations, the more difficult it had become to meet them. Working for the Quabbin Group was a rebound job. Like a recent widow, he'd taken it as much for the distraction from the loss of his own business as for the salary.

It was a death that never got discussed. The last of the refrigerated cases had been carted away over a year ago, and neither he nor Lily ever broached the topic of what had gone wrong at Station Break, what they might do differently in the future. It was as if they hadn't really failed, and there never would be a next

time. They could have saved the business if they'd put all their
energies into catering. There was little local competition. No
one in their league. But they'd been ambivalent about catering,
which always meant stashing the kids with Fran or his sisters for
most of a day and a night, always on a weekend at the end of a
long work week.

Jack leaned over the railing on the side and looked back at the
grayish-white wake. It all had to do with the kids. They'd tried to
make it work out for everyone. They'd stolen time, mixed family life with kitchen life, and thought they were one up on everybody else because of it. But it hadn't worked, and they'd been
forced to play the American game of one on one. One with the
kids all day, one with the job all day. And that sucked almost as
much as not having enough money.

But of course, nothing sucked as much as being deep in debt.
Every transaction was tainted when you owed a lot of money.
Every workday was retroactive. There was only the past, the
ironclad fact of the squandering, and the future, the gauzy possibility of solvency, redemption. The present, which most people
filled up with desire and satisfaction, had to be denied. When you
owed the kind of money they did, you couldn't covet a goddamn
thing.

Maybe that had been his problem as much as anything else.
No wishes could be fulfilled, so he'd stopped wishing all together. He'd organized his days and weeks and months around active-
ly abstaining. He suffered from the crabbed and inevitable fantasy that somehow the consumption that was life could be frozen,
put off, for a year or two, just until they could catch up.

He could just make out the wharf in Hyannis now. From
where he stood, it was impossible to tell if the lights running up
and down the beach on either side of the docks were illuminating waterfront estates or wet, one-room bungalows. He could
picture the cottages, chock-full of hardworking couples who'd
taken on double shifts for fifty-odd weeks so that they could

spend seven nights making love with the sound of the bay lapping just beyond the edge of the bed.

The sex and the money had run out at about the same time. After the shop had closed, he'd come home from a day at the Quabbin Group to find Lily working the toaster oven, making the kids dinner. He hadn't seen her in chef's whites in months. She never looked so promising to him as when she was dressed in a freshly starched jacket, the two rows of knobby embroidered buttons perfectly aligned with her breasts. She was different when she cooked. A kind of physical confidence flushed through her. It was the only time she walked purposefully on the ground, rather than on her toes, like someone habitually in doubt of her stature. The bedroom didn't compare to the nook in the back of the shop, where they had occasionally unrolled the deep blue rug purchased just for that purpose. Their whole life together had once been based on parity, and now it was gone. He wasn't particularly interested in having sex with someone whose life he would find it miserable to live. The synchronization of their interests and their abilities acted as the charged circuit that wrapped around their marriage. The possibility that they were interchangeable had been thrilling for Jack. But that possibility was gone. They had all but passed through one another's skin, and now they didn't even touch. For the first time it occurred to Jack that Lily must be mourning the loss every bit as much as he was.

He could hear the engine being thrown into reverse as the ferry began to dock. They'd made a terrible mistake, and he wondered if he had the power to even begin to undo it. Entering his bedroom tonight, Lily asleep in the cross-breeze of two fans, he wanted to be overcome with desire—for her and for the rest of their life together. More than anything, he wanted to be able to offer her that.

# Lily

In her sleep she heard the scritch, scratch of Mr. McGregor's hoe. The sound grew louder, and she realized that somebody was trying to break in downstairs. Filing the lock, that's what it sounded like. The sitter said that the phone had rung a few times during the evening, but when she answered, the person on the other end of the line had hung up. A wave of heat passed through Lily's already damp body. She knew she should pick up the phone and dial 911. Everybody would want to know how she could have let it happen. Why hadn't she called for help? What could she possibly have been thinking? She turned on the light, picked up the receiver, and pulled back the curtains from the window. There was a van in the driveway, Jack's van.

Lily grabbed a clean T-shirt from the top of the pile of unfolded laundry and went into the bathroom for some baby powder and a drink of water. She heard Jack drop his shoes by the front door and walk quietly up the stairs.

When she and Ben had left the diner this morning, he had asked if they could please just go to the movies. As she watched the baby-faced cartoon ghost from her own childhood materialize on the big screen, she realized that Jack would find Benjamin's behavior further proof that she was lacking as a mother. She didn't know how to talk to him about Benjamin outside of the adversarial framework that had sprung up so tightly around their marriage. She was engaged in a perpetual pretrial hearing of her character without the dubious relief of sentencing, let alone the chance for acquittal.

When the movie was over, Ben asked if they could see another. So they reentered the lobby, bought two more tickets, and stopped again at the candy counter. While they were waiting for the next movie to begin, Lily thumbed through her wallet for Lucy Balsaam's number. She had called Lily when she returned from Turkey. She'd been sorry she'd been unable to help them back in July, but glad to hear that everything had turned out fine. Lily refiled the card amid the money and the grocery-store receipts. Jack wouldn't want his kid going to a shrink on any kind of regular basis.

Only two people were seated in the theater. Ben stood at the top of the aisle, unable to choose a seat.

"Anywhere," she said after a while.

When a few more minutes went by, and he had not moved at all, Lily walked a little ahead and said, "This looks good." He followed her, slowly dragging his knuckles across the tops of the red metal seats. He wasn't talking to her, but at least he had the good grace, she thought, to pick a place where silence was appropriate, even demanded.

They sat side by side in the theater; he watched the screen and she watched his face. When he was younger, she'd been able to get the whole story just by looking at his face. It would be right there—if he was hurt or scared or angry, full of himself or of some brilliant, yet forbidden, plan. Of course, that's the way young children were—open, readable, accessible, vulnerable in every way. Hiding came unnaturally to them. Over time they learned how to cloak themselves, to stand behind doors, inside closets, soundless in the stretch of a shadow so that even their expressive young faces were cast in the shade. Adults fingered the secret nugget of themselves obsessively, privately, their whole lives. It had to start somewhere, sometime, age six, seven. Lily's mother had always mocked the mothers who cried at graduations. Growing up is what's supposed to happen to your children, she would say. "Could you possibly imagine anything more wretched than having someone remain dependent upon you your whole life?" Watching your children grow up was liberating, she said. Lily always wondered for whom. Her parents had never pried. They'd respected her privacy so much that she'd felt cut loose from life, alone and drifting.

Ben's eyes were glassy from a day spent staring at a screen. His breaths were shallow, few and far between. He didn't trust her anymore. He didn't trust her to protect him, to cherish him beyond her own demons. How had that happened? She couldn't spend one more second worrying about what Jack would think about sending Ben to a shrink. He needed a surrogate, someone he could tell every one of those secrets—the exquisite ones she hoped he'd harbor forever, and more important, the horrifying ones that ran alongside him, setting the pace, the ones that could chase you into oncoming traffic on the West Side Highway.

The  bathroom  door was ajar, and Lily could see Jack undressing—his shirt, his pants. Next he'd be getting his pillow and his sheet from the linen closet. She'd called Lucy at five, and had gotten the name of a child psychologist. Benjamin had an appointment lined up for Monday. She would simply tell Jack this is what happened. This is what needed to be done. She was the mother, and she'd taken the necessary steps.

"It's not so bad in here," Jack said. "The heat. It's not so hot in here."

Was he intending to sleep up here? She sat down on the bed.

"What happened? I thought you weren't coming home until tomorrow night or Monday?"

"I missed you," he said.

"No, really," Lily said. "Why are you home early?"

"I was worried about you. What happened last night . . . what you told me over the phone was pretty creepy."

"Yeah, well . . ."

"There's only a brunch tomorrow," he said, letting his torso fall across the bed so that he could reach her leg, place his hand on her knee. "I'd had enough, you know? Enough of one fucking shitty summer. Action was called for." He slapped her knee and laughed.

She nodded.

"We need to do something," he said, pulling himself closer to her.

What was this all about? Why was he touching her now that it seemed to matter so little? What he thought of her, whether or not he still desired her, was no longer relevant. She looked at him with a kind of contempt. He didn't know what had happened today with Benjamin, hadn't a clue, and his ignorance made him seem preposterous.

Jack kicked down the sheets with his knees and let one leg flop on top of the spread. He moved as if to put his head in her lap.

"Jesus, what did you do?" she said. Both of his feet were wrapped in strips of cloth.

He sat up and unpeeled the bandages.

"I've seen worse," she said, after a while. The tough skin of the soles had only blistered in two spots.

"It was just stupid." He followed her into the bathroom while she poked through the medicine cabinet. "I stepped into my own goddamn fire," he said, sitting down on the toilet seat lid and telling her the story.

When they went back into the bedroom, he lay down and she

sat at the edge of the bed with her back toward him. She looked at his foot, eyed a length of gauze, then cut the cloth with a pair of nail scissors. "This might hurt," she said, as she gently dabbed some ointment onto one heel. She bandaged one foot, and as she started in on the other, she began to tell him about her day, about their Benjamin.

He didn't answer, but she could sense him behind her as she worked. She could feel the heaving of his chest against the mattress, and long after she had slipped into bed beside him and turned out the light, she could hear him crying.

# Lily

The drugstore, the supermarket, and even the gas station had stocked their shelves with pens and pencils, notebooks, and extra-large bottles of Elmer's. The school bus route was mailed home, and the cafeteria menu for the first week appeared in the *Rooster*. The phone calls had stopped; the woman had lost interest in them again. The occasional leaf on the occasional tree had even turned color, and Ben had met twice with Carmella Tallent. She had called Lily after the first session and said that she wanted to see him twice a week for a while, given that school would soon be starting, a time of increased stress for all children. She said she liked to get to know a child a bit before talking with the parents, discussing strategies, accruing additional information. Ben "worked" well with her. He was open, articulate, and intelligent. She and Jack were very fortunate to have such a terrific kid.

Lily was worried about him. Greg preferred to set up his trains under the kitchen table rather than in the bedroom he shared with an older brother who could read chapter books but insisted on crawling into the bottom bunk with him now every night and once had even wet the bed.

Mostly, Greg was Captain Hook. As soon as he woke up, he'd put on one of Lily's old ruffled shirts and then he'd get the stapler and mend his black paper three-cornered hat. When he walked around with his fierce hook, a soup ladle, protruding from the sleeve of his blouse, Katie became Tinker Bell, Lily turned into Wendy, and Ben was invisible.

When Katie wasn't staring at Ben, she was busy bringing him raisins, cut-up pieces of paper, tennis balls, her boo-boo doll. She wasn't used to being ignored by the big brother who'd always catered to her. One night while Lily was on the phone and cooking dinner, Katie tugged on Benjamin's sleeve and pointed to the refrigerator, something she'd done a hundred times before when she was hungry or thirsty. He was drawing with markers at the kitchen table. It seemed to Lily that he kept drawing the same scene over and over again, the *Santa Maria* manned by Indians with campfire-like bombs exploding all around. When Benjamin ignored Katie, she stamped her foot and whined, which had always worked in the past.

"Just because you got burnt doesn't mean I have to care about you," he shouted. "I don't have to do things for you. I don't have to like you." Katie moved toward him with her open mouth, and just as she was about to bite him, Ben looked around, almost frantically, Lily thought, for a means of protecting himself. He reached for a marker, the one he'd used to draw the bombs, and began scribbling wildly in red on her forehead and over her eye and down her cheek. By the time Lily grabbed the marker from him he had just reached her throat.

Just before bed that night, Greg handed Lily a picture. "It's a card," he said. "It's a rainbow with birds and God and stuff. Things he likes. You can't see God," he said, pointing to a blank space on the paper.

"It's beautiful, honey." She held out the card for him to take back.

"You give it to him, Mum," he said.

"Well, don't you want to?"

He looked up at her, shoved his hands into the waistband of his shorts, and walked away.

The Saturday of Labor Day weekend was cold and rainy. The cookout they'd been invited to at Jean's was canceled. So they did what everyone else did, they went to buy clothes for school.

The mall was so crowded that they had to park in the spillover lot on the far side of Route 17. As they crossed the two-lane highway, Jack with Katie in the stroller and Lily with the two boys, a truck managed to splash them all. And when the whining ensued, Jack turned to the kids and said that if they all cooperated for the rest of the afternoon, he would take everybody to Pizzeria Uno for dinner. The only thing Jack hated more than shopping at the mall was eating there. Lily looked over at Jack and Jack looked over at Ben. Anything for Benjamin, she thought.

"I saw these in town the other day," Jack said, pointing to a table setting in the window of Crate and Barrel.

"We can't afford new dishes."

"Not for us," he said, leading them toward a fall display, plates overflowing with what looked like hay, set next to bandannas rolled up in horseshoe napkin rings. Katie leaned over the side of the stroller and grabbed some of the hay. Greg wheeled her away to distract her, and Ben followed.

Lily stared down absently at the brown crockery plates with the glossy white china centers, then looked over to where the children were standing, a few feet away in front of a display entitled "When in Rome . . ." Ben was tying Katie's shoe. "For work?" she asked, turning back toward Jack. "You couldn't run these through a dishwasher."

"Lilack's." He ran his finger around the deeply grooved lip of the plate.

Neither of them had talked about their old fantasy, their ideal restaurant, in over two years. Hearing him mention it now was as if he'd summoned a pagan god in whom they'd long ago agreed no longer to believe.

She looked at him studying the plates, and she felt a rush of hopefulness for which she was immediately ashamed. They were in no position to indulge in anything, especially unreality.

"It sets kind of a . . . rustic, earthy tone." He seemed to be looking for her to agree.

She nodded. "They're beautiful. Impractical, but—"

"No, Katie," Ben yelled.

Lily turned to see Katie lean over the edge of the stroller to reach the arm of an immense mock-up of a pasta machine. Ben moved to grab her hand, and as he did, he bumped an oil-and-vinegar set. The cruets hit the floor. Glass shattered. Green extra virgin olive oil flowed slowly and steadily onto a display of wrapped gift boxes.

"It wasn't my fault," Ben shouted.

Lily ran up to him.

"It wasn't my fault," he repeated, his voice rising and cracking as if he were going to cry.

"Don't worry about it," Lily said. "No big deal."

People in the kitchen gadgets section stopped and stared. A young man in an apron came over with a dustpan and broom and audibly muttered, "Jesus."

"It's all right," Jack said, staring at the mess on the floor. He picked up one of the boxed sets of cruets and turned it over.

"Are you going to make me pay for that, Dad?" Ben cried. "Do we have to pay for that? I can't pay for that. I can't. It was an accident."

"Benjamin," Lily said, putting her hands on his shoulders as if to force the emotions back inside. "It's all right."

"Everybody's staring at me. They know I did it," he yelled.

"We'll be in Sears," Lily said, opening her eyes widely at Jack. "In the boys' department."

They stepped out of the store and into the main concourse of the mall. "Would you like to push the stroller for me, Ben?" she asked.

Ben was behind them, walking slowly, his fists balled up and his chin to his chest. Greg was holding on to Lily's right leg. Every few seconds he would stop and turn to look at his brother. "I think he's gonna cry, Mum," he said.

"That's okay. He feels sad."

"Well, not if you're in second grade."

"Would you like to push Katie?" Lily said again to Ben.

"Yeah, right down the escalator."

Katie started screaming and kicking her legs in the stroller.

"Cut the crap, Benjamin," Lily said, startling herself. She'd planned on ignoring him, had even been sifting through her brain for a change of subject, but she just couldn't do it. "It was a piece of junk, Ben. It shouldn't have been piled that way, teetering on a tray. Kids break stuff all the time in stores." She was yelling now. "Just forget about it. Get over it."

She began walking a little faster, dragging Greg on her leg, not bothering to keep track of Ben. "Now, how many pairs of jeans do you think you'll each need?"

"I don't know," Greg said. "Seventeen?"

"Okay," Lily said. "That's good."

"See," Ben said, racing up from behind and grabbing onto one handle of the stroller. "You say 'Okay' to everything. You don't even listen. You don't listen to us."

"I was thinking," Lily said. "Thinking how long I could go without doing the laundry if we really did buy each of you seventeen pairs of pants." She could do it. She could control herself, keep from yelling at Ben, keep from feeling the need to shock him out of this vortex he'd been sucked into. She could walk up and down this mall all day and allow him to say whatever he wanted. She would maintain a consistent, upbeat, cheerful, semi-detached tone, if that's what it took. She couldn't make things better for him, obviously, so she'd have to settle for not making them any worse. She didn't know who to be with him. But clearly she could no longer be herself.

It was different for Jack. He could glide along for hours on a superficial plane, make joke after joke, pun after pun. He stayed with Ben in the boys' department, until enough pants and shirts and socks, the ones on sale, had been selected.

Lily took Greg and Katie into the toddlers' department and distractedly picked out clothes Greg thought would be "right" for the second year of nursery school. They bypassed the shoe store. They'd have to wait until the next pay period for that trip. In CVS they all bought notebooks and lunch boxes, although only one of them could write and would be eating lunch somewhere other than home. Lily consented to going into the pet store, something she hardly ever did. If depression had a smell, she thought, it would smell like a pet store.

Katie hopped from the stroller and pressed her nose up against the plexiglass that separated her from a St. Bernard puppy. Lily listened to the chirping, the bleating, the tussling of newspaper, and the sound of claws on metal all around her. The puppy licked the divider, and Katie pressed her own pink tongue up to her side of the glass.

"You shouldn't let her do that," Ben said. He was standing behind some other children, looking at a pile of white ferrets.

Lily smiled at him and shrugged.

"Maybe we should get one, Dad?" Greg said, lowering his arm down into the world of the St. Bernard puppies.

"Mom hates dogs," Ben said, not bothering to look in her direction.

"That's Mum for you," Jack said. "Wife, mother, dog hater."

Greg turned around and stared at her. "Someday could we?"

"Forget it. They'll never let us get a dog," Ben said, still staring at the family of ferrets.

"I don't hate dogs," Lily finally said. "Uncle David and I had Frank when we were little. He was a beagle."

agles are little dogs," Greg said.

/ell, we lived in an apartment."

"Dad had big dogs. This kind of dog gets very big, Dad, doesn't it?" he said, tapping on the glass.

"Too big," Jack said.

"Normal families have dogs, Greg. Believe me, we'll never get a dog," Ben said.

Jack gave Lily's shoulder a little squeeze.

"What kind of families?" Greg asked, still puzzled after a while.

"Just forget it," Ben said.

"What does 'normal' mean?" Greg said, turning around to Jack and Lily, as Katie gave the glass another once-over with her tongue.

"Regular," Lily said.

"Average," Jack said.

"What?" Greg asked. He pulled his cheeks apart with his fingers. "Do dogs laugh?" he said.

There was a long line outside Pizzeria Uno.

"Let's bag it," Jack said to Lily.

"I knew it," Ben said, kicking the base of a ficus tree.

So they sat on a green wrought-iron bench and waited for their name to be called. Lily wanted a drink. And then she wanted this to be over. She wanted to be walking out of the restaurant having survived the next hour, all of them together. No, that wasn't accurate. She wanted to survive the next hour with Benjamin.

In its entirety, time with children sped by. They grew up so quickly, forced you to acknowledge the passage of time in your own body's cells. But in its component parts, life with children could be made to stretch. Days, hours, even moments elongated to the point of grotesquery. The day was never over with Benjamin now.

She wondered if he would even be able to start school next

week. Maybe this trouble with him wasn't a phase or a reaction as much as an inception. Maybe he'd have to be carted off to one of those schools in the Berkshires, where he'd be housed with small groups of children who'd seen their fathers kill their mothers. She and Jack would spend every weekend until they died visiting him there. Every penny they earned would go to this place, where the psychiatric nurses and occupational therapists had discovered that allowing the children to help run a farm, feel responsible for the lives of animals, was immensely therapeutic. Maybe they *should* get a dog.

Lily fanned her face. She was drenched in perspiration down to the soles of her feet.

"What's the matter?" Jack asked.

She fished through her pocketbook for a sliver of a Xanax. "Do you mind . . ." she said, still looking, now in her change purse, ". . . if we just go?"

"You don't look too good," he said. "Hey, guys." He stood up and cracked his knuckles and then his back, making Katie and Greg laugh. "We're going to go get a movie, get a pizza, and we can all eat together in the living room, in the dark. Now what's a movie we'd all—"

"I knew it," Benjamin said, as they started to walk toward the exit.

It was drizzling and a dense, cool fog had settled all around the mall. It was later than Lily had realized. The parking lot was mostly empty and quiet, except for the sound of Katie's stroller wheels on the wet pavement and the occasional splash of Benjamin's foot landing purposely in a puddle. Jack was walking with Ben and Katie somewhere to the left in the mist. Lily could hear his voice murmuring to one or both of the children. Greg gripped Lily's hand. She sensed he was looking up at her, but she didn't know for sure. She had all she could do to keep walking and breathing.

If what had happened to Katie truly was an accident, then

what was happening now to Benjamin must be a bequest—bad genes or bad nurturing, depending upon how you looked at it, but a legacy all the same. His losing his equilibrium was either a disease he'd contracted via a microscopic chromosome, or one she'd infected him with because she'd been injudicious in allowing him to drink for so long from her cup. She could see now as they walked through the fogged-in parking lot that this damage to Benjamin was not simply a spin-off of what had happened to Katie. This unmaking of the boy she had once known was solely her own work, the product of her motherhood and her mothering.

The scream was so loud, so desperate, that at first Lily thought it was coming from inside herself. But it wasn't. It was coming from across Route 17, in the overflow lot. In between patches of fog, Lily saw the woman. Clearly, she was crazy. She wondered how they might avoid her. She was hysterical, very nearly ululating as she waved her arms wildly through the dusky fog. She was pointing. Lily looked behind her. No, the woman was pointing at her, jumping again and again, her shopping bag hitting the pavement each time she came down.

Lily looked over at Jack, about ten feet to her left. He had Katie in the stroller and he was running at Lily. Lily watched as he let go of the stroller, let Katie roll toward her, and ran in the direction of the woman. He headed straight into the traffic, cars going forty, forty-five miles an hour in the fog. He held up his hands as if he might really stop the vans and the sports cars, the wagons and the Jeeps. As cars honked and veered, flashed their lights, Lily saw that Jack was running toward a boy.

Benjamin was walking down the double yellow line in the middle of Route 17.

# Jack

Approach your victim head on, Jack remembered from the senior lifesaving course he had taken when he was sixteen. Talk to them, reassure them. Drowning people sometimes panic when being rescued. He had learned all these holds for subduing a struggling victim, and ways to disentangle himself in case a drowning person tried to drown him, too. Car horns were piercingly loud when you weren't in a car yourself. His heart pounded each time someone honked. He didn't know these people, these drivers. How could he trust them not to fuck up and kill his son? All he could think about now was that Benjamin might die. Whoever had said you didn't register fear in the face of imminent danger had lied, or else hadn't almost lost a child two months before. The worst case could happen, even to people like him and Lily, maybe especially to people like him and Lily.

Ben was walking slowly, arms dangling, head down, seemingly oblivious to the cars. He was dressed in dark colors, blue shorts, blue soccer shirt. The word "Winstead," outlined in white on his chest, and a few reckless spots of bleach on the back were all that illuminated him. Jack walked the center line, pivoting on one foot, then the other, trying to face the oncoming traffic, no matter what the direction. Ben's blond hair blew about his face every time a car passed. His oversized soccer shirt billowed up around his skinny torso like a sheet.

"It's Dad," Jack said. "I'm right behind you, buddy. I'm right here." Jack stretched his arm taut and reached out to feel Benjamin's bony shoulder beneath his wet shirt. Ben stopped and turned and let Jack pull him in close. He was still so little. How had Jack forgotten that? It was only in relation to Katie and Greg that he seemed big, but compared to Jack he was small, fragile, precious. They walked back toward the crosswalk single-file, Ben in front of Jack, Jack's arms draped over Ben's shoulders and down the front of his chest like a life jacket. A mixture of sweat and rain trickled down Jack's forehead into his eye. "I love you," he said. "Know that I love you."

The Jeep was forest green and the Honda was silver. Brakes squealed, rubber burned. The Honda slid forever, until metal hit metal. Traffic stopped. People got out of their cars. A yellow light spun closer and closer as a mall security car pulled up, illuminating a sparkling pile of red and white safety glass.

Blood was everywhere, it seemed, some of it Jack's, most of it Benjamin's. It was bitter to see that his boy was made of finite physical properties, and not the limitless stuff of Jack's heart and mind. Lily was there now, stroking Ben's head, murmuring to Katie and Greg, and talking to someone in a uniform. "You're going to be fine, just fine," she kept repeating, mostly to Ben, but occasionally, it seemed, to Jack as well. "You have a few cuts, that's all."

Jack sat down on the running board of the mall security vehicle, with Ben still in his arms, stretched partway across his lap. Ben said he was okay and begged them not to call an ambulance. A woman stepped into the bloody circle with a first-aid kit. She pulled on a pair of plastic gloves and pulled back on Ben's little-boy skin, the faint blond hairs all flattened down and pink with blood. The wounds would need to be probed, cleaned, stitched, she told them. In the meantime, she handed Lily some bandages for Benjamin, and told her to make sure to put one on the back of Jack's hand.

# Lily

Lily wanted Jack to have his hand looked at, too, but he refused. He pulled up to the entrance of the emergency room, and they helped Benjamin out.

"Call Dr. Tallent," he whispered, pulling her close. "Don't let the shrinks in there get near him."

The waiting room at Lincoln was filthy. Where the carpet wasn't worn through, it was bloodstained. The plastic chairs were nicked or gouged or broken. Lily had completely bypassed the waiting area that morning back in June when she'd been here with Katie. Tonight the triage nurse seemed in no hurry to help them. Lily took the clipboard full of paperwork and sat next to Ben, who had parked himself in front of the wall-mounted TV, his leg up on the chair beside him.

Momentarily, it occurred to her to lie, give herself and Ben another last name, claim she had no insurance. But they probably wouldn't treat him without proof that she could pay, and for that she would need to use her credit card, and then her identity as the former child abuser would be known. Besides, this world she lived in was small. They'd probably get the same nurse, maybe even Dr. Svanda.

261

"Does it hurt?" she asked, looking up at the television, as if she might make eye contact with him there, on the screen.

He shook his head.

"Good," she said.

The form asked that she describe the "onset of the illness or accident."

"I'm writing that it happened in a parking lot," she said softly to Ben. "That it was dark, the car pulling out didn't see you or the car it hit. Embedded flying glass."

Ben said nothing.

At least she was with him. At least she and Jack had been there when it happened. He hadn't been brought here by EMTs or police officers. He wasn't alone. There was comfort in that. There had to be.

She pulled Dr. Tallent's card from her wallet. It was a holiday weekend. She wouldn't be home. She'd have to leave a message. "Incident." Ben has had an incident, she said into the phone. He seems subdued now. He's getting stitches. She and Jack would take turns watching him for the rest of the weekend, sleeping outside his room each night, inside maybe, if that's what he wanted. School was supposed to start on Wednesday. Some decision would have to be made about that.

Ben sat ramrod-straight on the examining table as the doctor switched on the small lamp attached to his forehead and studied the wound. It was a different doctor, a resident. He didn't have many questions, and those he had he addressed to Lily. "I want to make sure we get everything out of here before we sew him up."

The nurse returned with a tray of instruments, and the doctor bent over Ben's left shin with a shot of novocaine and said, "Bee sting." When he was finally done mining, he handed Ben the small square tray filled with the little bits of bloody plastic and started stitching.

When they were all done, Lily called Jack to come pick them

up. She bought two sodas and a bag of Twizzlers from the machines in the waiting room, and then she and Ben went to sit on the bench outside.

The neon from the "Emergency Entrance" sign made their skin look green in the dark. Ben shivered, and Lily took off her jacket and put it around him. He made no move to shake it off. She had to say something to him, but she was scared it would be the wrong thing. Anything could cut him now.

"How come I don't have to stay?" he said, looking at her.

"Here?" she said, confused.

"You had to, right?" He sounded small and as young as he really was.

"When I had you, you mean?"

"No. When you were a girl, and it happened to you."

She stared at him, let him go on, hoping he was inventing all this.

"You had to go to a doctor like Carm, and you had to stay in a hospital when you walked in the middle of the road, like I did, right?"

"That was a long time ago, Benjamin. How do you even know that story, honey?"

"When we were camping with the cousins, I couldn't sleep. I pretended to sleep. I lay in the sleeping bag in the tent and I could hear Auntie Jean and Auntie Erin talking." He stopped and looked out toward the street. "Then I knew it was true—what I heard you say to Nana once, back when Greg and I had to talk to that doctor." He touched the tape on top of his bandaged leg. "A police car came to get you. That guy with the uniform at the mall, he was a kind of policeman, right?"

Lily nodded and stroked his bare arm. "Does it make you sad that I did that when I was a girl?"

He shrugged. "I don't know. You didn't want to be alive any- more, which means you didn't want us . . ."

"I didn't even know about you then," she tried to explain.

"But didn't you want to, I mean, grow up, and have us?"

"Well, I did. That's what I did."

"But only because the police caught you. What if they hadn't?"

"What if Daddy hadn't gotten you, today?" Lily said, after a while.

"I knew he would. I just knew he would. But your parents were already dead, right? Maybe that's why you did it, because you were sad about your parents?"

"What are you sad about, Ben?" she asked.

"Nothing," he said, sliding closer to her on the bench. "I'm just cold." He moved up onto her lap.

"Dad will be here any minute," she said, hugging him and staring out into the hospital parking lot. "I'll keep you warm, buddy. I'll keep you warm."

# Jack

Dr. Tallent's office reminded Jack of a tree house. It jutted off the second story of her home straight into the woods, and for that reason alone, he could understand why Ben liked coming here. The room was all knotty pine, with broad beams that ran the width of the ceiling. The windows were cut in at strange angles, framing views of the woods into circles or diamonds or trapezoids.

Jack wondered if maybe Ben didn't have just a little crush on Carm, as he called her. Each time Jack had met her, she'd slipped across the rough-hewn room draped in the kind of silk that made you want to touch her. She wore a flowery perfume that wafted around the woodsy office. When she was concentrating very hard she had the childlike habit of twirling her pen in her hair. And if that wasn't enough to captivate Ben, the entire waiting room and part of the office were lined with shelves full of what Lily called "kid tchotchkes."

"When I met with Ben back on Tuesday," Dr. Tallent said, "he mentioned that he didn't think you especially cared about him." Jack watched her flip through the pages of the small notebook, which she had slid into a leather cover just as the session began.

"He feels you don't talk much to him?" Dr. Tallent continued.

Jack looked over at Lily for corroboration.

"I don't mean to give that impression," he said.

"Of course not." Dr. Tallent crossed the legs of her silk pants. "He needs additional reassurance right now. We need to brainstorm as to how best to give him that."

"I've been telling him I love him. I mean, making a point to say it out loud."

Dr. Tallent nodded.

"Maybe he needs to see it. You might just need to show it."

Jack stared out the diamond-shaped window. It was getting darker earlier. There was just barely enough light left in the sky now to see a baseball coming toward you. "This is going to sound awful," he said. "But how do I do that? He knows me to be a certain kind of person, a certain kind of father, who behaves in a certain way."

"You might have to change?" Dr. Tallent reached down and fiddled with her gold ankle bracelet.

"I think we've all suffered here because of change. I mean, we've had nothing but change, and it's sucked—"

"That was external change," Lily interrupted. "I think what Carm means is—"

"I'm not suggesting you change because there is something wrong with who you are, Jack," Dr. Tallent said. "I'm talking about a shift in style to meet a pressing, immediate need your son has, that's all."

He nodded. "I understand. I just don't know how to do it. Do you know what I'm saying? I can't be fake. I mean, it won't work."

"Your son is exceedingly open, at least with me," Dr. Tallent said. "If he opens a subject, don't close it. Keep talking until he gives the cue that he's had enough. That's what he wants, that's what he needs from you."

What Jack wanted, what Jack needed, was for everything to go back, he didn't know exactly how far, but back to when they were happy. "Is this a short-term thing? I mean, eventually we'll be able to join up with our old selves?"

Dr. Tallent smiled. "I think there is a tendency," she said, "when there's a trauma, when there's been a trauma, such as the accident with your baby, to separate the events in our lives into 'before' and 'after.' Sometimes we even go so far as to separate ourselves, our identities, into 'before' and 'after.' It's natural. It's our means of protecting, conserving, but ultimately I think it's a fallacy."

"Because there is no more *before*," Lily said softly, as she turned toward Jack.

Dr. Tallent nodded.

"What are you talking about?" Jack said. "That's like saying the past wasn't real or true, somehow. That only the crappy present is what's real."

"What I'm saying is that our identity, our reality, shifts and expands, it's always changing. We get into a great deal of hot water emotionally if we make the assumption that reality is fixed or that there is one reality that everyone in a family shares."

"You're telling me I need to change for good."

"I'm telling you that the reality of your family life has already shifted and you both need to catch up with it."

This doctor was wrong, Jack thought. Not everything was vulnerable to change. There were fundamental, bedrock truths that, no matter how disfigured they might appear on the surface, were still recognizable, embraceable.

The night of Ben's accident, he'd dropped Greg and Katie with his mother and driven back to the emergency room, exhausted. A parking attendant had directed him all the way to the visitors' lot, forcing him to walk what felt like miles back to the emergency entrance. His back and legs and neck ached. For the three or five minutes it had taken to reach Ben he must have contracted every muscle in his body, and now he could barely

move. As he passed by the main entrance, he saw that the lights
that lit up the L's in "Lincoln" were out. A big masking-tape X
covered a crack in the lobby window. God, he hated this place,
doctors and nurses and patients in wheelchairs out in the parking
lot smoking in the rain. Everything and everybody was sick and
sorry-looking, including himself, with glass in his hair and blood
on his clothes.

He was afraid to see Benjamin. How could he father a little
boy who had gone somewhere he hadn't, knew something that
Jack didn't or couldn't know?

Lily and Ben were already outside the waiting room, sitting
together on a bench. Lily was holding him on her lap, his bandaged legs stretched out to one side, his hair mixed in with hers
as he lay with his head on her shoulder. Their eyes were closed,
and Lily was rocking him very gently, singing in a low voice.

This was all you could do and it was everything. Jack moved
in closer to them. This was the only truth you needed to know.

# Lily

Everybody was dancing, Lily thought. Katie and Greg were dancing around Ben, and Lily was dancing around the three of them, and Jack was just behind Lily night and day, bumping and grinding to a rhythm only he could hear. A few weekends after school had started, and with Carmella Tallent's consent, Lily finally agreed to leave the kids with Fran overnight so that she and Jack could go up to Vermont.

For the past three Sundays, Jack had driven into Harvard Square to Out of Town News and bought every northern New England paper that got sent down to Boston with its real estate and business sections still intact. He spent his evenings circling, clipping, and calling about restaurants up for sale. He'd race home from work, open the mail, and fan out color photos before her as if he were about to attempt a sleight of hand on their future. By the time they set out on their road trip, he had five sets of directions to restaurants that were on the market. He'd called ahead for a motel room in Fairlee and made dinner reservations at a restaurant in Hanover owned by an old coworker of his.

She knew it was a seduction, as was the surprise picnic along

the Charles, and the suggestion that she fill in for Cyn at the end
of September when Cyn took her vacation. She knew he was lur-
ing her, not so much toward a particular destination, a specific
plan, as toward change itself. She leaned back and allowed herself to succumb.

"Let's not talk about this in front of the kids," she said,
on their way back home. "Don't say anything to your mother, not
until we've been to the bank, had the house appraised."
Snowfields, as the restaurant was now called, was the only one of
the five places they saw still in business. They had spent most of
Saturday afternoon there, and Jack had insisted that they drive
back over this morning and walk around, before heading for
home. The restaurant was housed in a rambling old farmhouse,
which Lily was sure needed a lot of work. The couple who owned
it had raised their family in the living quarters on the second
floor. Lily had seen water damage on the ceiling of almost every
room. "It's probably a great big firetrap," she said. "Anyway,
we've got to go up in the off-season when they're doing a whop-
ping seven dinners a night. When the leaf peepers have gone and
the skiers haven't yet come."

"We need to do this, Lily." Jack took a long drink of his soda,
then wedged the can back between his thighs. "We need to throw
ourselves into this together, get all sucked up into it and over-
whelmed and scared and ecstatic. I hate this." He waved his arm
around the inside of the car. "Christ, I hate the way our life has
been eaten away by . . . what? By fucking shitty circumstance."

"Don't yell," she said. She'd been scared to go away with him
for the weekend, scared to leave Benjamin and scared that she
and Jack could manage only small amounts of intimacy.

"I'm excited. I'm not yelling," he said. "Don't shrug like that
at me."

"Well, what do you want me to do, Jack?"

"I want you to talk as loudly as I am in this car right now. I want you to take up a lot of room, more than your allotment. I want you to spill over—"

"What the fuck are you talking about?"

"We're cowering, and I hate it. I can't tell you how much I hate it. We're tiptoeing around Ben, around each other, around our whole fucking lives. And that's not who we are. It's like we're in the backseat," he said, turning around to look at the empty seat behind them, "and the car is roaring down a hill and no one's driving—and it's our car. It's our fucking shitbox."

"It's easy for you," she said, without looking at him. "But why would I want to be full of myself?" She pressed her nose to the window and watched a dairy farm fly by. "I want to be full of the kids. Sometimes I even want to be full of you. But it's impossible to try to fill up on myself without choking."

"How can you say that?" He leaned toward her and stroked her leg.

They'd come down out of the mountains. The trees were shorter here and the road was beginning to flatten out. "You weren't there when it happened. You don't have to—"

He reached over and put his fingers across her lips. She knew it to be an act of kindness, but she grabbed his hand away. "You can't flip a switch and say it doesn't matter anymore, just because it doesn't matter to you. It doesn't work like that. We can't just move on, excise the whole summer like it was some kind of benign tumor and skip ahead to the future." She turned now and shook her head at him in disbelief. "Benjamin ought to be a clue that we can't do that. We're saddled with this thing. It's what's taking up the room. It's sucking up the air in this car right now."

He was biting down on his lip so hard it was white. She knew he was going to tell her he understood, but she doubted he really could.

"You're wrong," he said. "You're so wrong, Lily. That accident is no match for us, no match for you. I watch you with the kids. And every day I see that the guilt is nothing compared to the love."

"It's not guilt," she said. "Just knowledge. Terrible knowledge."

It was late when they got home. The kids were asleep. As
Fran moved around collecting her things, Lily could hear Jack
cooking in the kitchen.

"So really," Lily said, as she helped Fran out to the car with
her bag, "how were they?"

"Good as gold. Truly." Fran opened her car door and looked
at Lily. "He's going to be fine, you know. He's not himself, but
he's going to be just fine."

"Did anything happen? You could have told me on the
phone." Lily heard the squeaking of baby bats in the distance.

Fran shook her head and got into her car. "Nothing happened.
In fact, we had a good time."

Lily watched Fran go down the driveway and then stood staring at the house for a while. She walked through the door, so
relieved to be home she began to cry.

"Thank you," Lily said. She dipped her finger into the
last bit of mushroom risotto on her plate.

Jack nodded, slipped down slightly in his chair, and scissored
one of her bare ankles between his feet.

The wind blew hard outside and the old screen in the window
above the sink rattled. The candles flickered, then flared. Jack
pulled his chair next to hers. He lifted her hair and kissed her
neck, the tops of her shoulders, the backs of her arms. He
reached over and swatted at the light switch. The kitchen was
now totally dark except for the light from the dripping candles in
the center of the table.

"What are you doing?" She laughed.

He tried to pick her up.

"Let's go upstairs."

The wind blew violently, and the screen in the window above

the sink pushed past the thumbtack that had been holding it there all summer. There was a clattering and then a splash as one edge of the frame dropped into the pot soaking in the sink.

Jack was at her feet now, his hand sliding up her leg, up under her skirt.

His eyes were closed, and she stared at him, trying to remember who she'd thought he was a month ago, a year ago, ten years ago. No one told you that about married love, that it constituted a continually, but not constantly, shifting perception of reality, that it was every bit as mutable and organic as a living being.

The floor was hard, the tile almost cold against her. Jack pulled a dish towel from the oven door and rolled it up under her naked hips. "I love you," he said.

She listened to the tree branches scrape against the windows upstairs. The spirea out by the open kitchen door whipped against the clapboards. He hadn't said he loved her in months, not even the other night in the motel. The wind blew from the woods, across the yard, straight through the unfiltered window. It sped across their bodies again and again. And, if she tried very hard, she could smell the cultivated scents of crab apple and grass, spruce and pine, and even more faintly, the original, moist smell of the soil, itself.

# Jack

Everything was laid out in front of Jack in small white monkey dishes, each of the ingredients he needed for making the first course, pan-roasted trout, already prepped. Lily was at the far end of the kitchen. She had trimmed the beef and was studding it with slivers of garlic and fresh rosemary. The water was at a rolling boil for the gnocchi. The oven creaked and popped as it cranked itself up to 450 degrees. The purposeful din in the kitchen made his eyes water. He stopped for a moment and listened to the sound of Lily's shoes as they sashayed under the counter, the rhythmic contact of her knife on wood, the slap of her peppered hand on the roast. Wordlessly they inspected the purple basil, tasted the vinaigrette, grated the cheese. All this industrious silence was their brilliant repartee.

Ben now met only once a week with Dr. Tallent. Sometimes Jack and Lily joined him. Once in a while they met with Tallent alone. More and more, it seemed to Jack that she was mining their psyches, and finally Jack called her on it.

"No, no," she said. She was only asking what she needed to know in order to help Benjamin. That was the object— Benjamin. She said this so often that Jack had actually, and inappropriately he knew, laughed out loud one night.

Tallent had thought his laughter a show of cynicism. He'd shaken his head and put a handkerchief to his eyes. All these people who worked with kids, the social workers, the child psychologists—so few of them had any sense of the absurd. It floored him. As they were driving home after that appointment, Lily had asked him why he'd laughed. He shook his head. She smiled and said, "I think she thinks you're insensitive." The tires of the Subaru hit the iron grating of Black Bridge. He wondered for a moment if he'd heard her correctly.

"You think I'm insensitive?" he asked as they reached the other side.

"On the contrary," she said, shaking her head. "I think it's all too much for you."

During the appointments they had with Ben, Jack was reluctant to talk. When he was in that office with his son he felt as if he'd stepped into someone else's version of reality. He wondered if that was how he'd feel twenty years into the future, visiting Ben in the apartment he shared with his girlfriend. Lonely. As those sessions unfolded he was shocked to see his son glance again and again at Dr. Tallent, as if she were his referent, his touchstone. The child was the instructor in this setting and the parent the one in need of remedial education.

In the sessions they attended without Ben, Tallent spoke to them of Ben's faulty belief system and the need, on the part of all three of them, to offer him a new one, a different possibility for himself. But as soon as the four of them got together, Jack invariably felt as if Ben were sitting at the right hand of God, and he, the father, were prostrate, repentant, silent before the son.

Jack scraped the pile of minced parsley into a small cloth and squeezed it dry. This week they'd mentioned to Dr. Tallent that they were looking into buying a restaurant up in Vermont. She appreciated their telling her, she said.

"Obviously, you're concerned with the effect this kind of change might have on Benjamin." She nodded and smiled at them. "Well, let me ask you," she said, staring at Jack. "What do you think?"

What he really thought was that for the past three or four months a number of professionals, mostly women, had been guiding, even dictating, the most intimate aspects of his life, and he wondered if the personal would ever again be private.

"We haven't put our house on the market yet," he said. "We haven't mentioned it to the kids, though they may have overheard us. . . . Lily and I have been discussing it a lot, at home. You know how those things go, kind of obsessional. . . ." The truth was that when they weren't talking about it, he was thinking about it. It reminded him, sometimes painfully, of the way he and Lily had talked about Benjamin when Lily was pregnant with him. It was an unquenchable need, the license to finally plan aloud the part of your life you'd secretly craved and that now appeared to be within your grasp.

"The impulse," Jack said to Dr. Tallent, "is not purely selfish, not all career-oriented. We both think the kids were happier back when we were working together. We certainly were. You'd have to tell us about the timing of switching schools."

Dr. Tallent nodded. "Your son certainly needs to continue treatment," she said, twirling the capped end of her pen in the fine strands of her hair.

"Sure," Jack said.

"He needs continuity right now—in as many aspects of his life as are possible. But more important, I think, he needs to be the focus." She smiled at them both. "Let's see how I can put this. You're a chef . . . he needs to be the entree. Not to the exclusion of your other children . . . but, for now, he needs to be the focus of your energies to the exclusion of your own professional lives. He's your project right now. And perhaps you could look at him as an endeavor as challenging as the business you're planning to start."

It wasn't yet sundown. Lily didn't want to start serving the Yom Kippur break-fast until then. Jack covered the fish and turned off the heat. He heard his family in the next room, his sisters and mother, his brothers-in-law, nieces and nephew, Lily and the kids. He could hear them laughing and shouting. They were playing charades.

Late yesterday afternoon he'd taken the kids apple picking. His mother had met them there. It was cool and shadowy by the time they found a row of trees with apples still to be picked. Jack lifted Katie onto his shoulders so that she could reach high up into the tree where it seemed the best apples remained. The boys had run up ahead, looking for a tree they could scale themselves.

"Do you think it's some kind of test?" Jack said after a while.

His mother stood below them, holding open one of the big white shopping bags supplied by the orchard.

"Or is God just punishing us?" he said.

His mother laughed and said, "You can't really think that?"

"I don't know," he said, pressing his palms into Katie's back so she wouldn't topple from his shoulders.

His mother looked down into the almost full bag. "You're just getting a fat chunk of real life served up to you, that's all. It's called growing up, Jack. You need to grow up."

He'd been telling himself the same thing every morning since the middle of August. It was a taunt he used to propel himself from his bed to his job. But that was easy, disingenuous even. It involved nothing more than a kind of relinquishing, a daily letting go of an idea of himself. This other maturation she was talking about, that Benjamin's doctor had implied, demanded that he embrace a portion of himself that had always been too small and slippery to grasp.

"I am grown up," he said to his mother, as he tossed an apple high into the air beyond where he stood. Then he ran, with Katie still on his shoulders, his feet seesawing over the rotten apples on the ground. He positioned himself perfectly, head tilted back, to receive the gift of the fruit, directly into his mouth.

# Lily

Katie climbed up onto a kitchen chair, struggling to free her legs from under the unfamiliar trap of a dress. Lily had the oven door open, the rack pulled out so that she could check the thermometer in the roast. She kept one eye on Katie as the baby's fingers walked across the table in the direction of the two Yahrtzeit candles.

Katie leaned forward to inspect the burning glass jars.

"No. No," Lily said. The candles were nearly out, Yom Kippur almost ended.

"Mine," Katie said.

"Those are special candles," Lily said.

"Hot," Katie said.

Lily nodded.

Katie tried to blow.

Lily shook her head. "For my mama and daddy and my nana," she said. "And this one is for baby Pearl." One of the nurses from the Shriners had called last week to say that they were having a memorial service for Pearl. She had died of pneumonia. It was in the *Globe*, the nurse said. Her mother was going to be tried for murder.

Katie pulled up her dress. Lily stared at the scar trailing up the front of her right leg from her ruffled ankle socks nearly to her knee. The depigmented skin was so shockingly white compared to Katie's natural color that Greg had wondered aloud whether they couldn't use Katie as a kind of light when it was dark. Lily had wanted to go to the memorial service. And she would have gone, had it been held anywhere but in that building.

"The candles help us remember them," she said to Katie, who tickled her cheek with the hem of her dress and settled her thumb deeply into her mouth, as if Lily were about to tell her a story.

"So long as we live, they shall live, for they are now a part of us, as we remember them," Lily said, reciting the one memorial prayer she knew.

Katie looked up at her, removed her thumb from her mouth, and stroked the side of Lily's arm with her wet hand. "Mama," she said softly. "Mama."

Lily bent down and kissed her daughter on top of the head. The cousins were calling Katie. She looked up at Lily once more, then scrambled down from the chair and ran out of the kitchen.

Lily had scavenged a ticket to Kol Nidre services the night before. *Avinu Malkeinu*, the cantor had sung, *inscribe us in the Book of Happiness. Avinu Malkeinu, inscribe us in the Book of Deliverance. Avinu Malkeinu, inscribe us in the Book of Merit. Avinu Malkeinu, inscribe us in the Book of Forgiveness.* The rabbi at the Reconstructionist Synagogue had cautioned them on Rosh Hashanah that it was the sins against their sisters and brothers, against the community, that they needed to atone for in the week before Yom Kippur. "It is the sins you commit in your interpersonal lives," she'd said, "that you need to work out with your friends and family, your spouses and children. The forgiveness must come from them, not God."

Guilt, apologies, forgiveness all bore very little relationship to one another in the real life of the soul. She was guilty of having broken the covenant she'd made with each of her three babies, the covenant to love them perfectly, keep them perfectly safe. That guilt was useless in summoning an apology. How did you apologize to children? And forgiveness, certainly that could only be offered to her once she had ceased to so desperately hunger for it.

Jack carried the marzipan top of her honey cake up from the cellar where she'd stored it in the ice chest. He poured each of them a glass of wine and watched as she unrolled the golden top onto the cake. He opened the small square container on the counter and gently, with his two forefingers, lifted the honey bee, replete with wings and a burgeoning striped body, which they'd fashioned together.

She'd done an awful thing in synagogue last night. She'd propositioned God. She laid out a proposal, a bargain. If he could make Benjamin fine, keep them all safe and happy and healthy, she would . . . give up . . . what? She'd relinquish . . . ? As she was threshing her mind for an adequate sacrifice, something to make God sit up and take notice, she realized that children made bargains with God, not grown-ups. Adults, wives, workers, mothers could only make bargains with themselves.

"We did it," Jack said, safely placing the sculpted confection in the center of the cake. "Let's put it out, on the sideboard."

"Careful," she said, watching him cross the hallway into the dining room. The cousins were running through the house, looping in and out of doorways. Jack's sisters and their husbands were in the living room looking at Fran's pictures from Canada. Lily walked past them all, following Jack and the cake. She had set the dining room this morning, a white tablecloth, the good plates, in the center a round challah with raisins.

"You should be very proud of yourself," Jack said. He laid the cake on the sideboard and kissed her on the cheek.

"Take a picture of it, Mom," Ben said, sneaking up behind them.

Lily shrugged and Ben ran from the room. She could hear him in the hall, hear his voice above the tapping of the girls' patent-leather shoes and the clinking of the ice cubes in the adults' glasses. She could hear him say, "Everyone, come in and see what my mom and dad made."